operation annulment

SHANNON MYERS

contents

First Printing: 2017

Print ISBN- 978-0-9975348-9-4

 Created with Vellum

also by shannon myers

(Killian and Ari's Story)

Wait For It

<u>Fictioned Series</u>

(Hayden & Jake's Story)

Protagonized

To getting what we need instead of what we think we want...

prologue

COMMANDMENT #1: THOU SHALT NOT COUNT THEIR DIAMOND RING BEFORE IT'S ON THEIR FINGER

Kate

I double-check my reflection in the rearview mirror, dabbing at the stray lip gloss that's settled near the corners of my mouth.

"Almost perfect," I mutter to myself.

Tonight is the night.

I'm almost positive that Benjamin is going to propose. It is our one-year anniversary, after all. One long year of waiting. One year of nothing more than chaste kisses.

So maybe he's a little old-fashioned and wanted our first time together to mean something—more men should take hints from him.

I've been patient.

Dakota and Jackson have been together for over a year now, but there is no way in hell that my little sister is getting a ring before me.

No sir.

Benjamin will propose tonight—he just has to— and I'll start planning a modest wedding with close friends and family. All those *Pinterest* boards are about to come in handy. Then, we'll settle down in south Lubbock and have two kids. Maybe we'll throw a dog in the mix, too. All that will be missing is the white picket fence, and that's only because I prefer an eight-foot-high security fence. It's better for the children.

Other than that, it's perfect.

He and I are amazing together. With his job as a physical therapist and my job as a licensed counselor, we'll have financial stability—something I lacked growing up. Our children, one boy, and one girl will be enrolled in the best private school in the area, and we'll take family vacations to exotic locations every year...

I might be getting a little ahead of myself. First and foremost, I need to sort out the wedding details.

I wonder if chocolate fountains are still in.

Benjamin said to come by around seven for 'dinner and a little surprise.'

I just hope that 'little surprise' weighs two carats.

I check the clock on my dash again.

Four fifteen.

I've got forty-five minutes to get his house ready for tonight. I can't wait to see his face when he comes home to find me in his bed, wearing nothing but lingerie.

I grab the overnight bag from the passenger seat, checking to ensure the lingerie is packed. It's a white lace number I picked up at Wal-Mart. I initially set out to find something at the mall, but Victoria's Secret is slightly out of my price range.

I've still got Dakota to think about. Retail doesn't pay that much, and God knows Jackson isn't helping out. He totally could, though, if he wanted to. His family is beyond rich.

I push aside thoughts of Jackson and Dakota before climbing out of my black Chevy Tahoe. It's the one splurge I've allowed myself over the years—granted, I bought it from a rental car company. The poor thing had been driven by God and everyone, if the mileage was any indicator.

It was like searching for a wife within a brothel, but beggars could not be choosers.

I shut the door with my hip while balancing my purse and bag in hand. I've got the lingerie, rose petals, and a bottle of champagne. I hope that once he sees all the trouble I've gone to, he'll drop to one knee and immediately beg me to be his wife.

I can't keep the smile off my face as I unlock the front door. Benjamin's house is pristine—no milk crates doubling as tables or second-hand furniture. Each piece was hand-chosen from *Pottery Barn* and *Restoration Hardware*. I place my bags on the mirrored console table in the entryway and remove my heels before running my fingers along the back of the brown leather sofa. The faint hint of cologne wafts up from a throw pillow. It's so deliciously Benjamin.

This is no bachelor's pad—it's a home fit for a queen.

And in a few hours, I'll be wearing the crown.

My hands still when I see the two glasses of red wine sitting on top of the vintage pallet coffee table on casters. It's not like him to leave anything out. I walk into the kitchen, but it doesn't look like he's been home yet. There is a small box sitting on the island, though.

A tiny yet very important velvet box.

I fight the urge to squeal and dance around. Instead, I calmly pick it up as if it's something I see every day. The box groans, and I glance around, suddenly afraid I'm about to be caught. The emerald-cut diamond is flanked by rows of smaller stones on either side. It's got to be two carats, at least.

I want to try it on but force myself to close the box and leave it where I found it. I'll have to work on my surprised face—maybe I'll practice it in the mirror a few times until it seems believable.

"Oh my gosh—Benjamin!" I whisper breathlessly.

It needs some work.

I've just picked up my bag when I hear a low groan from the main bedroom.

My mind races with possibilities—none of them good.

What if someone broke in and hurt him?

What if that second wine glass was for someone else?

It doesn't make sense, though. That's my diamond ring sitting on the island. If someone broke in, I think they would've snatched it up. And I'm sorry, but men who are about to propose to their girlfriends do not cheat.

I pad barefoot down the hall, my heart beating loudly. I push open the door and breathe a sigh of relief. Benjamin's just doing a home session with a patient—wait.

He's bent over the foot of the bed, breathing heavily, while a gorgeous man stands behind him. His dress shirt is unbuttoned, revealing a perfectly waxed torso. My brain scrambles to explain what I'm seeing. If this is a therapy session, then why is—

The man reaches down and strokes Benjamin's—

Oh God.

Thrusting. Groping. Moaning.

"Don't go through with this, Ben," he begs, his hands working him faster and faster.

Stomach roiling, I turn to escape, catching my elbow on the door frame with a resounding *smack*. I bring a hand up to muffle my cry, but it's too late.

They freeze before simultaneously turning toward the door.

"Jesus, Kate!" Benjamin lunges off the bed and scrambles across the hardwood floor, searching for his pants. "Don't freak out. It's not what it looks like!"

I note the company badge clipped to the man's collar, and my heart sinks.

No, it's somehow worse.

Because Benjamin isn't cheating on me with a random stranger, but a co-worker.

I'm a walking cliché.

A joke.

The laughingstock of Physical Therapy Associates.

Were they laughing at me behind my back? Poor naïve idiot thinks her boyfriend is being gallant by wanting to take things slow while he's busy screwing his assistant.

My cheeks burn with humiliation as I stumble back down the hall and out to my car. I make it three blocks before the numbness wears off, and I'm forced to pull over.

No love-making. No engagement.

Nothing but the soul-crushing reminder that no matter how hard I try, eventually, everyone leaves.

one

COMMANDMENT #2: THOU SHALL NOT MOPE OVER WHAT COULD HAVE BEEN BUT EMBRACE WHAT IS

Kate

"Tell me again, how long are you planning to drag this out?" Benjamin asks from his perch on the arm of the chair in my bedroom, restlessly fidgeting with his tie.

"I don't know," I admit while applying another coat of mascara to my lashes. "It's not like I meant for this to drag on as long as it has. I thought I'd meet someone else and—" I wave a hand between us. "—this whole thing would just work itself out naturally, you know?"

My grandmother called not long after I discovered Benjamin and Connor—*in flagrante delicto*. The words were right there, on the tip of my tongue, but I couldn't do it. She's had me on this pedestal since I was a child, and I can't imagine how she'd react if I ever dared to climb down.

The situation would be different if Nan and Pops were just our grandparents. But after my father's death when I was six, they were forced to become so much more. Over the years, my memories of him have grown fuzzy, making it hard to separate fact from fiction. I can remember his tattoos, specifically a spider web, and tracing the colorful ink with my fingertips when he would tuck me in at night.

My mom struggled to care for us on her own for a few years before dropping us off on our grandparents' porch when I was sixteen and my younger sister, Dakota, was twelve. Overnight, we went from struggling financially to being made to feel like burdens for simply existing. Pops tried to step in as a father figure, but Nan was adamant that her child-rearing days were over, claiming that mothers do not abandon their children.

Early on, I learned that taking on the role of mother with Dakota was the best way to keep the peace and avoid Nan's wrath. Nan became more affectionate if I worked hard enough to present our lives as perfect and lacking nothing. Knowing both were temporary, I did my best not to let her praise or criticism affect me, but I did try to stay in her good graces for Dakota's sake.

So, maybe it was wrong, but I was willing to go to any lengths to keep up the charade. I did some digging into Physical Therapy Associates' strict policy on workplace relationships between supervisors and subordinates—a violation that could cost Benjamin his job if his supervisors found out—before offering him an ultimatum. He would continue to attend family events and play the role of the doting boyfriend, or I would go to his company about the relationship.

It was a win-win for both of us. He'd keep his job, and I would continue to float merrily down the River Denial for as long as possible.

As a therapist, I recognize this is an unhealthy pattern of behavior likely stemming from a deep-seated fear of abandonment and rejection.

But if it ain't broke...

"This is it," Benjamin says with a sigh. "This is the last time."

I open my mouth, but he shakes his head, silencing my objection.

"No. Let me finish. I took a job in Colorado. Connor and I are moving up there at the end of the month."

My pulse races—not at the thought of him leaving, but at Nan discovering the truth. Sure, this was a temporary solution, but I mistakenly assumed Benjamin would be willing to play along for as long as I needed him to.

He wraps his arms around my shoulders and turns me to face him. "I love him, Kate. You and I—it wasn't right."

I swallow past the sudden lump in my throat. "But-but- you love your job! How can you just give that up?"

He smiles at me, much like one would a small child. "We need a fresh start. A training facility opened up this year—Survivor's Gym—and they need PTs and assistants. Plus, the owner, Travis, seems really cool."

"I'm happy for you," I manage, ignoring the sting of tears behind my eyelids.

Despite the image that's been forever burned into my memory, I mean it. Benjamin deserves to be loved for who he is, and we weren't right for each other. We were just trying to check off boxes on someone else's to-do list.

"Stop letting Norma Cross dictate everything you do," he continues, lifting my chin and forcing me to look him in the eye. "It's not like she's paying your bills, so stand up to her. Then, I want you to get the hell out of your comfort zone and find a man who deserves you —not someone you think she'd approve of."

I let him pull me into a rough hug. He's right. It's time to come clean.

First thing tomorrow.

* * *

"So, Benjamin, how are things going at work?" Pops asks, his fork hovering in front of his mouth as he waits for an answer.

"Actually, Richard, I've got some news—Aghhhh!"

I roll my eyes. Sensing he was about to blow my cover, I slid my salad fork off my plate and under the table, giving his thigh a gentle nudge. Not anything that warranted a scream like that.

"Good Lord, are you okay?" Nan's voice is filled with concern, but her expression remains neutral thanks to the sheer number of injectables in her face.

Not that she would ever admit it.

I'm honestly surprised it still moves.

"Sorry about that. Charley horse," Benjamin forces out through gritted teeth before turning to Pops. "And work is going well—really well, in fact."

I move to nudge him again with the fork, but he easily pries it from my grasp before I can make contact.

"I'm up for a promotion," he says, his features tightening as he turns toward me. "I'll be traveling to our affiliate offices around the state more, but I think this could be a good move for my career."

He's shown up to every Sunday dinner for the past year, where we eat off Nan's finest china and present a version of ourselves that doesn't exist in reality.

I'd run away to Colorado too...

"I hate to eat and run, but I have an early day tomorrow," I announce, pushing back my chair. The heel of my shoe catches on the rug as I stand, sending me and the chair crashing to the floor.

"Mary Katherine, what on earth?" Nan exclaims as she rushes over.

"I'm fine," I insist, my shoulders curling over my chest as I wave off her help. "I think my shoe was the only casualty."

"What is this, duct tape?" she asks, picking up the broken heel for closer inspection. The black rubs off on her fingers, and she shakes her head in disgust. "Did you color these with a marker? I'd say it's time to buy yourself some new shoes, missy."

My lips flatten as I admit, "I can't really, um, afford that right now, Nan."

As it turns out, my sister makes more with a high school diploma than I do with a master's degree, which would have been nice to know before I took on student loans.

"And that is why I have always told you girls that you have to work hard for what you want because why?"

"Because there are no handouts," I mutter.

Never mind that I've had these shoes for ten years. I got through graduate school by getting creative with permanent markers and tape. I can fix them again once I get home.

"Norma, leave it. The girls didn't come here for a lecture. Come on. Let's get you up, Katydid." Pops helps me to my feet while Benjamin grabs my purse.

Dakota gazes down at the intricate design on the rug, carefully avoiding making eye contact with me. Which honestly makes me feel like even more of a colossal failure.

"Hey," I say, limping over to where she stands. "I love you, you know that?"

"I love you more." She pulls me into a bone-crushing hug before lowering her voice. "Next paycheck, we're getting you some new shoes."

"Stop. I'm supposed to be the one taking care of you," I whisper, blinking back tears.

"You do."

It doesn't feel that way, though.

"I didn't realize things had gotten this bad," Benjamin says when we arrive back at my apartment building. "If I'd known—what I'm trying to say is that if you need money, I can help."

Most of the drive was spent in complete silence, which gave me time to contemplate all the ways I don't measure up.

"It's not that bad," I lie. Benjamin reaches for my hand as I'm getting out, stopping me. "I just need to up my patient load for a little while. Seriously, I'll be fine."

He carefully weighs his words before admitting, "Listen, for what it's worth, I did love you. And I hate seeing you like this. Promise me you'll call if you change your mind or need anything?"

His clenched half-smile and overall awkwardness are too much, and I offer him a tight nod before bolting across the parking lot. I don't want to fall apart—not in front of someone who's only being nice because they feel sorry for me.

I don't want anyone's pity.

By the time I reach my apartment, my bare feet are filthy, and I tiptoe down the hall to avoid transferring anything onto the carpet. I run a hot bath and turn on the small CD player on top of the hamper before climbing in, letting Mama Cass's voice take me to a better place.

As she begs her lover to dream a little dream, I swipe at the mascara-laced tears coursing down my cheeks and try to sing along. My voice is severely off-key, something that only makes me cry harder.

I cry until I'm hiccupping, and my nostrils are clogged with snot.

I cry until the water turns cold.

I cry until I can't even pinpoint what's making me sad anymore.

two

COMMANDMENT #3: THOU SHALT TRUST THE UNIVERSE

Kate

"He bent me over the island and lifted up my skirt before dropping to his knees like he's about to worship—wait. What was the question again?"

Carla begins every session by recounting how her husband discovered her affairs before digressing into her favorite topic.

Sex.

"I asked if you regret Jackie finding out about your affairs," I tell her before taking a sip from my coffee mug.

She mashes her lips together and offers a shaky nod. "I do. I was too blind to see what I had when I had it, and if I could go back, I wouldn't have wasted so much time being angry at him for leaving me."

Having documented this story more times than I can count, I doodle another heart in my notebook and once again question my decision to take Carla Snyder on as a patient.

It was meant to be a simple favor to a former therapist in our practice when she was offered a job in Denver. Amelia's notes indicated the patient displayed bipolar tendencies, but I'm convinced Carla is a textbook sociopath, and I'm just the sucker who got stuck with her.

"I love him." On cue, she sucks in a ragged breath and buries her face in a tissue—like Jackie's decision to leave the marriage is recent and not something that occurred three years ago.

Her performance might have been more convincing had I not heard various versions of this story in the past. In one, she wasn't cheating but simply trying to get a drunk man home to his wife. In another, the man came on to her and refused to take no for an answer. On more than one occasion, I've questioned whether any of these men exist.

To her, life is a game of chess, where every move is calculated. She might be able to conjure up a few tears for sympathy, but she won't feel remorse over her actions. She's just not capable of it.

"But he was so sweet. I could barely get out of bed and face the day, yet he was there, holding my hand through it all."

It appears we've moved on to the miscarriage she suffered right after she and Jackie got married. *Also false.*

There has been one instance in the past six months when I felt she was being candid with me. The rest have been rehashing a fairy tale that likely exists only in her head.

In that session, she admitted that she faked the pregnancy in a desperate ploy to get him to commit. Once they were married, she staged a miscarriage. She spoke in a monotone, reciting the details as though they happened to someone else.

"It wasn't easy, but I managed to wrestle the keys from him before helping him into the back seat. I thought I'd let him sleep it off—you know, sober up a bit before heading home to his wife because I'm a good friend."

And we're back to her best friend's husband, David.

How is this woman fighting men off with a stick, yet I can't get so much as a handshake after a lunch date? Even Dakota managed to find a man who resembles her favorite comic book hero just by going to the gym.

I nod at the appropriate times while Carla waxes poetic about her latest conquest. Then, I take a deep breath and envision what I want my life to look like.

Spiritualists call it the law of attraction or manifestation, but it's really nothing more than combining cognitive reframing techniques with creative visualization.

If I want to change the pattern of bad first dates, I have to envision exactly what I want and make myself feel as though I've already gotten it.

Positive thought. Positive emotion.

Like attracts like.

"I see," I murmur, both to Carla and myself. My thought patterns dictate my experiences. Instead of fixating on what's missing in my life and settling for less out of fear, I need to focus on attracting a man who is worthy of my time and energy. Next to the hearts and squigglies lining the page, I write:

Musts:
Clean-shaven
Dark blond hair
Blue eyes
Tall
Doesn't curse
~~Rich~~ Financially abundant
Helps people
~~Well-endowed~~ Has a big heart
~~Actually wants to have sex with me~~ Sexually generous and open to exploring new depths of pleasure with me

"So, I told him, 'Go on to Seattle, baby. Live your dreams. I'll drop you a line when this little one shows up.' Well, he took one look at my hand on my stomach, and suddenly, med school—are you listening?"

"Of course." I drop the pen and meet Carla's gaze. "Do you feel that Jackie would have gone to Seattle had you not been pregnant?"

"How the fuck should I know? I never had to find out," she replies with a careless shrug. "Can you believe back then he didn't have a single tattoo? He said it wouldn't be professional to start med school with tattoos. Graduated summa cum something but wouldn't ever let himself enjoy it. I mean, look at me. I graduated cosmetology school and had a damn good time doing it."

"Tell me about your time in school," I say, discreetly checking my watch when she's not looking.

Forty more minutes.

I run the pad of my index finger over the list. It's a good start.

Everything's about to turn around. I just know it.

three

Kate

I can't believe I've been wasting my time at Spin Cycle classes while all the gorgeous—and, more importantly, available—men congregate at Dakota's gym.

There's no sign of my dream man yet, but I have a good feeling he's here, just waiting for a dark-haired beauty to waltz in and sweep him off his feet.

Obviously, he'd have to do the sweeping. I'd look ridiculous doing it.

Maybe we'll bump into each other while filling our water bottles at the fountain. He'll offer an apologetic smile and insist I go first, to which I would reply—

"Dakota, who did you bring with you today?" The stocky man directs the question to my breasts while smoothing a hand over his Better Bodies t-shirt.

Not him.

I believe I was very specific on the height part.

"I'm Dakota's sister, Kate." I automatically offer him my hand, operating off the childhood programming that prioritizes friendliness over self-preservation.

"Kyle," he replies, grasping my hand tightly in his damp, meaty palm. "Were you looking for a trainer? I had a client no-show, so I'm available."

Dakota pauses her search for Thor to roll her eyes. "Oh, gee. I can't imagine why they didn't come—what with you being such a stellar trainer and all."

Ah, the jerk who got my sister hurt.

"I'm sorry. You said your name was Kyle?" I ask, wrinkling my nose when he doesn't release my hand.

His smile stretches even wider. "Yeah, but you can call me whatever you want to, beautiful."

He's a cocky little shit, I'll give him that. I wonder how many women actually fall for that line.

"Hmmm..." I tap my finger against my lip as if mulling over nicknames. "Doucheface has a nice ring to it, don't you think?"

Dakota claps a hand over her mouth, trying and failing to mask her snort.

He drops the smile and my hand before turning to her. "Real mature. Just because you weren't satisfied with your training doesn't mean you have to talk shit behind my back. Kate, how about this? I'll give you your first session for free; let you make an informed decision and all that jazz."

"Oh, sweetie. That's cute," I say loudly while patting him on the shoulder. "But I'd prefer someone who looks like he knows his way around the free weights, if you know what I mean. And one more thing. If you ever speak to my sister that way again, I'll jerk a knot in your tail so fast your head will spin. Am I clear?"

Kyle sputters through most of the alphabet, his face growing redder by the second.

Satisfied that he's been thoroughly emasculated, Dakota and I leave him gaping like a fish by the front desk and head for the stairs.

"I've been waiting for someone to put that prick in his place since I met him."

I turn toward the speaker and immediately suck in a sharp breath, feeling the blood rush into my cheeks.

He's definitely not the one.

Not even close.

I think I would remember requesting thick brown hair that's disheveled in a way only men can pull off without looking like they just rolled out of bed. Gorgeous, whiskey-colored eyes that soften when they meet mine. And tattoos... I would definitely remember asking for those. Every visible part of him, from the neck down, is covered in swirls of colorful ink. I can't help but wonder if the parts I can't see are adorned in a similar fashion...

But he's nothing like the man I conjured up on a legal pad. Everything about him is wrong, so why can't I look away?

"You have my eternal gratitude," he says with a low chuckle. My heart does a somersault when he walks toward me, eager to revise our list to something matching his description. "I'm Nate."

He extends his hand, and I latch onto it with a breathless, "Kate."

I feel like I just grabbed hold of an electric fence and wouldn't be the least bit surprised if the lights above our heads burst, showering us in glass.

Dakota taps me on the shoulder, but I can't hear a thing she's saying over the thrumming in my veins.

"Does it feel warm in here to you? We should tell someone," I murmur, gazing into his eyes like we're in a movie—one where the camera moves in on the couple, and everything else fades away. I've seen it play out hundreds of times but never experienced it for myself before.

Screw the list, universe.

My eyes roam over his broad chest and—*holy biceps, Batman!* This man could easily sweep me off my feet without breaking so much as a sweat. Thank you very much.

His brows furrow. "Are you okay?"

A quick glance confirms Dakota is long gone, yet I'm still inexplicably holding on to this man's hand like my life depends on it. I let go and try taking a couple of deep breaths to clear my head.

The weird fluttery sensation in my chest is perfectly normal, as are the thoughts of pushing him down on that bench and straddling him.

It's been a long time since I've been this close to a man. Correction: I've been this close to a man *who doesn't bat for the other team.*

An incredibly long and lonely time.

What is Better Bodies' policy on sex in the bench press area?

I take a step back and then another. Before I know it, I'm up at the top of the stairs in the cardio area while Nate stands frozen—and somewhat shell-shocked—below.

Dakota's on one of the treadmills near the back, and one look at her quivering lip and crestfallen face is enough to send my libido back into hibernation.

"Sorry for... whatever that was back there," I say as I climb onto the treadmill beside hers.

She continues staring straight ahead as if I'm not there, making me feel like the world's worst sister. Now I remember why I haven't bothered pursuing another relationship since Benjamin.

Dakota comes first. Dakota will always come first.

"So, what's the plan?"

She mashes the emergency stop button and cracks her neck from side to side. "The plan is to get through this workout and get on with our day. Come on. That's enough of a warm-up."

"I take it things didn't go well with Thor?" I guess, trying to keep pace with her.

"Who?" she asks, her ponytail flicking back and forth like an agitated cat's tail.

"Zane? Big Guy? The man of your dreams?"

"Oh," she says with a heavy sigh. "Him. Yeah, he acted as if he didn't know me, so it appears I'm the butt of yet another one of the universe's jokes. Cool, right?"

"Maybe there was a work emergency? Yeah, that's it. Somebody downstairs dropped a barbell on themselves, and he's working to free them. No one else has the strength of Thor, so obviously he had to step in. He's obligated. Blessing and a curse, all that strength."

"Yeah. Maybe. Let's just get this over with, okay?" She's trying to pretend he means nothing, but her wide eyes and furrowed brow tell a different story altogether.

"What's the deal with that?" Dakota asks as we take the stairs back down, nodding to where Nate hangs from the pull-up bar.

His mouth splits into a wide grin when he catches me out of the corner of his eye. He pulls himself up effortlessly before winking at me.

Okay, now he's just showing off.

The hair on the back of my neck rises even as I lift my shoulder in a casual shrug. "Him? Nothing. He was just thanking me for the whole Doucheface thing. That's all."

She nods at my answer and goes over to a stack of containers in the corner. "Yeah, I figured as much."

See? Even my sister doesn't see this going anywhere. It would be entirely out of character for me, that's for sure. Nothing more than a temporary lapse in judgment. Well, that, and he's nice to look at.

God, I want to do more than just look...

I shove my lustful thoughts aside when my sister, probably the most uncoordinated person on the planet, begins setting up metal steps for box jumps.

This is worse than the time Nan hid all the junk food on the top shelf in the storage room. Dakota waited until she left to run an errand and then stacked box upon box to reach it.

I came in just in time to witness her fall from the shelf with an armful of Chips Ahoy. She landed on Pops' toolbox, knocking the air out of her lungs. While gasping for her next breath, she kept a death grip on the cookies.

"Are you sure you don't want to start with something—I don't know—easier?"

Dakota shakes her head and flashes a confident smile. "I've got this. Seriously, working out has helped tremendously with my balance issues."

Balance issues.

Well, that's one way of putting it.

After watching her demonstrate her newfound agility by completing a couple of jumps, I reluctantly agree to join her.

"We're going to go to ten for this first set," she orders as though she's been training people her entire life.

Nate suddenly jumps down and begins walking over. My cheeks flame again as I try to think of something clever to say. I step around the box to meet him.

He runs his fingers lightly down my arm and I silently thank Dakota for picking this gym. Then his hand freezes and he glances over my shoulder. "You've got to be fucking kidding me. Stay right here, babe."

Babe?

I may swoon. The blood in my veins seems as confused as I am right now. One minute, it feels as if it's all rushing to my head, and with that one word, it begins moving south.

"David, you son-of-a-bitch. I've been wondering when you'd show your face here." Nate moves away from me and toward two men who have just walked in.

I give both men a once-over. *Seriously, do they vet the men who apply to work out here?* Maybe they only allow models.

I tune out the argument the three of them seem to be having, lost in thoughts of a gym full of fragrance ad models.

I envision myself throwing a diamond earring down in front of them and seductively saying, *"These have always brought me luck."*

You know, if I owned diamond earrings and looked like Elizabeth Taylor.

"What's going on? You were fucking my wife. That's what's going on."

I snap back at the word *wife* and stare at Nate's back.

Wife?

Seriously, Universe?

He's married?

Well, I'm glad I didn't give up my diamonds.

Nate continues talking as though he didn't just drop a bomb on me. "Yeah, you thought you got away with it, didn't you? Jess told me everything. You got her pregnant and then abandoned her. She's sitting in prison now over some bogus charges you leveled at her. She lost your baby in a fucking prison cell!"

I freeze as something pricks my brain. This sounds vaguely familiar. My rational side is demanding that I storm out of here, while the other is struggling to piece together how I know this story.

Maybe I saw it on the news?

The man with dark blond hair steps in. "Nate, calm down. I'm not sure you have the whole story."

Now, he's exactly what I envisioned. Blond hair and deep blue eyes. He's got a bit of scruff, but hand him a razor, and he'd fit the bill quite nicely. Maybe the universe meant for me to find him? I catch the glint from a wedding band on his left hand and sigh.

Or not.

"I divorced her knowing she cheated but never imagined that it was with this low-life. Did Elizabeth leave you over it? I hope so. I do." Nate seems seconds away from ripping off his shirt and transforming into the Hulk.

Gone are the second thoughts. I am now entirely convinced that Nate is not the one. The guy just screams emotional baggage.

No. Literally.

He is literally screaming about his baggage.

four

COMMANDMENT #5: THOU SHALT NOT DEVIATE FROM THE PLAN

Kate

I'm insane.

Yep. I should probably have myself committed.

Within a half-hour of meeting me, the man admitted he was married and divorced, and I'm now letting him walk me to my car. Granted, he wasn't exactly volunteering that information, but as loud as he was talking, it was a little hard to miss.

"So, are you seeing anyone?" Nate asks, his eyes hopeful.

"No, but—" I pull my lower lip between my teeth, debating how to address the elephant in the parking lot. "Your *situation* seems complicated."

He huffs out an unamused chuckle and shakes his head. "It's really not, and I've got the divorce decree to prove it. What you saw back there was closure. My ex-wife and I are completely done, though."

I look to Dakota for help, but she and Zane appear to be locked in a rather heated discussion.

"Let me take you to dinner," Nate adds, pulling me back to the conversation. We can start over—pretend that this morning was a fluke."

I glance back at Dakota. "I don't know. My sister—"

"Is old enough to fend for herself for a night," he finishes with a smirk that should be illegal.

As much as I want to blow him off—*because, hello? Waiting for the universe to send the man I requested*—I can't fight the grin tugging at my lips.

"You've got this all figured out, don't you?"

"Just need your number, babe. Then, I'll be golden."

I rattle it off before I can talk myself out of it.

"Got it," he says, entering it into his phone before checking the time. "Crap, I'm late, but I'll call you later tonight?"

"Sure. Have a day—a good day, that is. I hope you have a good day at work, I mean."

Smooth, Mary Katherine. Real smooth.

So much for playing it cool, as if giving a man my number is something I do often. I focus on a patch of concrete, kicking a stray pebble with the toe of my running shoe.

"Have a day," he echoes with another grin before slinging his gym bag over his shoulder. "Alright then. I'll talk to you later."

"Yep. Talk later. On the phone, that is. Not in person, obviously. Not that I don't want to see you again—I do. Why am I still talking?" A flush spreads up my throat and into my cheeks. Instead of fumbling my way through yet another awkward attempt at conversation, I turn and bolt across the parking lot toward my sister, with the sound of his laughter ringing in my ears.

* * *

I reward my three box jumps with French toast and bacon. It was one of the strangest workouts I've ever done, not counting when I signed up for a Bikram yoga class. Once the room heated up to the point I could smell the alcohol that the guy in front of me drank the night before, I was out.

My phone buzzes against my thigh, and I discreetly look down to see a text from an unknown number.

> Katy girl, it's Nate. You've run away from me twice now. I'd take offense, but I'm starting to think you might be as socially awkward as your sister is clumsy—yeah, I was there for the 'treadmill incident.' When can I see you again?

My heart beats just a little faster, and my palms grow clammy. While Dakota rambles on about something our cousin said, I tap out a quick reply.

> Kate: Maybe I'm just not into you...

He immediately starts typing a reply, but I ignore it and focus on Dakota. She's going on about unicorns, and I try to feign interest, but as my phone vibrates again, I can't help myself.

> Nate: Your eyes told quite a different story at the gym. I think you're into me, and it scares you.

I swallow past the lump that's formed in my throat. I want to tell him that he's quite the egomaniac, but he hit the nail on the head. I just don't know how to process what I'm feeling.

I channel my inner therapist. This is nothing more than a sure sign of sexual repression. I've been in a dry spell, so it makes sense that I would be attracted to a man who is the complete opposite of what I find ideal. Lust is clouding my judgment at the moment.

What if I didn't fight it?

Maybe I should take him up on his dinner offer, have a one-night stand, and then return to my regularly scheduled programming. Then,

I'll be ready for whomever the universe wants to send my way. I just need to get rid of these repressed feelings.

It's entirely out of character, but I'm twenty-six years old. I need to do something out of character or risk spending my life alone. If I were in a Jane Austen novel, I would have been written off as an old spinster by now.

With that in mind, I reply to his text.

> Kate: Maybe you're right...or maybe you're just a narcissist. I'm free tomorrow night if you want to find out which.

"What the heck is going on with you?" Dakota asks, narrowing her eyes at me over her forkful of biscuits of gravy.

My grip falters on my phone, and I narrowly avoid dropping it on the black and white tiled floor of the café. I've been conversing with her for several minutes, but I've been so caught up in Nate's texts that I couldn't tell you what we've been discussing.

I try to play it cool. "What do you mean? I'm eating breakfast."

She doesn't buy it and launches into a spiel about how our grandmother would react to someone like Nate. It's sobering, to say the least, but she's not wrong.

Nan would take one look at Nate's tattoos before writing him off entirely.

No tattoos.

No leather jackets.

No motorcycles.

No facial hair.

No nicknames.

Those have been the rules for as long as I can remember. I have always found them more than a little strange, yet I followed them regardless.

"Let's talk about why you—the queen of self-control—were blushing and stammering like you'd never seen a man before."

I rearrange the salt and pepper shakers as I mull her words over. "It's stupid, but it was just nice to flirt with someone, you know? Even if said someone is the very definition of emotionally unavailable." The lie slips easily off my tongue, but Dakota isn't biting.

"So, you didn't give him your number?" she asks, blue eyes narrowing in suspicion.

I turn to face the window, trying to hide the warmth in my cheeks. "It wasn't like that. I was just saying something to get him to leave."

She huffs out a laugh. "Puh-lease. You're going to respond to him when he texts, aren't you?"

I slyly hold my phone up and take a bite of bacon. "I already have."

"Of course you did," she says with a sigh. "Because only you can fix him, right? You'll tame his wild heart and get him to settle down. Then, y'all will get married and have lots of babies—babies who insist on stick-on tattoos to look like Daddy."

She laughs, but I can see Nate coming home from a long day at work and building Lego houses on the floor in the living room with the kids. I can picture him stroking my swollen belly as we lay in bed at night and squeezing my hips as I ride him, his deep voice calling out my name as he comes...

I shiver and contemplate telling him I want to meet tonight... or in the next hour if he has the time.

Screw what I said earlier, universe. I want that.

"Kate—no. Snap out of it. You're the smart one here. I was kidding! There is no way it would play out like that. Dude is still very much hung up on his ex, and that is not what you need in your life right now. It'd be like Benjamin 2.0, except with another woman and not a man."

"Enough, I get it," I say, swallowing hard as she takes a proverbial pin to my balloon. "It would never work, so let's drop it and finish eating. I've got my first patient in an hour, and I still need to shower."

I wait until I'm back at my apartment before reading Nate's text.

Nate: You've got yourself a deal. I should probably mention this upfront, but I'm never wrong.

Crap... I'm in big trouble.

five

COMMANDMENT #6: THOU SHALT KEEP THINE SISTER IN THE DARK

Kate

> Nate: I thought we'd grab a bite at the strip club and then get matching tattoos for our date tonight. Sound good?

I grin as I read the text before telling myself not to read too much into it.

It's just a one-night stand.

Knowing doesn't stop the butterflies from fluttering in my chest, though.

> Kate: Nah. Too fancy. I was actually thinking McDonald's, and then, if we have enough time, maybe we can hit up a biker bar afterward.

> Nate: You're the boss, darlin'.

"You just couldn't leave well enough alone, could you?"

"I don't know what you're talking about." I shove my phone in the back pocket of my jeans and put some plates in the cabinet, pretending I don't see my sister glaring at me from the other side of the kitchen.

I regret my decision to help Dakota move into her new place because she's spent most of the day trying to set me up with the realtor who helped her find the house. Well, when she's not sneaking off to make out with Thor.

So far, she's grilled Jeremy about his love life and admitted she's worried I'll die alone.

Real subtle.

Little does she know... been there, done that. He and I slept together after a chamber of commerce event, and I may or may not have dodged his calls ever since.

"I'm talking about Nate, Mary Katherine!" She drops a hand to her hip with a huff. "Covered in tattoos? Has ex-wife drama? Does any of this ring a bell?"

"Are you really lecturing me right now? Because I don't have to help you unpack."

"You're lecturing me now?" I raise an eyebrow.

She scrapes a hand over her face before taking a deep breath. "He's no good for you, Kate. We talked about it at breakfast yesterday. I don't know how you're so good at counseling people, yet you go out of your way to sabotage yourself. What's wrong with Jeremy?"

"He brought breakfast for everyone, Dakota. Please don't make a big thing out of it," I beg, feeling the start of a headache blooming behind my eyes.

"No. He's totally into you, and it's as if you're blind to it."

"Oh, I am very much aware of how Jeremy feels," I bite out through gritted teeth. "And I do not sabotage myself."

She cocks her head to the side with a snort. "Yeah, what would you call what you're doing then—self-flagging?"

"*Self-flagellation?* I guess I can say with extreme confidence that I am not flogging myself."

I want to shake her by the shoulders and scream that she has no idea how many times I've forfeited my happiness in favor of hers—the times I went without so she could have. "Also, who died and made you relationship queen? Zane pretended you didn't exist yesterday, and I didn't try to tell you what to do."

"That was more of a misunderstanding," she says, rubbing at the back of her neck. "And I'm not trying to tell you what to do. I just want you to be happy, and I think Jeremy could make you happy."

No, Jeremy would make *Nan* happy.

1. *Successful career.*
2. *Luxury vehicle.*
3. *Owns his own home.*
4. *He w*ears custom suits every day of the week, regardless of whether he's working.
5. He volunteers at the hospital in his free time.

Minus his beard and the tattoos he keeps hidden beneath those custom suits, he's perfect. But with his shaggy red hair and bright blue eyes, I imagine he'd have her eating out of the palm of his hand within minutes.

Jeremy is the whole package, yet no matter how hard I try, I can't seem to conjure up any feelings beyond friendship.

Zip. Zilch. Nada.

"Drop it, Dakota," I grumble as my phone vibrates. "Hang on, my office is calling. Hello?"

"Hey, Kate. It's Nicole. Listen, I've got an emergency session in a couple of hours, and I was wondering if you still have information on that new treatment facility up in Amarillo."

Nicole is more than just a co-worker. She's my best friend. We met during grad school when she was my instructor and have remained close ever since. Other than Dakota, she's the only friend I have.

"Hey, if it's an emergency and you can't do it, I understand. I'll need to run by my apartment and change, but I can be up there within forty-five minutes."

She laughs. "Ah, I see you're not alone. Let me guess... I know it's not Nan since you're not speaking to her right now. Dakota?"

I smile. "You got it. Let the patient know I'll be up there as soon as possible."

"Uh-huh," she says with another chuckle. "Call me back when you can."

I end the call before turning back to Dakota. "I've got to head into the office—"

"You're leaving?" she splutters before pointing to the stacks of boxes surrounding us. "But what about all this?"

"Sorry. Work emergency," I lie, lifting my shoulder in a half-shrug. "But I bet Jeremy could get these unpacked in no time, what with him being perfect and all."

"Biscuits and gravy, Kate!" she exclaims, throwing up her hands. "I didn't mean it like that. I just want to see you happy. You deserve it after everything you've been through. Just don't leave upset, please. I'm sorry."

I sigh and pull her into a hug. I couldn't stay mad at her even if I tried. No matter how much we bicker, she's always the first to apologize, and it's like she's eleven years old again, running after our mother's car, screaming, *"I'm sorry! I'll be better!"* as she drove away.

I'll never understand why my mother ran from her responsibilities and abandoned us, nor would I ever tell Dakota that she still calls to check in on us from time to time.

As far as my sister knows, it's us against the world, which is probably for the best.

"There's no need to apologize. It's been a long day, and we're all a little cranky. How about this? I've got some free time tomorrow afternoon. I can help you finish unpacking whatever's left, okay?"

"Okay," she mumbles into my hair, squeezing me tighter. "I'm really sorry I hurt you."

"We're good, kid," I assure her. "I'll see you tomorrow."

Zane stops me on my way out. "Watch this," he mutters before waving to someone across the street. "Hey, neighbor!"

Instead of returning the greeting, the man makes a jacking-off motion with his hand and goes inside.

"Wow, he seems... nice," I say, biting the inside of my cheek.

He raises an eyebrow. "Oh, yeah. I bet he's baking a batch of cookies to welcome your sister to the neighborhood as we speak."

"I don't know—" I pause to dig through my purse for my keys."—he seems more like a magic brownie guy to me."

"You heading out? Did the interrogation get to you?" Zane asks, getting off the porch swing to follow me to my Tahoe.

"Yep, and please. I can handle my sister just fine, thank you very much. Are you planning on sticking around?" I ask, fishing for information.

He really is a gorgeous man—all long blond hair and muscles. I just hope he's not stringing Dakota along with his hot and cold behavior.

"Is she still unpacking?" he asks, dodging the question.

"She was grabbing a quick shower—she said she wanted to wash the moving dust off." I pull my lower lip between my teeth as I figure out how to ask him about his intentions without it turning into an inquisition.

His easygoing smile fades. "Something on your mind, Kate?"

"I—" I brush my hair off my forehead with a sigh. "I just want to know you're serious about her. That's all. Dakota's been through a lot, and I don't want to see her get hurt again."

"Anything else?" he asks, moving his hands to his hips like Dakota does when she's got an attitude.

"Yeah," I say, jutting my chin up at him. "You break her heart, and I will destroy you. *Capisce?*"

He nods and holds the car door open for me. "Understood. Have fun on your date."

"As far as Dakota's concerned, I'm dealing with a work emergency and not having dinner with the gorgeous man from the gym at The Cellar Door. Oh, and we never had this conversation."

"What conversation?" he replies with a wink.

I think I like him already.

six

COMMANDMENT #7: THOU SHALT NOT DISCUSS THE EX

Kate

Modern rules dictate that a woman should always bring her own vehicle or have Uber on standby when going on a date or risk sneaking out of his house at the crack of dawn, looking like a wet koala bear.

Clearly, I'm out of my depth if I'm sitting in my SUV, researching how to have a one-night stand instead of sprinting to the tall, dark, and tattooed hunk waiting for me in front of the restaurant.

My one and only experience with Jeremy left a lot to be desired, so I'll take any help I can get, even if it does come from an article titled, *Fuck Like A Man*: *The Art of the One-Night Stand*.

I check my makeup in the rearview mirror before nodding to my reflection. "One night. You'll get rid of these repressed urges and be back to normal in no time."

Who knows, maybe I'll even find Jeremy desirable after this. It would sure as hell certainly make things less complicated.

As soon as I step out of my SUV, the fragrant scent of sizzling steaks hits my nose, reminding me I missed lunch. I pause to smooth a hand over my off-the-shoulder little black dress and adjust my cleavage.

One night or not, I plan on making a lasting impression.

Where my sister's curves are more evenly distributed, mine are more... top-heavy. During our teen years, Dakota was notorious for coming into our shared bedroom while I was changing. Instead of slipping back out, she would don an Australian accent and creep around the room like she was hosting a nature show.

"Crikey! We're going to be doing some exploring today. We've got some nice hill country with adorable little gazelles roaming about," she would say while gesturing to her own chest before cupping a hand over her brow and turning to me. *"Just beyond these hills, you'll find Mt. Kate. The terrain is rugged and treacherous, but the visitors never seem to complain."*

I smile at the memory and sweep my dark hair, styled in loose waves, over one shoulder before crossing the parking lot.

Nate turns when he hears me approaching, and I stumble to a stop, suddenly ravenous—not for a fifty-dollar steak—but for him.

"McDonald's wasn't taking any more reservations for tonight. I hope this is okay." His eyes move from my head down to my feet, and his throat bobs in a slow swallow as he admits, "You look amazing."

If I thought seeing him in a fitted t-shirt and athletic shorts was intense, it has nothing on the sight of him in a white dress shirt and black slacks.

It's one night.

Don't get attached.

His brows pull together, and I know I should say something to break the awkward silence, but I'm distracted by the way his shirt molds around his muscular frame.

"I could eat you for dinner," I murmur before grimacing. "I mean, I could eat dinner with you because you look very nice. Stop laughing!"

He presses his fist against his lips. "Let's start with dinner first, though, yeah?"

"Obviously," I say, trying to laugh it off despite the heat flooding my face.

Nate holds the door for me before leaning down to whisper, "So, not a narcissist. I'm glad we cleared that up." His teeth graze the shell of my ear as we approach the hostess stand, and I suck in a breath.

One night. I can do this.

* * *

I can't do this.

There's no way that one night will be enough. Nate is nothing like I expected, which is surprising considering I've made a career out of figuring people out.

Once we've ordered, Nate addresses the elephant in the room. "I'd like to discuss what happened yesterday."

I swallow a sip of water. "Yeah. That was interesting?"

He holds my gaze with the confidence of a man with no secrets. The only indication he's uncomfortable is the restless drumming of his fingertips against the tabletop. "First, I just want to say thank you for agreeing to go out with me. I get that there's a certain stigma surrounding divorce and a—I don't know—feeling like maybe you've failed."

"I can understand that." My fingers itch for my notebook, but this isn't a session, and he's not my patient. I settle for a nod and consider taking another drink of water just to give my hands something to do.

His shoulders relax, and he spins his water glass in a slow circle before adding, "It's like, you take on the role of provider and husband, and once it's gone, it takes this piece of your identity with it if that makes sense."

"Do you ever talk to her?" I ask, fighting to keep my tone neutral.

"Sporadically here and there, although I couldn't tell you why... which sounds bad."

"What about your mother?" I ask, scanning the restaurant for our server. This conversation calls for a bottle of wine... or ten.

"What about my mother?" Nate asks, glancing around as if looking for clues.

"Um, are you two close?" This is way too personal for a first date, much less a hook-up. Then again, so is any discussion involving an ex.

"Yes... are you close with your mother?"

The therapist in me is trained to avoid his question by asking him another. "And what about your father? Is he in the picture?"

"If you're asking if my parents are still together, the answer is yes," he says, rubbing the back of his thumb along his brow.

I nod absently, mentally trying to arrange the pieces in a way that makes sense. "How would you describe your mother—hard to please? Domineering? Overly involved?"

An overbearing mother who undermined his sense of autonomy as a child would explain why he felt as if he had lost his identity in the divorce. It would also explain why he continues to maintain contact with an ex who, from what little I know about her, seems highly toxic.

"Jesus, Katy girl. I expected questions, just not about my family. Are you always this inquisitive?" he asks with a forced laugh. "My relationship with my mother is entirely normal. She's pretty easy to get along with and lets her adult children make their own decisions.

I trace the wood grain pattern on the table with my fingernail as we slip into an uncomfortable silence. This is why I blackmailed Benjamin into hanging around for as long as I did. I suck at small talk and tend to jump off the deep end while everyone else is splashing in the kiddie pool.

"How about we start over," Nate suggests before reaching across the table. "I'm Nathaniel Davis, but everyone calls me Nate."

"Mary Katherine Quinn," I say, my breath catching as our hands connect, sending a current of white-hot heat through my body. "But everyone calls me Kate."

"Does anyone ever call you Katy?" he asks, pinning me with his intense gaze.

I shake my head. "Just you."

"Good girl," he says, stroking the inside of my wrist with his thumb. "Tell me about yourself, Katy girl?"

"W-what do you want to know?" I ask, distracted by the petting.

The corner of his mouth curves into a wide grin. "Everything. Like, off the top of my head, what makes you laugh? What makes you cry? What are you afraid of? Do you have a favorite color? Do you see yourself staying in Lubbock, or do you dream of moving somewhere else someday? Do you like getting dressed up and going out on dates with guys who ask too many questions, or are you wishing you stayed home?"

"Oh, I definitely wish I stayed home," I say, smiling so hard my cheeks ache. "That's a pretty impressive list. You really threw that together off the top of your head?"

"Completely off the cuff. Now, tell me something I don't know about you."

"Um, my favorite movie is *Die Hard*," I reply, choosing the least invasive question from his list.

Nate lets out a low whistle and leans back into his chair, crossing his arms over his broad chest. "Surprising me already, Katy girl. I did not peg you as an action movie connoisseur."

"What's yours?"

"*The Notebook*, obviously," he says with a straight face. "All that angst and longing really does it for me."

"Liar," I say through giggles, unable to recall the last time I felt this carefree. "Tell me."

"*Just Friends* with Ryan Reynolds," he admits as our food arrives. After assuring our server everything looks perfect, he cuts into his steak and asks, "So, what do you do for work?"

I scrunch up my nose. "Therapist. I counsel people for a living, find out what makes them tick."

He smirks. "There it is. I've been sitting here trying to find the connection between my ex-wife and how it could possibly relate to my relationship with my mother. Were you a fan of Freud, babe? Afraid I've got an Oedipus Complex? No, I bet you're more of a Karen Horney follower. I ended up divorced because of Womb Envy, yeah?"

Holy cow. The man knows his psychology.
Not only is he gorgeous, but he's smart as well.
And I am going to fall head over heels in love with him...

seven

COMMANDMENT #8: THOU SHALT NOT DINE AND DITCH

Nate

T his woman is going to be the death of me.

Nothing about tonight has gone as planned. The plan was to keep it casual and get to know her. But one look at her in that fucking dress, and suddenly I'm confessing things about my marriage that I've never told anybody.

When she began peppering me with questions about my parents, I naturally assumed she was unhinged. The pretty ones almost always are.

Finding out she's a therapist should have come as a relief. Instead, it left me with a hard-on that even Freud himself would side-eye.

"What about you? Wait, no. Let me guess." She taps a finger against her mouth with a mischievous smile, and my slacks grow even tighter.

What are you doing to me, Katy girl?

"You work as a tattoo artist. You loved art as a boy, but your father wanted you to follow in his footsteps and take over the vineyard. You turned to tattooing to rebel while still following your dream."

Damn. If the whole counseling thing doesn't pan out, she'll make a killing writing fiction.

"So close," I respond with a mock wince right as she takes a drink. "I have conflict with my father because I'm secretly in love with my mother."

She promptly chokes on the water. "You did that on purpose," she rasps between coughs. "Also, you might consider seeing one of my colleagues."

This is what was missing from my marriage. The mundane, nothing particular conversations that show you who a person really is underneath the surface. Jess and I had the physical aspect down but never could perfect the emotional side of things. By the time I realized things weren't what they seemed, it was too late. This time, I'm looking for a partner—someone in my corner, for better or worse.

What about Kate, though?

While she playfully diagnoses me with a variety of mental illnesses, I study her, trying to gauge whether she sees me as a casual fling or something more.

She tucks her lower lip between her teeth and smiles, and I wonder if it's too soon to ask for another date.

My phone buzzes against my thigh, and I fight back a groan, wishing I could let it go to voicemail. Unfortunately, I'm on call tonight, so I've stuck with water even when the conversation demanded something stronger.

"I've got to take this," I tell her before answering.

"Dr. Davis, this is Rachel at the transfer center. We've got a trauma case coming in."

"Got it. I'll be there shortly." I love my job—just not tonight. Tonight, I want to be someone who stays up late and gets to know Kate.

Kate's face falls when I return the phone to my pocket and flag down our server for the check. "Is everything okay?"

"Yeah, I'm on—" I stop myself. To her, I'm Nate Davis, a struggling tattoo artist and aspiring vintner. When I've discussed my career in the past, it changed their perception of me. Suddenly, all they could see were dollar signs instead of a person. "I've got to go. Family emergency. Can I call you tomorrow?"

She pulls her wallet from her purse and fumbles for her debit card, refusing to make eye contact with me. "Sure. Sounds good."

I place my hand on her arm, stopping her. "Hey, put that away, and let me buy you dinner."

Her nostrils flare, and she mashes her lips together before asking, "Was that your ex-wife?"

I hand over my credit card and wait until he leaves before turning back to her. "No, it wasn't. It's work stuff."

Kate's cat-like green eyes narrow to slits. "You just said it was a family emergency. Now it's work?"

I mentally kick myself. "It's our family business. The vineyard? Surely, you didn't already forget."

"Thanks for dinner, Nate," she says, getting up. "It was nice meeting you."

I hastily scrawl my signature and a thirty percent tip before running after her.

"Babe, wait up. Let me explain." She doesn't slow down, and I'm forced to grab her arm. "Wait, please."

"I don't know what this is, but I'm not in the habit of going out with men who can't even be honest about why they're cutting a date short," she hisses before yanking free of my grip. "If you're going to meet your ex, that's fine. But don't lie—"

I grasp her cheeks in my palms and silence her argument by slanting my mouth over hers. A better man would have waited until she finished, but she didn't seem close to a stopping point.

A soft moan drifts past her full, pouty lips as they part for my tongue. Her hands move to the lapels of my shirt, frantically tugging me closer.

"Do you think if I was going to meet my ex, I'd do this?" I murmur, nipping her bottom lip with my teeth.

She shivers and presses her fingers to her swollen lips before admitting, "I'm scared, Nate. I don't want to get hurt."

I tuck her head beneath my chin and stroke the goosebumps on her arms. "I won't hurt you."

I only hope it's a promise I can keep.

eight

COMMANDMENT #9: THOU SHALT NOT DRINK AND SEXT

Kate

It's been two weeks since the world's most awkward date. Two weeks since Nate left me dazed and painfully aroused in a parking lot after the best kiss of my life.

I might have assumed he was blowing me off with the work excuse if it weren't for the daily texts. And these aren't just any texts—no.

These are texts that no self-respecting woman should respond to, texts that leave me aching and take everything I thought I knew about relationships and turn it upside down.

> Nate: I can't get you out of my mind, Katy girl.
> I've got to see you again soon. The things I've
> got planned for that mouth of yours…

I blush just thinking about them before going back to rowing with a frustrated growl. All the pent-up sexual tension is taking a toll on my mental state, leaving me in a perpetual state of wanting that all the vibrators in the world can't fix.

Did I join my sister's gym to spend more time with her? Absolutely.

Do I scan the parking lot whenever I come, hoping to spot Nate's car? No comment.

Dakota's gone completely still on her machine, hands gripping the cables while she stares into space.

"Earth to Dakota," I sing when she shows no signs of snapping out of her stupor anytime soon. "What happened to 'We're rowing until our arms fall off?'"

She jerks and pulls herself forward before stopping again. "Why are we doing this to ourselves?"

I couldn't even begin to guess. Rowing on a machine is an incredibly dull workout.

"Agree. Pancake time?" I suggest with a hopeful grin.

She grabs my calf as I move to stand, tugging me back down. "No. I mean, why are we chasing after men who clearly aren't interested? I've thrown myself at Zane for the past few weeks, and he politely turns me down each time. You're hung up on a man who has an unhealthy obsession with his ex-wife. Why?"

My heart drops down to the rubbery mat at my feet. I've tried to accept that he's busy with work, but the truth has been staring me in the face the entire time. His ex is still involved in his life to some degree —he admitted as much at dinner—and I'd bet my next paycheck she's the reason we haven't gone out again.

Well, maybe not my entire paycheck, but, like, a couple of dollars.

Nate may be texting me daily, but I don't know him. Not really, anyway. I know his work is demanding, but not what he actually does. I know he's a damn good kisser, but not why he's kept in contact with the woman who broke his heart. And the worst part is, he seems perfectly content to keep it that way.

I swallow past the sudden dryness in my mouth as the universe provides a much-needed cosmic tit slap to the face.

"You're right—why should we wait around night after night, just hoping they'll show up and take us roughly against the wall while telling us what a dirty, dirty girl we are? If they can't see what's in front of them, then screw them! You and I are going out for drinks, and they can sit at home, waiting for us to call. But we won't because we'll be out, drinking alcohol and meeting new men— better men." I clear my throat, aware I said much more than I meant to.

Dakota's eyebrows are hovering near her hairline. "Wait—that's not exactly what I was—"

"Awesome," I interject, reaching for my water bottle. "I'll pick you up at eight."

And if this doesn't work, I'll recruit Jeremy to take my mind off Nate.

I'm getting desperate here.

* * *

"This article says tequila shots are the best way to forget your troubles."

"Seriously?" Dakota asks, adjusting her glasses as she leans over to peer at my phone screen. "That seems a little, I don't know, hardcore for our first time. I was thinking more along the lines of Coors Light or maybe one of those wine spritzer things."

"It's not our first time," I argue, despite agreeing with her logic. "We've had drinks before."

"A glass of champagne at weddings doesn't count," she mutters while tugging at the top of the strapless dress I insisted she wear. "Don't text Zane back. Don't wear the Deadpool shirt and jeans. I gotta be honest here. So far, I'm not loving 'Girl's Night.' I sort of envisioned something a little more—I dunno—fun."

That makes two of us.

> Nate: Okay, I'm starting to worry. Text me back… please.

I gnaw at my thumbnail before placing my phone face-down on the bar.

Not tonight, Mr. Davis. Not tonight.

"What'll it be, ladies," the bartender asks, his eyes dropping to the deep v of my dress.

I plant the toes of my heels on the footrail beneath the bar and lean across, giving him an even better view. "We're thinking of tequila shots," I say, toying with the ends of one of my curls. "But I might need a few pointers."

His grin turns wolfish as he grabs a bottle of tequila, some salt, and a couple of limes. He takes my hand and casually strokes the back with his finger.

"Lick right here," he says, his gaze darkening as he watches my tongue sweep over the skin. "Now, we add the salt."

"Yeah, that seems super unsanitary," Dakota notes as he pours it onto my hand, her nose wrinkling in disgust.

I have got to get some alcohol into this girl, or this night will be over before it's even begun.

"And then what?" I ask in a breathy tone that makes me sound like an airhead.

He releases my hand to pour the shots before sliding them in front of us. "You're going to lick the salt, knock back the tequila in one drink, and then suck on the lime wedge. Lick. Slam. Suck."

He runs his tongue over his lower lip as he says it, and I feel... absolutely nothing.

I turn to Dakota. "Ready?"

"I don't know," she says, pursing her lips. "Don't all the bad drinking stories start with tequila?"

"No, they start with someone being too much of a scaredy cat to drink a shot—"

"Take a shot," the bartender corrects with an amused grin. "Don't drink it. Just knock it back."

"You heard the man, Dakota. Just knock it back and live a little," I declare before raising my shot glass. "To not chasing."

* * *

My reflection moves in and out of focus in the bathroom mirror, and I grip the sides of the sink to steady myself. When the first shot didn't help take my mind off Nate, I ordered another round.

And then another.

What was it Luke had said—that tequila sneaks up on you?

That was the bartender's name, right?

Or was it Levi?

I wet a paper towel with cold water and press it to my flushed cheeks, silently willing the room to stop moving so I can think straight.

My phone buzzes against the scarred laminate countertop.

Nate. Again.

> Nate: I can come to you, or you can come here, but I won't sleep until I know you're okay.

Leave him on read. That was the rule.

But that was before the liquor turned my body into one large erogenous zone. Before tonight, I'd never understood the appeal of drinking. I always thought people used it as an excuse to act out and let their shadow side run free.

But I get it now.

I feel buzzy and relaxed and—"Horny," I mumble before slipping into a stall and locking the door behind me.

The warmth in my face migrates lower as I work my dress up over my hips and tug my panties down.

Torture.

That's what this man has been doing to me for two weeks. Torturing me with promises he hasn't kept.

I bite back a moan as I slide my fingertips through the sticky strands of arousal clinging to the insides of my thighs before deciding it's time for a little payback.

> Kate: I want to come for you.

For the first time, I'm free to say or do anything I want without repercussions. It's exhilarating.

I suck my index finger into my mouth and push my lips into a pout before snapping a photo. I could leave it at that—add the image to a hidden folder and call it a night—but I want him to hurt like I do.

> Kate: Tell me, is this what you had planned for my mouth?

> Nate: Where are you?

"Uh, uh, uh," I say with a grin before slipping my arms out of the straps of my dress. "That's not how this works, baby."

Feeling bratty, I yank the cups of my strapless bra down and tease my nipples until they tighten into aching points.

> Kate: Just thinking about your hands on my body...

> Nate: FUCKKKKKKKKK...

> Nate: Wait—is that a bathroom stall?

> Nate: Are you in a bar?

> Nate: Katy girl, tell me where you are right the fuck now!

"What's the matter, baby?" I groan, adjusting the camera angle as I dip a finger into my body. "Don't like being strung along?"

> Kate: See what you do to me... what you've been doing to me for weeks?

> Kate: But you're too busy, so I guess I'll just have to find someone else who's man enough for the job.

His reply comes through almost immediately.

Nate: You can tell me where you are, or I'll drive to every bar in the Depot District.

Nate: But know that when I find you—and I will find you—I'm going to take you back to my place and tie you to my bed.

Nate: Then, I'm going to take my time proving to you that I am the only man for the job.

Nate: Over... and over...

Nate: Katy girl, I'd go ahead and cancel any weekend plans you have because it's probably going to take a while until it sinks in that this thing between us is far from over.

Nate: We're just getting started.

I let my head fall back against the stall with a dull thud, feeling strangely out of breath. Not because of the texts or the images they conjure up. Not at all.

"It's just the tequila," I say, righting my dress, even as shivers dance across my skin.

nine

COMMANDMENT #10: THOU SHALT REMAIN CLOTHED WHILE OPERATING A MOTOR VEHICLE

Nate

> Nate: Last chance, babe. Where are you?

> Kate: You want me? Come and find me.

A second later, an image of a cocktail napkin comes through, and I pound my fist into the steering wheel with a low growl before making a U-turn. Thanks to the logo emblazoned across the front, I now know exactly where she is.

But that's not what has me on edge.

That would be the hastily scribbled phone number beneath the logo. "Who the fuck is Liam, Katy girl, and why is he giving you his number?"

It's not like I wanted to press pause on this thing between us, but with a full caseload at work, I didn't have another choice. Besides, the last time I put a woman first, it damn near cost me my career before it had even begun.

After finding a place to park down the street, I walk in and spot

Kate almost immediately. She's draped over the bar, chatting animatedly with the bartender. His eyes keep bugging out of his head. Given the way she's bent over, I imagine he's getting quite the eyeful of her cleavage.

Not as good as the one I now have saved to my phone, fucker.

I pick up their tab while staring the bartender down before turning to Dakota. "Do you need a ride home?"

She blinks up at me through narrowed eyes before shaking her head slowly. "Zane's on his way," she says.

"Okay, I'll just stick around until he gets here. Is that alright with you?"

"Whatever. Knock yourself out," she mumbles while scrolling through her phone.

"I need a ride... lots of them," Kate says with a giggle, resting her cheek against her fist. "Hey, you found me!"

"Told you I would. Now, how much did you have, babe?" I ask, brushing the strands of hair off her face as I peer into her eyes, searching for visible signs of intoxication.

"Not nearly enough to forget you," she admits with a soft sigh.

Well, that explains the empty shot glasses.

Once Zane arrives for Dakota, I lead Kate out of the bar and toward my car, still trying to gauge how drunk she is. She's not slurring her speech, and her pupils aren't dilated. And despite the sky-high heels, she navigates a curb and slides into the passenger seat without a problem.

"Are you mad at me?" she asks quietly after several minutes of silence.

"Mad?" I glance over at her as I merge onto the interstate. "Not exactly, but what the fuck were you thinking, Katy girl?"

She pushes her lips into a pout. "Is it the pictures? I thought you'd like them."

Like them? I fucking loved them.

"It's not the pictures," I force out through clenched teeth before discreetly adjusting myself.

Kate tracks the movement before observing, "It looks like you liked them."

"Mmm-hmmm—Jesus, Kate! What the fuck?" I gasp as she palms me over my jeans.

"It feels like you liked them," she says, gently squeezing my cock as if testing its weight. "A lot. So, what's the problem?"

This woman.

I don't know whether to tan her ass or pull over so I can fuck her senseless.

"The problem—" I groan as her grip tightens and try redirecting her hand to my thigh. "—is that you've been avoiding me instead of being honest about how you're feeling. And the drinking—"

"You want honesty, Nate?" she asks as she unbuttons my jeans and slides the zipper down. "How's this? For the past two weeks, you've dominated my every thought. And no matter how many times I touch myself, it's never enough."

"I'm sorry. Work has been—" I swallow and grip the steering wheel a little tighter as she frees my cock from the confines of my boxer briefs. "Kate, we can't."

"Can't what?" she murmurs as she swipes a bead of pre-cum from the tip. Once she knows she has my full attention, she brings her thumb up to her mouth and sucks it clean. "Mmm... you taste good."

Who is this woman?

What happened to the uptight therapist? Where the hell did she go? I could really use her voice of reason right now.

"Please," I beg. For what, though, I'm not entirely sure.

"Relax," she whispers, wrapping her fist around the dark, swollen shaft. "Let me make you feel good."

"I—" I groan as she takes me into her warm mouth. A car honks as I drift into their lane, and I jerk the wheel, fighting to stay focused on the road. "Fuck—Katy, sweetheart, you gotta stop!"

Instead of listening, she takes me deeper. I mash the accelerator to the floorboard as her throat convulses around my cock. The speedometer quickly climbs toward 120mph, and I can see the headline now: *Local Surgeon Crashes Car While Receiving Road Head.*

I take the next exit and pull over onto the shoulder of the road before letting my head fall back against the seatrest. "Stop, stop, stop."

She pulls off of me with an audible *pop* and looks up at me through heavy-lidded eyes. "Am I doing it wrong? It's my first time."

I mash my fist to my lips to muffle the sound of my groan.

Hold it together.

Do not come on her face.

"Just—" I take a deep breath and gently guide her back into the passenger seat before tucking myself back into my jeans. "Just stay right there. Okay?"

Kate jerks her chin in a nod before turning toward the window. I think she's pouting until I hear the deep breathing.

She's asleep.

Meanwhile, my dick's hard enough to cut glass over here.

Great.

ten

COMMANDMENT #11: THOU SHALT TRUST YOUR GUT

Kate

"Here we are," Nate says, helping me out of the car.

"Your house—it's, um..." I swallow hard as I take in the spinning metal shelves and bare walls, feeling like I'm on the merry-go-round from hell. "It's nice."

"Well, this is just the garage."

Thank god.

"Right. I knew that." I squeeze my eyes shut, trying to remember whether it was The Modern Gals Guide to Casual Sex that suggested complimenting a man when you visit his home for the first time or Nan.

Shit, what am I supposed to say—"You have a huge cock, Nate, and I appreciate you letting me go down on you?"

When Nate loops an arm beneath my knees and growls, "Jesus fucking Christ, Katy. That mouth of yours," I realize there's a possibility my internal dialogue wasn't so internal after all.

He carries me to his bedroom and tosses me on the bed before stripping off his t-shirt. I push myself onto my elbows to watch as he tugs his jeans down over the v of his hips, committing the sight to memory.

I knew Nate was in shape, but watching his well-defined muscles ripple as he undresses is on an entirely new level. Dark bands of ink wrap around his torso and trail down his thick thighs, and I don't know that I've ever seen a more beautiful canvas in my life.

His nostrils flare as he stalks toward me, and my stomach clenches in anticipation.

"Come here," he growls through his teeth, grasping my ankles and tugging me toward the side of the bed.

I lose my balance and fall back against the mattress with a breathless giggle. "I like seeing you go all caveman on me."

"Then, you're gonna love this, babe." He pushes my dress up past my hips and tugs my panties to the side before kneeling before me.

He plants his palms on the inside of my thighs to hold them open before pressing his lips to my skin. "Fuck, Katy girl. You're so wet for me."

I shiver under his intense gaze. I don't know what things will be like in the morning. There's nothing beyond this moment, with all the lights on and him staring up at me like I'm a goddess he wants nothing more than to worship.

He kisses the inside of my thigh, higher this time, before asking, "Is this okay?"

My lips part with a soft sigh, but I'm no longer capable of complicated things like producing words, so I settle for a nod.

His fingers brush over my clit before sliding one into the slick heat of my body, and my hips instinctively roll forward, seeking more.

"So fucking tight. You still with me?"

I bob my head up and down, but I'm burning up. I free my arms from the straps of my dress and reach back to unclasp my bra, tossing it aside with a ragged exhale.

Nate makes a sound of approval before burying his face between my legs like his only purpose in life is to please me.

I arch my back and moan against the hand I've clapped against my mouth, shuddering as his beard scrapes over my sensitive flesh. He strokes my tight bud with the flat of his tongue, sending goosebumps racing over my skin and tightening my nipples into hardened points.

My inner muscles clench and flutter wildly around his fingers, and he exhales a soft laugh against my core. "I think she likes it."

Like it?

The man is a damn sex magician. And his tongue—sonnets should be written in honor of his tongue.

He switches positions and tempos, and with a sudden sinking feeling, I realize the pressure building inside me isn't an orgasm.

Nope. It's vomit.

"Don't do this to me," I moan, pleading with my body. My palms grow sweaty and numb as the blood migrates south to my stomach.

Nate immediately pulls back with his hands raised and eyes wide with alarm. "I'm stopping. You're safe—"

I shove past him and into the attached bathroom, dropping to my knees in front of the toilet as the tequila makes a sudden and violent reappearance.

"Go away," I groan when Nate knocks at the door several minutes later.

He ignores me and enters the bathroom armed with a bottle of ibuprofen and a glass of neon orange liquid.

My dress is still haphazardly bunched around my midsection, and I tug at it before giving up and lowering my face back to the toilet seat. "I'm disgusting."

"Nah," he says, offering me the glass before sitting on the tile beside me. "Gatorade. It'll help replenish the electrolytes you just lost."

"What are you a doctor now?" I ask with a weak laugh before squeezing my eyes shut and muttering, "Oh, god. I'm never drinking tequila again."

"First time?"

"Yep. And last."

His fingertips stroke lazy circles over my back. "Almost every bad drinking story begins with tequila."

"Ugh, I know that now," I say, smacking my lips with a grimace. "I sort of hoped I'd be the exception." I take a couple of sips of Gatorade before lurching forward to retch again.

Nate holds my sweat-soaked hair off my face as my body purges the alcohol and everything I happened to have eaten over the past five years.

"I'm gonna go out on a limb here and say that you're probably not going to be the exception when it comes to tequila," he quips once I'm finished.

After brushing my teeth with a spare toothbrush, I swap my dress for one of his t-shirts and let him help me into bed.

I'll just wait for him to fall asleep before ordering an Uber to take me home.

His body molds around mine like a warm blanket, and I melt into his embrace with a wide yawn.

Maybe I'll close my eyes.

Just for a couple of minutes.

eleven

COMMANDMENT #14: THOU SHALT NOT STAY THE NIGHT

Kate

I wake up to a pounding headache and an unfamiliar room. Memories from last night come back to me in bits and pieces, and I bury my face in the pillow with a muffled scream.

I did that while he was driving?

And then he... and then I puked.

My phone buzzes from my purse, and I drag myself out of the empty bed to grab it.

"Hello?" I rasp, sounding like a cross between Stevie Nicks and Elle King. I resist the urge to belt out "Edge of Seventeen," at least until I'm back in the safety of my apartment. I think I've humiliated myself enough for one lifetime.

"Mary Katherine," my grandmother snips. "Is there a reason you're not answering your door right now? I've been waiting outside for fifteen minutes now. Did you forget our lunch date?"

"Crap," I mutter, glancing down at the oversized t-shirt I'm swimming in. If there was ever a time to panic, it's now. Instead, I lower my face to the shirt, breathing in his scent like I'll never get another opportunity.

Which, let's face it, I won't.

"Mary Katherine? Hello?" Nan's grating voice is like ice water to my libido.

"Yeah, Nan," I mutter while massaging my aching temple. "I'm here. Listen, I had a work thing this morning. I can't do lunch."

What time is it?

Who doesn't have a clock in their bedroom?

Nan clears her throat. "Why are you lying to me? Where are you? I'm coming to meet you."

I gasp and wrap the comforter around me while searching for my clothing. "Um, Nan—I'm not sure that's a good idea right now."

I find my bra on the nightstand and my underwear hanging off the lampshade, but no sign of my dress.

Jiminy Christmas, what is happening to my life?

"Mary Katherine!" Nan screams into my ear, and I pull the phone away, clenching my teeth in frustration.

"What the hell, Nan? I'm going to be deaf!" I cover my mouth, instantly wishing I could lasso all the words and put them back in my mouth. I've never talked back to her in my life.

Her voice is deceptively calm as she asks, "Where are you, Mary Katherine?"

Now's the time to be honest. Come clean about Benjamin and tell her about Nate. I look around again, but the house is silent. Then again, Nate's not here right now, so maybe now isn't the time.

The seconds tick past in silence. I need to tell her something, or she'll have the police out searching for me. I take a deep breath.

Tell her about Nate.

"I spent the night with Benjamin, Nan."

Or, you know, just lie your face off some more.

I close my eyes and wait for the barrage of insults undoubtedly coming my way.

"I hope you used protection," she says with a sigh. "Tell Benjamin hello for me. We'll just see you both tomorrow for Sunday dinner."

I hang up and stare at the phone in shock. Maybe I'm not the only one who drank too much last night. I fall back onto the pillow and throw my arm over my eyes to block out the late morning sun.

Everything hurts, and I'm dying.

And where is Nate?

I take his t-shirt off long enough to put on my underwear and then venture out into the living room. A quick check of the house confirms my suspicions—he's gone.

Maybe he leaves, so it's not awkward. I guess this is something he does a lot. The thought of him with other women has my stomach in knots. I find my dress on the bathroom floor and slip it on.

I catch sight of my reflection on the way out and stop in my tracks. I look terrible. My face is pale, and my hair is sticking out everywhere. I fish a ponytail holder out of my purse and assemble my hair into a messy bun.

It's not great, but it'll work until I get home. I imagine the author of The Modern Gal's Guide to Casual Sex would probably shake their head in disappointment, but in my defense, I didn't plan on going home with him or anyone else last night. I grab my heels under the bed and slip them on, resisting the urge to snoop through his things.

In my rush to escape the scene of the crime, I don't stop to question whether he has a security system, something I regret immensely once I open the front door and an alarm starts blaring.

Who sets the alarm when they've got a houseguest?

After staring blankly at the keypad for half a second, I bolt down the front steps. My heel catches on the last step and breaks off, sending me tumbling onto the sidewalk with a groan.

Knowing the cops are likely already en route, I plant my palms against the pavement and scramble to my feet. Like a modern-day Cinderella, I leave the broken heel behind because I cannot afford to be arrested.

Tears spill onto my cheeks as I limp down the sidewalk. An older woman stands on her porch, watching my speed walk of shame with a furrowed brow.

"Don't mind me. Just doing my daily run in heels," I mutter, angrily swiping at the tears.

I make it two blocks before I'm forced to ditch the remaining heel and pause long enough to catch my breath. There's a strong possibility my SUV has been towed from the bar, and I have no idea where I am in relation to my apartment.

There's a street sign at the intersection up ahead. From there, I can order an Uber or Nicole—literally anyone but Nan or Dakota.

A vehicle approaches from behind, and I lower my head, letting my hair form a curtain around my face. Maybe they'll see me and assume I'm someone from the neighborhood, just out enjoying a morning stroll.

Barefoot. In a mini dress. In one of the more prestigious subdivisions in Lubbock.

Yep, I definitely won't stand out.

"There you are!" Nate calls through the open passenger window. "I thought I'd make it back before you woke up."

He looks like a million bucks, while I look like I've been run through a trash compactor. I self-consciously smooth my tangled hair, avoiding his penetrative stare. "Yeah, I'm just heading home now."

"Were you going to leave without saying goodbye? Wait, did you think I left as like a—I don't know—a hint for you to do the same because—" His phone rings through the car's speakers, and he holds up a hand before answering. "Hello?"

"Mr. Davis?"

He switches to the call to his phone. "Yes, this is him. You can cancel that. Yeah, the door didn't shut all the way. Oh, it's—" he pauses to lower his voice. "Ringo Starr. Yep, thank you."

As much as I want to keep what remains of my pride intact, I can't help but ask, "Would your alarm passcode happen to be Ringo Starr, by any chance?"

He brushes the non-existent dust from the gearshift, refusing to look at me. "Maybe."

"And that would be because..." I trail off, my mouth lifting in a wide grin.

"Because... I like The Beatles, so sue me," he admits before rubbing his thumb over his lower lip. "Want to tell me why you're running away?"

My heart stills at the wounded look in his eyes. "I thought you left. I didn't know if you were in the habit of taking women home and having them show themselves out the next morning or what. Where did you go?"

He nods to the drinks in the cupholders and grabs a brown paper bag from the passenger seat. "Greasy food and caffeine, the cure-all for even the worst hangovers. I left a note next to the bottle of water and aspirin on the nightstand, but I'm going to go out a limb here and assume you didn't see it."

"Um, no, I didn't see it," I admit quietly, feeling like a complete fool.

"If you want to leave, I'm happy to give you a ride home, but I'd really like it if you stayed—"

I climb across the passenger seat and give him my answer by pressing my lips to his mid-sentence.

Nate is nothing like the man I envisioned when I made my list, but maybe the universe doesn't give you what you want.

Maybe it gives you what you need.

And I definitely need more of this man.

twelve

COMMANDMENT #15: THOU SHALT NOT TAKE A CALL FROM THE EX-WIFE

Nate

When I wake up, the sky is dark, and the living room is lit only by the soft glow of my television. I rub the sleep from my eyes and stretch my arms, gradually becoming aware she's no longer curled against me.

"Kate?" I wait for a response, but the house remains silent.

She's gone again.

I'd thought the movie marathon and cuddling on the couch would erase the idea that this was just a one-night thing, but it's becoming increasingly clear I should have gone with my original plan and handcuffed her to the bed.

Because I'm not sure I can give her up.

Having her here feels right in a way that seven years of marriage never did.

The sound of running water grows louder as I move down the hall, and I stop in front of the half-open door to my bedroom, releasing a rough exhale when I see the trail of clothing leading to the bathroom.

A cloud of steam billows over the top of the oversized shower, fogging the glass and obscuring my view. While Kate hums softly to herself, I make quick work of my T-shirt and jeans and gently place them on the counter before joining her.

"Found you," I say, careful to keep my voice low so as not to spook her.

She spins around with a yelp, her hands automatically moving to cover herself.

"Hey, it's just me."

The tension in her shoulders melts instantly, and she slowly lowers her hands back to her sides with a shaky laugh. "Sorry, I was trying not to wake you."

With a low growl, I push her back against the wall before dropping my lips to her throat. "You didn't, although you definitely should have."

She shivers and grips my shoulders a little tighter as I suck the thin flesh between my teeth. "Nate..."

The corner of my mouth lifts when I see the mark I've left on her gorgeous skin. *Mine.* "What do you want, darlin'? Name it, and it's yours."

"You," she says, blinking the water from her lashes before guiding my guiding my mouth to hers.

I trace the seam of her lips with my tongue, and she obediently parts them, letting me in. "Good girl," I growl, grazing her bottom lip with my teeth. Despite the rough nature of our kiss, there's a softness there that's been missing.

Kate watches through hooded eyes as I trace the pout of her lips and the line of her jaw with my fingertips before moving lower to her full breasts.

"Is this okay?"

"Yes," she hisses when I duck my head to latch onto the sensitive peak of one nipple before moving to the other. While she loses herself to the sharp pull of my mouth, I skim my palm down her flat stomach and between her folds.

"So wet," I murmur before sliding two fingers into her body. She sucks in a breath and clamps down around me like a vise. Before she can fully adjust, I add a third and thrust even deeper, and her eyelids flutter open in surprise.

"I'm—"

"Come for me, Katy girl," I demand, closing my teeth around her puffy pink nipple and changing up the angle of my thrusts. She comes apart with a guttural groan, shuddering violently as she drenches my hand in her release.

I suck her juices off my fingers and stand, wanting to beat my chest in victory.

Mine. Mine. Mine.

The word plays like a drum beat in my head as I lift her boneless body and notch myself at her entrance.

"C-condom," she stammers, placing her palm against my chest. "We need a condom."

I open my mouth, prepared to argue why we didn't need one.

#1: I need to fuck her bare, the way nature intended.
#2: See #1.

The thought of filling her with my seed and making her mine forever has me ready to blow. I'll dissect the pathology behind my behavior once the blood's returned to my head.

For now, I force myself to put her down long enough to grab a condom and wrap it up before sliding inside her wet warmth with a low growl.

My jaw tightens as I sink deeper, stretching her body around mine. It's taking every ounce of strength I possess to remain in control. I use the glass wall for leverage, reveling in how her green eyes lose focus as I lick the drops of water from her lips and chin. I don't know how long we stay like that. For all I know, it could be minutes, hours, or days.

"Fuck, babe," I pant against her mouth. "You're taking my cock so well."

An embarrassed flush sweeps over her face, and I squeeze the curve of her hips in warning. "Look at me. You. Are. Fucking. Perfect." I thrust deeper with each word until her head falls back against the glass, and moan after moan spills from her pretty lips.

"Right there, right there, right there," she babbles as her fingernails sink into the flesh of my upper back. "Please—"

Instead of going harder, I switch to slower but deeper strokes. She rocks forward to slip her tongue between my lips, and goosebumps immediately spread over her skin.

"Oh—" Her pebbled nipples scrape against my chest, and she cages me in with her thighs before coming with a hoarse scream.

I bury myself deep, bellowing words of praise as I come so hard I see stars.

Fuck. I've never had this before.

Kate continues clinging to me as I shut off the water. When I try setting her on the rug so I can grab a couple of towels, her legs buckle.

"Okay, I've got you," I say softly, carrying her over to the counter before reaching for the towels. When I turn back, she's sobbing quietly into her hands.

Fuck.

I sling a towel around my waist and wrap the other around her shoulders, suddenly struck by the fear that this might have been her first time.

"You're okay." I stroke a hand through her damp hair before asking, "Was this, uh—was this your first time?"

Please say no...

She offers me a soft smile before shaking her head. "No."

I feel a slight sense of relief, immediately followed by anger that someone else has seen her vulnerable like this.

That's not psychotic or anything.

"I'm sorry. I don't know what's wrong with me. I just—I didn't know it could be like that."

"Neither did I," I admit

"So, you're not a virgin?" I ask, peering down into her eyes.

She smiles through the tears and shakes her head again. "No. I'm sorry to disappoint you."

"I'm not disappointed. That was—fuck—that was amazing."

And it was. I was married to a woman for seven years and never felt a connection as strong as the one I have with a woman I met two weeks ago.

* * *

While Kate gets dressed and dries her hair, I try to find something for dinner. Unfortunately, my refrigerator is in the same sorry state as when I checked this morning.

"Takeout it is," I mumble as I search the couch cushions for my phone.

JESS: 10 MISSED CALLS

Jess: Please call me back

Jess: It's an emergency

My thumb hovers over her name, and I gnaw at my lip before stepping onto the back porch to return her call.

"I'm sorry," Jess says when she picks up. "I didn't know who else to call. It's getting worse. I passed out this afternoon and hit my head on the nightstand and had to get ten stitches at the hospital."

I check the French doors, watching for any sign of Kate. "I'm sorry to hear that, Jess, but why are you calling me?"

"The hospital won't release me without someone to take me home," she says, sniffling. "I wouldn't have called you, but I don't have anyone else."

Her voice sounds so small, and I feel like an asshole. I needed to pick up dinner for me and Kate anyway. It might not take too much of my time to swing by and get her on my way home. "Fine. I'll be there in twenty," I bark before ending the call with a muttered curse.

73

If I want a future with Kate, I need to cut ties with Jess. But why do I feel like she's got my balls in a vise?

The house feels strangely empty when I walk in, and I immediately head for the bathroom to find it empty.

The open window only adds to the sinking feeling in the pit of my stomach.

Kate heard everything.

thirteen

COMMANDMENT #14: THOU SHALT NOT HOOK UP WITH A GUY WHO'S CLEARLY IN A RELATIONSHIP, EVEN IF HE SWEARS HE'S NOT

Kate

"Katy girl, you've been avoiding me for—let's see—seventeen days, eighteen hours, and forty-seven minutes, give or take. I know why you left, but I'm asking that you at least hear me out before walking away for good. Please..."

I listen to the voicemail while gathering up my things to leave for the day, ignoring the painful tightness in my throat. It's one of countless he's left in the weeks since I left, but I'm not ready to talk.

Still, it doesn't stop me from replaying his voicemails over and over like a masochist. It's like I can't help but rip the scabs off and let myself bleed out all over again.

I've almost made it to the door when my office phone rings from my desk, forcing me to turn back. "Hello?"

"Your five-thirty is here," the office manager chirps. "As soon as he's finished filling out his paperwork, I'll send him up."

"Five thirty?" I echo with a frown. Are you sure it's mine, Stacy? I didn't see anything on my calendar.

"I added him in yesterday after Carla called to cancel. It should have synced to your calendar and sent you a reminder, but maybe there was a glitch in the system. The poor guy's been trying to get in for weeks, so it was perfect timing."

"Let me check," I murmur, pulling my cell phone from my purse. "Yep, here it is. Chris Brander. I don't know how I missed it."

So much for my regularly scheduled sob fest while listening to Celine Dion in the car.

I unpack my things, trying to pinpoint why the name sounds so familiar.

Chris Brander... Chris Brander... Chris—*that conniving bastard!*

Chris Brander is the main character from the movie *Just Friends.*

Nate's favorite movie.

Before I can buzz Stacy to tell her to cancel, the door opens, and Nate walks in, looking hotter than any man has a right to in his solid black suit.

"Hey," he says as he folds himself into the armchair I typically sit in.

I stay behind my desk, praying that it hides my wobbling legs. "You know I can't actually counsel you, right? Fake name or not, it just wouldn't be right."

He nods and leans forward to rest his forearms on his thighs. "I know, but I needed to see you. You won't take my calls—"

"Because there's nothing to say, Nate." My voice cracks at the end, and I swallow hard, refusing to let him see me fall apart.

"There will always be something to say when it comes to us," he argues before taking a deep breath. "

I can't. If I admit that overhearing him on the phone with his ex-wife was only part of why I left, I'll also have to tell him about my family drama.

Like my sister being arrested and having to reach out to my estranged mother for bail money only to learn she's in deep with the local biker gang.

Nope. I am nowhere near ready for that conversation.

There would be a Nate-sized hole in my office door before I even got to the part about Thor being an undercover cop who was investigating Dakota the entire time she thought they were dating.

"I've been a little busy," I finally say, which is technically accurate. "And I don't have the mental capacity to work out whatever we had between us. I just can't focus on that right now."

"Have."

My brows furrow. "What?"

"Whatever we *have* between us. I'm here now," he says before glancing at his watch. "And I've got an hour and a half to hear anything you want to tell me."

He gestures for me to sit down, but I shake my head. "Nate, I can't. My time is reserved for paying patients."

"Oh, I'm paying for this," he mutters dryly, the corner of his lip lifting in a slight smile. "I've been paying for it since I met you."

"I'm not a whore."

"Jesus, Kate. I didn't mean it like that." He rakes a hand over his face with an exasperated groan. "I don't think you're a whore, but I would like you to hear me out."

"Fine," I bite out. "The floor is yours for the next hour and a half."

"Will you at least sit down?"

"You're in my seat."

Nate briefly closes his eyes as if praying before moving to the couch. "How about now?"

I sit and cross my arms over my chest, pretending the heat left behind from his skin doesn't make my pulse flutter. "Go."

He nods before looking down at his hands. "Taking a call from my ex-wife was quite literally the stupidest thing I've done. Believe me, I've already gotten an earful from my family, and I regret hurting you like that."

"So you didn't pick her up?" I ask, pinching my lips together to keep them from trembling.

"I did," he admits with a grimace. "But I swear, nothing happened."

I lift my chin. "Yeah, I'm not interested in sharing. Been there, done that, and gotten the emotional baggage as a souvenir."

Nate moves around to sit on the coffee table in front of me before reaching for my hands. "Give me another chance. Let me prove to you that there's no one else."

He nudges my legs apart with his knees, forcing my skirt up toward my hips. Instead of putting some distance between us or calling for a time-out, I close my eyes and breathe in his scent.

I pride myself on my ability to stay in control, yet I feel like a ship caught in a hurricane he's around—entirely at the mercy of his waves.

His hands move over my arms as if trying to warm me up. The proximity is making my brain short-circuit. All the reasons for staying away from him seem ridiculous and petty when his face is inches from mine.

My downfall comes dressed in a suit and smelling like sandalwood. I try to remember what I'd planned to say to him when I first walked in, but my mind goes blank.

I wrap myself around his torso, pulling him closer. "I want you."

No. Bad Kate.

"Is that a yes?" he asks, tracing my knuckles with his thumbs.

"Yes." My tongue darts out to lick my dry lips, and his eyes narrow in on the movement.

"Fuck, Katy girl," he murmurs. "It's taking everything in me not to spread you out across your desk." His lips curve into a sly grin. "But that would be wrong."

The image of him taking me on my desk short-circuits my brain and leaves me aching with need. I wrap my fingers around the end of his tie and tug him forward to whisper, "Show me."

fourteen

COMMANDMENT #15: THOU SHALT CATCH FLIGHTS, NOT FEELINGS

Kate

"Remind me never to get involved with someone I met at a gym again," I snap into the phone while gnawing on a hangnail.

"Ooookay," my sister, Dakota, says, drawing every letter of the word out. "Seeing as to how Nate is technically the only person you've ever picked up at a gym and, like, the only relationship you've been in, not counting Ben—"

"Ben is completely irrelevant to this conversation," I cut in, about as eager to discuss my ex-boyfriend as I was to discover him in bed with the head of the finance department hours before he'd planned to propose to me. One year later, it was still too soon.

"Right, so why are you and Nate calling it off this time?" Dakota asks, a note of boredom creeping into her tone. Given that I've supported her through a break-up, helped her move, and then bailed her out of jail—all within two months—she owes me one.

Or a thousand.

"For starters, we have nothing in common."

Well, almost nothing. We seem to share an interest in having sex with each other.

On my desk at work.

At my apartment.

In the hot tub at his place.

But, obviously, I'm not about to admit any of that to my sister.

I clear my throat and thoughts before moving on to my next point. "Not that it would matter if we did after last night. I felt like he'd been off lately, but I thought maybe he was just busy with work or something. I should have listened to my gut, though, because do you know what I found in his bathroom cabinet?"

"Um, towels?" Dakota guesses, not even bothering to mask the sound of her yawn.

"Yes," I admit before taking a second to unclench my jaw and breathe. "But next to the towels was a bottle of perfume and a pretty pink toothbrush. How do you explain that?"

"Maybe the perfume belonged to his sister or mom, and they accidentally left it after coming for a visit? And there are a lot of men who like pink, so the toothbrush can hardly be considered evidence."

A male voice pipes up in the background, and Dakota explains my predicament with the same enthusiasm one might have when going in for a root canal.

"Here, talk to Little Ricky. He's a man and knows how they think."

"But I don't—"

"Hail Mary, full of grace. How's it hangin'?"

I don't want to discuss my love life with my sister's neighbor and new best friend. A man who shared the history behind his name within seconds of meeting me but was suspiciously vague when I asked what he did for a living. I want my sister to give me the same attention I've given her over the past twenty-two years.

"Rick," I force out through gritted teeth. "It's Kate. As I've told you at least a hundred times by now. May I speak with Dakota again, please?"

He laughs easily. "Nah, Caparina's gettin' ready for the gym. I hear there's trouble in paradise. Tell ya boy all about it."

For reasons I cannot fathom, Little Ricky refuses to call us by our real names. Dakota never bothers to correct him, though she obviously has no idea what Caparina means. Meanwhile, I've wasted more time than I care to admit trying to determine if his nickname for me is a football or Catholicism reference.

Against my better judgment, I lay out the case against Nate, starting with the nagging feeling that something is missing to finding 'female shit' in the bathroom, as Little Ricky so eloquently put it.

"And you're sure they weren't there before?" He asks after a brief pause. "You said he was married before, maybe his ex moved out and left some of her shit behind."

I consider it before remembering the most damning piece of evidence. "I also found a pair of panties wedged between the couch cushions."

He lets out a low whistle. "*Caparina*, get your *culo* back in here. Hail Mary's got actual problems this time—"

"What do you mean, *actual problems*? I'm not calling for fake problems."

He laughs like he thinks I'm joking. "Okay, Hail Mary. Whatever you say. Personally, I feel you need to take a chill pill most of the time."

"Don't tell her that," Dakota tells him before taking the phone. "Kate, what do you have for me? Do I need to add him to the list? Come on, a girl needs a name."

I massage my temple with my free hand. I should have called my co-worker and best friend Nicole instead of my sister. "No. He doesn't need to be on your list. Will you stop with the Game of Thrones talk?"

"Let me know if you change your mind. Ooh, real quick, have you seen our grandmother lately?"

In the background, Little Ricky cackles maniacally.

"Um, no. Seeing her isn't high on my priorities right now, kid. I'm still trying to come to terms with the fact she was stealing from us the entire damn time we lived with her."

"Thought so. Just one small favor? If you see her, ask her if she's feeling royal lately—maybe work something about me into the conversation, if needed. What do you think, Little Ricky? Implicate ourselves or work like the group Anonymous? You know, 'we are legion.' I think that might be more terrifying for her. Scratch that, Kate. Just ask her how she likes the dye job."

I groan. "What did you do to her hair? I thought we were going to discuss things before you began punishing people. I seriously just called for some advice."

"Uh, we discussed it," Dakota says, clicking her tongue against her teeth. "You didn't make the meeting. As for the advice? I'd say your chances of having an honest, long-term relationship with the man are about as good as my chances of getting back together with the undercover cop sent to ruin my life. What do you think, LR?"

"Oh, Hail Mary. You're completely fucked on this one."

I hang up with a growl and pace my apartment. Once, after one too many happy hour martinis, Nicole speculated that my father's death and mother's abandonment were the reasons behind my sky-high standards in relationships.

As much as I want to deny it, her assessment rings true. I leave people before they can leave me because I never want to feel pain like I did when they told us my father had died. I don't want to relive watching my mother drive away after dropping us off on our grandparents' front porch.

These were the same grandparents who would go on to steal the money our mother sent every month. The money would have been enough to cover clothes, cars, and college.

I stumble to a stop beside the couch, struck by the possibility that the twenty-five thousand dollars that appeared in my bank account overnight isn't an error after all.

My mother had been gutted to discover we never received a dime of the money, but to wire thousands of dollars to try to make up for years of neglect?

Never gonna happen.

If I call and report it, the bank should be able to reverse the payment. I gnaw on my bottom lip when it occurs to me that I could also do something completely irresponsible, like spend it.

After the crap with Nate, I need to get out of town and clear my head and heart. And what better way to get over someone than by taking a vacation—somewhere fun—like Vegas?

At least what happens there stays there, which would be a delightful change of pace from the neverending problems that seem to keep piling up on my doorstep.

Deep down, I know it's one more example of me running from my problems, but I'll save the psychoanalyzing for after the trip. To hell with responsibility and gorgeous men with perfect, orgasm-inducing dicks.

I deserve a break.

fifteen

COMMANDMENT #16: THOU SHALT NOT CONFUSE A ONE-NIGHT STAND FOR THE ONE

Kate

O h god, I did it again...

I groan into the pillow, unable to determine whether the constant buzzing pulling me out of a dead sleep is coming from my phone or my aching head. The harsh taste of booze lingers on my tongue, leaving me fighting a sudden wave of nausea.

Mistake. Such a mistake.

I swore that last time was the last time and now look at me. Just look at me—barely clinging to consciousness in a body that's primarily composed of booze.

The buzzing continues, and I peel my arm off the mattress with a soft whimper before carefully reaching for my phone.

"Never drinking again," I croak as I blindly swipe at the screen. "H-hello?"

"Kate?" My mother's voice sounds strange, and for a moment, I prepare myself for a lecture on the dangers of leaving town without telling anyone. Just as quickly, the more rational part of my mind sluggishly chimes in to remind me that I'm a grown woman who can do what she wants. Sort of.

"Listen, your sister's up at the hospital with Zane. He was shot earlier tonight, but he's going to be okay. He's out of surgery and resting in a room now, but Dakota wanted me to let you know."

I suck in a sharp breath and struggle to sit up before the pain in my head kicks in, forcing me down again. "Oh my god. I can meet you there. Just let me throw some clothes on—"

And get rid of the hangover from hell.

"Katydid, take your time. Do you need me to book you a return flight?"

"A return flight?" I echo, forcing my legs over the side of the bed. "What do you mean?"

"From Vegas," she says before quickly correcting herself. "Or wherever you are."

I frown, knowing it isn't a random guess. "How do you know—"

"That doesn't matter. Just get here, and we'll talk, okay? I love you, baby."

She ends the call before I can question her further, and I exhale a heavy sigh. Because I should have known I couldn't skip town without someone noticing. Clearly, she has people watching my every move.

As I stand, my shin collides with the corner of the nightstand, and I bite back a curse before stumbling over to the window. The strip is a kaleidoscope of colors against the still-dark sky.

So much for a weekend of irresponsibility and room service. My twelve-hour reprieve from reality—and men in general—is over before it's even begun.

I sigh heavily and shove my tangled hair off my face, catching several long strands on my ring.

My ring...

Time seems to slow down as I lower my wide eyes to the obscenely large diamond on my left hand, convinced I'm seeing things. But this is no hallucination. The gem winks in the light coming from outside, sending sparkles across the glass.

How? A sudden heaviness fills my chest as I try and fail to piece together last night's events.

"Fuck, babe," a deep voice groans from beneath the mound of blankets on the bed. "Never drinking again."

I fall to my knees on the plush hotel carpet with a strained gasp.

What in the actual hell did I do last night?

"Nate?" I croak, folding my arm across my stomach. "Is that you?"

"Who the fuck else would be in your bed?" he growls, kicking off the comforter.

I peer down at the offending object on my finger, feeling lightheaded.

"We—we might have a problem."

It means nothing.

Maybe I saw the ring and decided to use my newfound funds to treat myself.

"Yeah, we do, Katy girl," he says with a low chuckle. "Why don't you come back to bed so we can solve it?"

"I'm not—" I swallow past the lump in my throat. "I'm not talking about sex."

"Babe, we're in a hotel in Vegas for the weekend. Let's get romantic."

I inspect my left hand again on the off-chance the ring happened to disappear in the last ten seconds. "Oh, we got romantic, alright."

"What? What are you doing over there?" Nate rolls over and slaps at the nightstand until he finds the light switch, flooding the room with light.

I wince at the sudden brightness, blinking through watery eyes until he comes into focus.

The mattress groans as he swings his leg over the side of the bed and cracks his neck from side to side. After raking a hand through his medium-length dark hair, he stands with a yawn and stretches his arms overhead, either unaware or unbothered that he's completely nude.

And completely aroused.

The sight of his cock bobbing against his abdomen as he pads over to me provides a momentary distraction from the problem at hand.

On hand.

He rubs the sleep from his eyes and scans my body, silently assessing the situation before asking, "Are you sick?"

Worse, I think...

As much as I want to reassure him that, physically speaking, I'm in tip-top shape, I can't seem to find the words. Instead, I can do little more than stare in transfixed horror at the black titanium band on his left hand before an uncontrollable shudder sweeps through my body.

"No, we didn't," I whisper, shaking my head in a slow back-and-forth sweep of denial.

Nate reaches for me before visibly paling when he sees the ring on his finger. His brown eyes immediately move to my hand, and he swallows hard. "We're—"

"Don't say it," I plead before he can finish, hugging my knees to my chest. Saying the word will make it true, and it's not. "We didn't. It's just jewelry. It doesn't mean anything."

But the evidence says otherwise.

sixteen

COMMANDMENT #17: THOU SHALT SEEK ENTHUSIASTIC CONSENT THROUGHOUT

Nate

Fuck. She doesn't remember.

The woman who just hours ago appeared as sober as a judge was, in fact, so intoxicated that she'd forgotten our nuptials.

Which also means she was too intoxicated to give consent to any of it. The marriage. The spontaneous sex in the elevator. The mindblowing blowjob on the balcony. The—*well, you get the idea.*

Get to know her better... I said.

Take things slow... I said.

I glare at the marriage license sitting on the nightstand. I'm not a hundred percent sure, but eloping feels like the fucking opposite of all of that.

There has to be a way to fix this, but my mind is blank at the moment.

Well, not completely blank. It's helpfully reminding me that I know next to nothing about this woman or her family. I flee to the bathroom to splash cold water on my face.

As I take in the love bites on my neck and the condoms littering the counter, I can't help but think it's Jess 2.0.

"This is your fault," I mutter to my dick, still painfully hard despite having every reason not to be. "You get that, right?"

"Nate?" Kate taps a finger against the door. "Are you talking to someone?"

Just my dick.

We're finally having a long-overdue heart-to-heart. The bastard's been doing whatever he pleases without considering the repercussions.

"No," I lie before asking, "Are you okay?"

"Um, not really," she says, her voice rising. "I think I'm freaking out. No, I know I'm freaking out. Can you come out, please?"

Reluctantly, I open the door. I'd much rather stay in here until I have a plan.

"I can't remember anything—"

"Nothing?" I ask, trying and failing to keep the rising panic from my voice.

"No—well, I remember asking you to come with me and the flight here. I vaguely remember dinner... and then nothing." She buries her face in her hands. "I have to go home. Dakota's in the hospital, and Zane—he got shot. I never should have left."

I freeze. "Zane got shot? By whom?"

"Maybe in the line of duty?" she guesses with a shrug. "I don't know the details."

"Babe," I say gently. "Zane's a trainer at the gym, not fighting on the front lines. I know you had a lot to drink—"

"He's an undercover cop and the entire reason my sister was arrested for drug possession a month ago," she blurts out before slapping a hand over her mouth.

I thought Jess had drama. I also thought being married to someone who ran on chaos was the worst mistake of my life.

This though?

This is like Jess on steroids.

I need a drink—or, better yet, several drinks.

New plan.

Mainline whiskey to deal with this situation. I scan the room for the minibar. At first glance, the room appears to be without one, but my persistence pays off. It was disguised to look like a cabinet. Inside, there's a mini bottle of Johnnie Walker Black, and I don't even blink before knocking it back.

"Isn't that stuff really expensive?" Kate asks, watching me through wide eyes.

"Do I look like I give a fuck how much things cost right now?" I soften my tone before adding, "I've got the money to cover it and the room. We're good."

And that rock on your finger...

As if reading my mind, she glances down at the ring. "This has to be five grand, at least. Do you have the money for that, too?"

"It was twenty, and yes," I explain before she cuts me off with a shrill shriek.

"You spent twenty thousand dollars on this ring? Why? Why would you do this?"

I've been asking myself the same thing for the past several minutes. See, I'd always imagined my first big purchase being a condo in Vail or a matte black G-wagon, but the second I saw the ring, I knew I wanted it on her finger.

Her voice jumps from octave to octave, moving dangerously close to shattering the empty bottle in my hands. "Calm down," I groan. "It's going to be fine."

"Fine? Fine? Look around you, Nate! None of this is fine!"

Well, maybe not fine...

"We're married, and I know nothing about you other than the fact that you have a couch full of lacy underwear and perfume in the bathroom. You're emotionally unavailable, yet I somehow took that as a challenge. I've never met a tattoo artist who could drop twenty thousand dollars as if it were nothing. I mean, I've never met a tattoo artist, but I can't imagine they have gobs of money lying around."

While she continues her disjointed rant, I drop onto the edge of the mattress and rub at my throbbing temples. Jesus, it's like an ice pick to the brain every time she opens her mouth.

I chuckle. "Katy girl, I don't think I ever told you I was a tattoo artist."

She stops pacing and turns to face me, flexing her toes against the carpet. "Yes, you did. Our first date. We were having dinner, and you said—"

"No, you said I was a tattoo artist, struggling to break free from the shadow of my family and their vineyard. Remember?"

"But... but," she splutters, her jugular vein pulsing wildly against her neck. "You didn't correct me! You let me believe you were a tattoo artist! Why would you do that—oh god! It's drugs, isn't it? You're a drug dealer. I can't be around anything else illegal. I can't do it." She collapses into one of the oversized chairs, gasping for air.

A drug dealer?

Anything else illegal?

What the fuck is this woman into?

"Look at me," I command, trying to pull her away from the panic attack she seems committed to having. "I'm not a drug dealer, okay? I'm a surgeon."

She blinks rapidly at the news before shaking her head. "Stop. I know you're trying to lighten the mood, but a doctor, really?"

I stare blankly at her until her smile fades.

"Oh my god, you're serious. I—so you cut people open and stuff?" Kate's nose wrinkles as she says it. It makes her look adorable, something that's not helping my current situation.

"Yeah, I 'cut people open and stuff.' You seem disappointed. Would you rather I was a drug dealer or tattoo artist?"

Her reaction is not quite what I expected. It's the exact opposite of the response I've gotten from other women when giving my occupation.

She studies the pattern on the arm of the chair, refusing to look at me. "No. I—I'm just surprised, I guess. You just don't—"

"Don't look like a doctor," I finish, unable to keep the bite out of my voice. "Got it. In your perfect little world, Kate, it'd be unheard of for someone with tattoos to go out and make something of themselves."

"No, I didn't mean it like that," she pleads, coming over to where I sit. "I'm just incredibly hungover and extremely confused.

I dodge her attempts to hug me and start throwing on clothes. "Let's just get our shit together and get back to Lubbock. We'll sort this whole mess out there."

She sucks in a sharp breath. "When you say sort it out..."

"An annulment. It'll be like it never happened."

I see the devastation on her face before she can hide it. Maybe I'd consider staying married in another world where I never met Jess.

Kate and I barely get along now, though. This doesn't bode well for a long and happy marriage.

"An annulment," she repeats the words quietly to herself.

"What? You've got a better idea?"

She swallows hard. "No. I think it's probably for the best."

* * *

"Folks, we seem to be experiencing a bit of turbulence, so we're going to leave the seatbelt sign illuminated for the time being. Please remain seated until we turn those off again." The plane rocks forcefully as if to punctuate the captain's warning.

I left Kate in the hotel room and went downstairs to the bar, where I drank as much whiskey as I could stomach. The best part? The bartenders didn't chastise me about the cost or scream at the top of their lungs.

The cab ride to the airport was also uneventful. Kate sat silently with her body angled toward the window, which suited me just fine. The less we said to each other, the better. After spending a small fortune on tickets home, I left her at the gate and fled to another bar until it was time to board.

The plane could be freefalling from the fucking sky, and it wouldn't bother me at all. That stomach in your throat feeling? I live for that shit.

It dips again sharply, and Kate squeezes her eyes shut with a soft whimper. She's gripping the armrests so hard her knuckles have gone white.

"Kate, it's going to be fine. You know that, right?" I keep my voice low and calm. I'm not sure if I'm referring to the extreme turbulence or our sham marriage. Maybe both.

"Mmm-hmm..." She nods, and a tear slips from the corner of one eye. It catches on her lashes before dropping onto her cheek, reminding me of that night in the shower and weakening my resolve.

She shakily reaches toward me, only to drop her hand back to the armrest when the plane rocks.

I pry her fingers away from the seat and lace them through mine. "It's okay. Deep breaths."

"I'm scared," she whispers, keeping her eyes shut as more tears slide down her face.

"I've got you," I murmur, stroking the back of her knuckles with my thumb.

Even terrified, the woman is stunning. There's just something about her that brings out my nurturing side.

Kate continues taking deep, controlled breaths until her shoulders relax. Instead of releasing my hand, she squeezes tighter before nodding to herself. "Thank you."

Those two words change everything. Words bubble up in my chest

"What if we didn't get the annulment?" I ask, peering into her watery eyes. "What if we stayed married?"

She mashes her lips together. "Do you want that?"

"Give me sixty days. Sixty days where we give it a shot. We don't make any decisions until then."

The sudden smile that lights up her face surprises me almost as much as her next words. "Let's do it."

seventeen

COMMANDMENT #18: THOU SHALT NOT EXPECT EXCLUSIVITY

Kate

"Do you want to move your furniture or leave it for now?" Nate asks as he surveys my tiny apartment.

"Maybe a few of the smaller pieces?"

"I'll see about renting a truck," he says, tapping his phone screen.

I'm moving in with him.

He said that if we were going to try and make everything work, we should probably live together. I'm still keeping my apartment—he insisted I not give up my lease until we were confident it would work. It's a big commitment, but the thought of playing house with him just feels right.

If I work hard to hide the drama in my life, he'll see how good we could be together. I cannot fail at this.

It may be a trial marriage, but I can see it lasting forever. We just need to focus more on each other and not let the past get in our way. I am so much wiser than I was a few days ago. It's as if the blinders have been removed, and I can see our relationship more clearly.

I was jumping to conclusions before. As his wife, I need to give him the same benefit of the doubt he'll give me.

He lifts a box, and his forearms tighten.

That's my husband.

Dr. Husband...ooh, I like that a lot.

At least the universe honored part of my request—the man's a doctor.

He catches me staring and winks. "See something you like, Mrs. Davis?"

Mrs. Davis?

I could get used to the sound of that.

"Always, Mr. Davis. Are you getting hungry? I could order us some food."

He places the box near the front door and cracks his neck. Just as he does it, there's a knock. He shoots me a puzzled look, and I shrug.

Nate unlocks the front door, and all hope for a drama-free sixty days flies out the window.

Jeremy is standing there, holding a big bouquet of roses. I should mention that I hate roses. It seems I always end up getting pricked by the thorns.

Speaking of pricks...

He glances at Nate briefly before returning his full attention to me. "I was out of town on business when you called, but after hearing your message, I cut my trip short," he says.

My message?

"But I didn't call you—"

"Jeremy! It's Kate! So, I've been thinking... we should go to Vegas together. We could spend the weekend in bed, recreating our first date, if you know what I mean. Sex, Jeremy. I'm talking about sex."

In case I wasn't convinced drinking is the worst idea in the world, this voicemail has ensured that I'll be sticking to nonalcoholic beverages for the remainder of my natural life.

A muscle under Nate's eye twitches as he rubs at the stubble on his face before chuckling—not in a 'my wife is just adorable' way, but more of a 'trying to decide where to bury her body' laugh.

Oh, this is bad. Really, really bad.

"You called him first? So, what was I? Your backup plan? Cute, Kate. Real fucking cute."

Jeremy slides his phone into his pocket before approaching him with narrowed eyes. "What are you, her parent?"

Shit. Shit. Shit.

Nate mashes a fist against his mouth as if trying to rein in his temper is taking everything in him. "Parent? Try husband."

So. Bad.

It was almost as bad as when Dakota convinced herself she was Spider-Man and scaled our swing set. She reached the top and stood up in victory before promptly falling and breaking her arm.

"You got married, Kate?"

"Surprise!" I exclaim, weakly lifting my arms above my head and wishing the carpet would swallow me whole.

Jeremy's eyebrow shoots up, and he takes a step back, probably deciding how fast he'll have to sprint to outrun Nate. "Okay. Well, I'm going to go—"

"Better yet, take her with you," Nate interjects coldly. "You're the one she wanted."

"Nate," I protest, but he holds up a hand, silencing me.

"Nope. Go on. I hope you have a really nice time together," he growls before brushing past me and out of the apartment.

I'm not a fan of this side of my new husband. He expects me to hear him out when he calls up his ex. But, god forbid, he actually show me the same courtesy when I make a mistake.

Hey, Universe? I asked for a man who would fight for me, not pawn me off to the first guy who shows up...

I blink back the sting of tears and grab my purse from the side table before turning to Jeremy. "Let's go."

"Yeah, I'm pretty sure he wasn't being serious about us going out," he says, placing a hand on my shoulder.

"You think?" I snap, shrugging away from his touch. "I'm going to Dakota's. All of this feels like too much, and I can't—" My voice breaks off in a loud sob.

He pulls me into a rough hug, not freaking out that I'm getting snot all over his dress shirt. "I'll take you. You're clearly in no shape to drive."

Why couldn't I have just had feelings for him?

I look for Nate's BMW as Jeremy guides me to his car, but the parking space is empty.

"Maybe on the way, you can enlighten me about this marriage," he adds. "Because the last time I checked, you were single. Hell, your message last night made it pretty damn clear that you were available."

I dab at my eyes with the back of my hand before climbing into the passenger seat. "We got married in Vegas. End of story."

"Somehow, I doubt that," he mutters before starting the car. "Were you two dating, if you don't mind me asking?"

I stare blankly out the window, watching the headlights from passing cars as they pass. "I don't know what we are."

"Married, Kate. Married is what you are."

Touché.

eighteen

COMMANDMENT #19: THOU SHALT NOT BURDEN HIM WITH YOUR PROBLEMS

Kate

"Do you want me to wait here or go in with you?" Jeremy asks as he pulls up in front of Dakota's house.

"Oh, you've already come this far. Why not join in on the chaos?"

Jeremy locks the car as I run up to the front door. Before I can knock, the door is wrenched open.

"Oh, it's just you, Kate. Come on in." I'm not even sure how he's out of the hospital, but Zane stands before me in nothing but a pair of jeans, his arm in a sling.

I step back in fright, my heels connecting with Jeremy's toes. He grips my shoulders to steady me. "Zane, you scared me to death. Were you crouched by the door, waiting for someone to show up?"

He laughs easily. "You can never be too careful. Jeremy, good to see you."

Jeremy steps around me and follows Zane into the living room. "It's Good to see you, too, Zane. You're looking a little worse for the wear, though, man."

Zane sits down on the arm of the couch. "Yeah, I took a bullet last night. Do you want a beer?"

Jeremy nods and holds up his hand. "I'll get it."

I try to rationalize why the same man who got my sister arrested is now acting like he owns the place.

"Say it, Kate. You'll just combust if you don't."

I glare at him. "I would not. I'm just a little confused about why you're here." I look around the room. "And where is my sister?"

"Right here. Sorry, I was in the shower." Dakota's hunched over, running a towel through her wet hair. When she stands up to face me, I gasp.

Her nose is covered in a bandage; black and blue bruises peek from underneath. Her eyes are swollen and bruised as well. It looks like she was beaten.

She gives me a confused look. "What? What's wrong?"

I point at her. "Your face! What happened?" I spin around to Zane. "Did you do this to her?"

She starts laughing. "Kate, Big Guy would never do anything to hurt me—"

It's my turn to laugh. "Really? So, him having you arrested and charged with drug possession was just an expression of love. Look, I know that trauma can make things murky, but this man—"

She puts her hand over my mouth. "This man is the best thing that's ever happened to me."

Zane beams with pride, and I want to kick him in the shin. Jeremy wanders back in with two beers and takes a seat next to him on the couch. "What'd I miss?"

Zane leans over to him. "Nothing. Cap's getting to the good part right now."

I turn back to Dakota and shake my head.

"No, Mary Katherine, don't you dare shake your head at me. You're going to listen to everything damn thing I have to say. Sit." She pushes me into the chair and continues, "Do you remember Jackson?"

I roll my eyes and mutter, "Of course, I remember Jackson."

She smiles. "Good. That would have been a headache to have to rehash. So Jackson showed up at the gym last night and insisted I get in the car with him—something about Zane, I think. Anywho, so I got in the car, and it was a setup. He admitted that he was behind my arrest. He took me to his warehouse but wasn't counting on the fact that he was dealing with a woman who possessed the training of Black Widow. I disarmed Bill just as Zane showed up to 'rescue me.' I didn't need a hero, though—"

Zane clears his throat. "There you go again with the air quotes, babe. I thought we talked about that."

She purses her lips. "Yeah...right. Sorry. Zane showed up to interfere, and he got shot in the skirmish. It was a big skirmish—guns blazing. If I hadn't been there—"

"Dakota shot me, Kate," Zane says dryly.

"That's not been proven, Big Guy." Dakota places her hands on her hips in mock anger, and I'm glad I'm sitting down.

My head is a fishbowl of nonsensical information right now. Dakota's ex-fiancé kidnapped her and was the mastermind behind her arrest. The guy was barely capable of tying his shoes on his own.

"Was this part of your whole *'A girl needs a name'* plot? Did you shoot him because he was on your list?" My head hurts as I try to figure it all out.

"You had my name on a list, babe?" Zane stands up and comes over to her.

She nods. "Yeah, but that was before I had all the facts."

He leans down and kisses her on the nose. "I'm honored that I made your vengeance list."

I close my eyes and shake my head. Maybe I'll shake loose something that explains what I'm seeing because this is unbelievable. This kind of stuff doesn't happen in real life.

"So Dakota, you shot Zane—but who broke your nose?" Jeremy takes a casual sip from his beer as he reclines on the couch, one ankle crossed over his knee. As if gunfights and drug deals are everyday topics of conversation.

Her eyes light up. "Right, I can't believe I left that part out. I broke my own nose. Jackson got to waving the gun around like a moron, and I stumbled over my own two feet. I made close friends with the gravel."

Jeremy nods and takes another drink.

Maybe I need a drink to make sense of all of this. I leave the three in the living room and walk into the kitchen. My mother and Little Ricky are sitting at the kitchen table, watching something on his phone. A bowl of cereal sits in front of him.

He laughs and takes a big bite before noticing me. "Holy shit, Hail Mary. I thought I heard you in there. How's it hanging?"

My mother smiles nervously.

"What are you two doing here?" I'm confused enough as it is. I don't know that I'm mentally capable of handling anything else tonight.

"Hail Mary, I'm always here. You know that." He rubs his flat stomach. "I got a little hungry, and Caparina has the best cereal. What are you doing here?"

I place my hands on the kitchen counter and lean over, using it to support myself. "I—are you high?"

"Kate, asking people if they're high is not polite," Mama chastises.

"I'll get to you in a minute. Little Ricky, answer the question."

He takes another big bite, elaborately licking milk off his lip. "Hail Mary, I was up late last night working and couldn't relax, so I partook of the herb. It's all-natural, with none of the harsh side effects of Ambien."

I slide down the front of the fridge and hug my knees to my chest. "This is psychosis—disorganized thinking and hallucinations."

"Is she talking to herself, Celia? Hail Mary, you're thinking of peyote—not psychosis." Little Ricky pauses something on his phone.

"You said you were working late. What were you doing?"

My mother places her hand on his arm and shakes her head. "Don't."

He grins widely and then places his hand where she can't see it—

his thumb and pointer finger in the shape of a gun. The blood leaves my head, and I slump forward, trying not to pass out.

Dakota walks in and stares at me. "Come on, Kate. Quit moping on the floor."

I stare incredulously at her. "You're joking, right? You were so upset with me earlier, and now you're acting like all this is fine. You shot your boyfriend after getting kidnapped. Mama is watching cat videos with the stoner over here. I'm sorry, I'm having difficulty keeping up with everything in front of me."

Maybe I should place myself under a mandatory seventy-two-hour hold or until I can make sense of my life, whichever comes first.

Little Ricky takes another bite of cereal, oblivious to everything around him. "Caparina's emotions will be all over the place until the second trimester."

Second trimester?

I look up at Dakota, and she bites her lip. "I was going to tell you..."

Well, Zane's presence makes a lot more sense. So, there's one thing I've managed to piece together. The enormity of it hits me, and I start crying. "How? When?"

She sits down next to me. "I found out last night in the ER, and when two people really love each other—"

I hold up my hand. "Stop. I get it."

She's only twenty-two. Zane hasn't been in the picture that long. What if she ends up like our mother, raising kids alone because Zane takes off? Or worse, gets killed in the line of duty? My dad dying was so hard on us financially.

I'd have to support her and the baby.

Sweat breaks out on my forehead, and I focus on breathing to keep from hyperventilating.

"Kate, I have something I want to discuss with you." Mama stands up and comes over.

Just as she opens her mouth, Jeremy and Zane walk in. Dakota's kitchen was barely made for two people to fit. We've managed to cram in six.

Jeremy looks over and gives me a sad smile. "Kate told you guys she got married in Vegas, yeah?"

Why?

Universe, I thought we had a good thing going...

My mother pats my back lightly. "You got married, Kate?"

I place my head on my knees and suck in a ragged breath.

Dakota stands up and goes over to Jeremy. "Congrats. I have a brother now."

Little Ricky cracks up and mutters under his breath. "You're so dead, Jarvis."

He's obviously talking to himself.

I'm about to that point myself.

When Dakota hugs Jeremy, he shoots me a panicked look and blurts out, "She didn't marry me..."

Dakota whirls on her heel and stares daggers at me. "God of thunder, Kate. Tell me you didn't do something as stupid as marrying that asshole!"

I stand up. "Well, it's time for me to go."

She shoves a hand into my chest, and I wince. "No, you don't, Mary Katherine. I need details!"

I grind my teeth together. "You just called my husband an asshole, Dakota. You don't get to make demands now. Jeremy, let's go."

"If you're married to Nate, why are you here with Jeremy?"

I grab my purse from her coffee table, ignoring her on my way to the front door.

"Kate, stop. Don't leave like this. Let's talk. You can tell me how the wedding was."

She tries to stop me, and I shrug her off.

"Kate—Dad's alive."

I stop and turn back. Everyone is standing around Dakota. Mama nods as if confirming everything.

"My dad died," I say the words slowly, hoping the truth will sink in.

Mama shakes her head, and Little Ricky laughs. "Nah, Hail Mary. Your padre is my boss."

Oh my god.

My dad is the president of the motorcycle club. I look at my mother. "So, your husband is my dad?"

She nods. "Kate, I wanted to tell you—"

I shake my head. "Wow, I'm hearing a lot of that tonight. I need to get out of here."

This means that my father is an incredibly dangerous man. This is so much worse than I previously thought.

I kick off my broken-down heels and run out into the front yard with Jeremy right behind me. He tries to grab my arm but misses and grabs the strap of my tank top, ripping it.

It's the final straw in what's been an absolute banner day.

I sink onto the damp grass and wail. Jeremy scoops me up in his arms and carries me to his car.

"It's alright, Kate. I'll get you home." His words are just another reminder that I'm not even sure where home is anymore.

I cry into his chest. "It should've been you. It would've been so much easier if it were you."

He buckles me in and then goes around to get into the driver's seat. "Easier isn't always better, Kate."

I sniffle. "You just heard all that, and you're not fazed by it. Nate would have run immediately."

Jeremy doesn't take his eyes off the road. "Every family has baggage. This is real life—I've yet to meet a perfect family. You've just got to find the person you don't mind sharing the baggage with."

I nod and continue weeping silently. My emotions are all over the place. I need a solid eight hours of sleep and then a couple of pots of coffee.

He clears his throat. "How long have you been in love with Nate?"

I'm distracted when I blurt out, "Since the moment I met him." I then cover my mouth and shake my head. "I mean, I'm not in love with him. I don't know why I said that. We couldn't even make dating work—"

He cuts me off. "Kate, I saw the way you looked at him tonight. You never looked at me like that. You love him."

I can't love him.

I hate him.

Don't I?

* * *

I slip my key into the lock with shaking hands. I can't stop crying. I've tried, but my body is insistent on purging. Jeremy offered to come up and stay with me, but I needed to be alone.

Nate leaps off the couch as I flip on the light, and I scream in terror.

"It's just me." He blearily blinks at me, and then his eyes widen.

I hastily wipe at my tears as he stalks over to me.

"Jesus Christ, Kate! Did he touch you? Are you hurt?" He begins running his hands up and down my arms, and I start crying again.

"Talk to me, babe. Did that motherfucker hurt you? I never should have left you. It was a dick move." He fingers the strap of my tank, and I realize how I must look.

I place my hand over his. "It's not what you think. He was trying to stop me from running out of my sister's house, but he accidentally caught my shirt." I hiccup as another sob forces its way out.

He holds me at arm's length. "And you were running out of your sister's house because…"

I take a shaky breath. "Because of my d-d-dad." I lose control of my emotions again, and he pulls me into his chest.

"Okay, babe. You're going to have to start at the beginning."

I wipe at my runny nose and streaming eyes. "I can't, Nate. You'll just leave. It's too much—even I can barely wrap my mind around it."

He leads me over to the couch and covers me with a blanket. "Did we or did we not promise for better or worse, Katy girl?"

I stare blankly at him. "I don't know, Nate. I can't even remember getting married."

He cracks a small smile. "Fair enough. I do recall that most wedding vows include those lines. So, humor me, and tell me what's got you so upset—before I decide to track down the asshole who ripped my wife's shirt and beat the shit out of him, accident or not."

My pulse quickens at his words. "Jeremy didn't mean to do it."

He nods. "Yeah, you've said that. It doesn't change how I feel. Start talking, babe. I've got to be in surgery all day Monday, and a broken hand will make my job a hell of a lot harder."

I take a deep breath. There it is again—this urge to pour my heart out. I don't understand it. When I told him Dakota had been in jail, he bolted from our hotel room as if it was on fire. There's no way I can tell him everything I learned tonight.

He'd never stay.

I just got the sweet side of him back—and call me selfish, but I want more. I like this protective husband, hell-bent on ensuring his wife is okay. I don't want the guy who sees me as nothing but baggage —or, god forbid, his ex-wife.

I need to save the drama for my mama—or father, as the case may be.

I bite my lip and try to organize my thoughts. "My dad passed away when I was young. Since the stuff with Dakota, my mother's been—around more. I don't know what it was about tonight that triggered all of this, but the grief just washed over me. I'm sorry I worried you; I'm just a wreck."

It sounded a lot better in my head.

Nate surprises me by pulling me back into his chest and squeezing my back. "Oh, Katy girl. God, I fucked up tonight. I all but shoved you into that prick's arms. Then you had to deal with your grief alone—"

"Well, Jeremy was there—"

He cuts me off. "Like I said, you were all alone. I'm sorry I reacted like I did; old habits die hard."

He holds me on the couch until my tears dry and my breathing returns to normal.

"Let's get you to bed." He lifts me in his arms and carries me into the bedroom. Suddenly, sleep is the furthest thing from my mind.

He sets me down near the foot of the bed, and I begin stripping off my clothes as I walk over to the dresser.

"Babe, what the hell are you doing?" His voice doesn't sound as steady as it did in the living room.

I look over my shoulder. "I'm changing into my PJs... what are you doing?"

With that, I unfasten my bra and drop it on the dresser, taking my time to find something to sleep in.

He sits down on the bed. "Uh...same."

My jeans are the next to go, and Nate leans forward as if hypnotized.

I place a hand on my hip. "You're not changing..."

He doesn't say a word as he reaches behind his head and pulls his shirt off in a way that only men seem capable of doing. Then he stands up and unfastens his jeans, slowly working them down over his hips.

I bite my lip to keep from grinning when he kicks them across the carpet. With the way his boxer briefs are tented, there is no denying that I affect him.

I lose all interest in finding clothes and move closer to him, needing to touch his skin. My fingers lightly stroking his pecs is enough to break his trance, and he roughly grabs my wrists.

"Let's stop for a second."

I croak out a weak "Okay" before sinking into the comforter.

He begins pacing in front of me. "I just want to slow things down and get to know you better," he says.

I gesture toward his boxer briefs. "Are you sure about that?"

He groans and runs his hands through his hair. "No, Kate. I'm not sure, but I already know you physically. I know you have a freckle right here—" He touches the spot under my left breast. "And I know how you like me to touch you—" His hand drops down my stomach, and my pulse quickens. "I know the sounds you make when you're close."

His fingers slip under the lace band of my panties before he pauses.

The blood rushes in my ears, and I give a small moan. Nate smirks at me. I'm close, but he's not even touching me yet.

He pulls his hand free and takes a step back. "You know what I don't know?"

I shake my head, drunk from his touch.

"I don't know what you were like as a kid...what your favorite food is...your best friend growing up. Any man can fuck you; I want to know you. I want to own your secrets. If we want this to work, we've got to take things slow, yeah? Let's focus on the next sixty days, though—get to know each other."

I nod, still not entirely sure what I've just agreed to.

He confidently walks over to my dresser and tosses me a tank top and shorts. Once I've changed and gotten under the covers, he slides in behind me, pulling me back against his chest.

His lips press gently against my temple. "I'm sorry about your dad, Katy girl. I would have liked to have met him and done this whole thing properly, you know?"

"Yeah," I whisper the words because I'm afraid the truth will slip out if I speak any louder.

He wraps his arm around my waist. "We make quite the pair, you and me. I've never lost anyone close to me like you have, but I know about loss. Sometimes, the littlest things just break you, reminding you of what you had. The scars you thought were healed are ripped wide open again. You try to tell yourself that time heals everything, but why does it hurt so badly if that's the case?"

I think of my life and how everything has changed overnight. My former life wasn't anything extraordinary, but the loss still weighs heavily on me.

As sleep pulls me under, I can't help but wonder if he's referring to his ex or someone else.

nineteen

COMMANDMENT #20: THOU SHALT NOT MARRY INTO A FAMILY OF HUCKSTERS

Nate

I walk into the physician's lounge for breakfast before my next case. I left Kate sleeping in bed, grabbed a quick shower, and ran out the door. We spent all day Sunday getting her moved in with me. There's still a lot left at her apartment, but she's got enough to get through the next sixty days.

My first case was at six-thirty, so it was still dark when I pulled up outside the hospital. I expected work to feel as surreal as my personal life was at the moment, but it didn't. It felt completely normal to be in the hospital, doing what I loved, even as nothing else in my life was going according to plan.

I grab a coffee and a sausage biscuit from the buffet before finding a table in the back corner of the room. I chart my first case on my laptop in between bites of food. Just these simple acts leave me feeling much more like myself.

Almost as if nothing happened.

My phone buzzes from the clip on my waist, and I see it's a text message.

Kate: Good morning. I hope you slept well and made it to work on time. I've been thinking about what you said Saturday night and want to know your favorite meal. Maybe I could make it for you for dinner.

At the mention of Saturday night, images of her standing in nothing but her underwear flood in, and I exhale slowly.

Easy, Nate.

Do not get a hard-on in the middle of the physician dining lounge.

I tap out a quick reply.

Nate: Good morning to you. I slept well. Lasagna is my favorite meal.

It doesn't come across as affectionate, but I'm not sure we're there yet.

Are we?

I can't think about that right now. I need to get downstairs for my next case. I toss my stuff in the trash and head to the elevator. Just as the doors close, I catch a flash of blonde hair.

That looked like Dakota.

I get off the elevator and step around the corner, out of sight of anyone getting off. Sure enough, the doors open a few seconds later, and Dakota walks out.

She immediately begins looking around before approaching the nurse's station.

"Yes, excuse me. I'm looking for a man with blue scrubs and lots of tattoos. He just got off the elevator before me."

One of the nurses, Monica, makes eye contact with me, and I shake my head.

What the hell is she doing here?

Monica gives Dakota a bored look. "And you are?"

She giggles. "How silly of me. I'm Dr. Quinn, Woman of Medicine."

I damn near bite my tongue in half, trying to hold it together. I don't think she has any idea that she just referenced a nineties television show featuring Jane Seymour.

Monica appears to be choking. "Dr. Quinn? Are you kidding me right now?"

Dakota frowns. "I was worried that my reputation as a ball-buster would precede me. Do not be afraid. I'm not here to fire anyone."

Another nurse pipes up. "Dr. Quinn, Medicine Woman?"

Dakota nods. "Close. Woman of Medicine is my official title. Now, I was pulled off the tennis courts and told to get up here—I don't like wasting my time. Roderick is strict with my lessons and takes my leaving very seriously."

My eyes are streaming at this point. I don't know what medical shows she's been watching, but I've never met a doctor that talked like that. It's like a cross between *Little House on the Prairie* and *Downton Abbey*.

I can't take it anymore. "What are you doing up here, Nancy Drew?"

Monica checks the computer and interrupts before Dakota can answer. "Dr. Davis, your patient is in pre-op."

Dakota's face turns bright red. "Y-you're a doctor?"

I wrap my arm around her shoulder and steer her away from the nurse's station. "So are you, Dr. Quinn, Woman of Medicine."

She laughs weakly. "I had to say something so they'd take me seriously. Why does that sound so familiar?"

I shake my head. "It was a television show, way before your time."

She bites her lip and glances back at the nurse's station. "Did they catch on, you think?"

"Nah. I think you fooled them. So, are you stalking me?"

Her smile returns. "No, well, yes. It's complicated. I was here to get paperwork from my new doctor." She pats her stomach.

"Are you—" I don't know how to finish the question and ensure that my balls remain attached to my body.

She cocks her head to the side. "Kate didn't tell you? Yeah, I'm about six weeks along. I expected she would've told you. Congrats on the marriage, by the way. I can't see any way that could fail. How dumb do you have to be to get married in Vegas?"

I resist the urge to call security and smile instead. "About as dumb as someone who gets knocked up at twenty-two. You do know how that happens, right?"

She clenches her teeth, looking a lot like Kate as she does it. "Yes, I know how that happens. I don't understand how you tricked Kate into going to Vegas to marry you. And if you two are so happy, why didn't you know I was pregnant?"

I glance down at my watch. "Sorry to cut our little reunion short, but I have to be in surgery. Also, I didn't know you were pregnant because Kate's been pretty broken up over stuff with your dad. Nice talking to you."

I've made it three feet when she responds. "Yeah, finding out your dad's alive is pretty nerve-wracking. And just so you know, Jeremy is the one my sister should be with. He was there comforting her when she found out. Where were you?"

My teeth are going to crack under the pressure I'm putting on them.

Her dad's alive.

Why wouldn't she say something? Why would she lie?

And just how the fuck was Jeremy comforting her?

I pass Monica on my way into pre-op. "Call security."

* * *

I grab my bag and toss it over my shoulder. My last case ran over—I went in for a routine gallbladder removal. I could do this surgery in my sleep, but I was off. I nicked the mesenteric artery and had to reopen him, repair the artery, and then sew until my motherfucking hand wanted to fall off. I almost lost the patient because my head wasn't where it needed to be.

And now, I'll be about an hour late for dinner.

"Nate."

I'm so lost in thought that I almost miss the voice.

Almost.

I turn, and there's Jess, curled up in a chair in the ED waiting room. She looks like a shadow of her former self. Her eyes are rimmed in dark blue circles, and she's lost a lot of weight since I last saw her.

When was that?

The last time I saw her had to have been the night I picked her up from the hospital and let her stay with me. It was just over a month ago, but it might as well have been years.

"Jess, what are you doing here?"

She struggles to smile. "I'm having trouble keeping anything down, so I came in for fluids."

"Are you sick with a bug? Or is this related to the headaches you were having?"

She nods. "It's the headaches. I had an MRI done on my brain, and they found lesions."

She says it as though it's nothing more than a bump or bruise. I shouldn't care—she broke my fucking heart—but I'm suddenly that twenty-two-year-old kid again when it comes to her.

I sit down in the chair next to hers. "Are they looking at surgery? Or chemo? What's going on? Who's your surgeon? I can see if there are some strings I could pull."

She smiles sadly. "Nate, I'm fine. We're not together anymore. Go home. I'm sure you've had a long day."

I look down at my shoes, spinning my wedding band as I try to think of something. She looks at it, and I swear, her face pales even more. "I uh—I got married over the weekend, Jess."

Her smile disappears, and she stiffens slightly. "Wow, congratulations. I guess I always knew it would happen one day. I just convinced myself that it would be a long time from now."

"I'm sorry—"

She cuts me off. "Why are you sorry, Nate? You don't owe me an explanation. I wasn't any good for you. I just got so preoccupied with the next best thing I missed what was right in front of me the whole time. What is it they say—hindsight is 20/20? I'm sorry for what I put you through while you were trying to make a better life for us."

I can't sit here and listen to this shit. Shit, she should've said three years ago. I stand up and walk back through the doors again, stopping one of the nurses.

"You've got a patient out there—Jess Davis. I just wanted to see if we could get her into a room and start an IV."

She consults her clipboard. "I was just going to get her, Dr. Davis. Is she your patient?"

I shake my head. "No, just someone I knew."

I decide to leave the building through the side door. I can't go back out there and see her like that. She never once apologized for anything in our marriage—it was always someone else's fault. She's fucking with my head again, and I can't be a part of it.

I have Kate to think about now.

My wife.

The woman who lied to me about her father. Why would she keep that from me?

And what kind of a man fakes his death?

twenty

COMMANDMENT #21: THOU SHALT CHOOSE DATES THAT REQUIRE LITTLE CONVERSATION

Nate

I pull into the driveway next to my brother's truck. He's known for dropping by unannounced, and it doesn't hit me until I park in the garage that Kate's here now, too.

Fuck.

I didn't exactly reach out to alert my family that I was married. I take a deep breath and open the door.

"Well, well. If it isn't my big brother?" Garrett leans back in one of the dining room chairs, an empty plate in front of him. And in typical Garrett fashion, he's chewing on the end of a toothpick.

We share many of the same features and were often mistaken for twins when we were younger. Then I got tattoos and grew out my facial hair while he remained clean-cut and tattoo-free.

"Garrett, I didn't know you would be stopping by tonight."

He winks at me. "Your lovely bride was home and invited me to stay for dinner. We tried to wait for you—" he pats his stomach, "but it was impossible to resist."

I open my mouth to reply just as Kate walks in. Her hair is piled up on her head, and she's wearing a baggy sweatshirt that's slipped off one shoulder. In a word, she looks amazing.

Her face lights up when she sees me, and she comes over and wraps her arms around my waist.

All my frustration from seeing Dakota and dealing with Jess evaporates.

Kate stands up on her tiptoes and presses her lips against mine. I'm sure she meant it as a peck, but I lock my arms around her back and devour her.

The sound of a throat clearing pulls us apart. Garrett's now got his feet propped up on the table. "So, now that you're home. How'd you end up married without any of us knowing about it?"

Kate reluctantly lets go of my t-shirt. "I'm just going to get you a plate. I'll let you two catch up."

I swipe his feet off the table and sit down across from him. "We went to Vegas—it was a small ceremony. I did the 'big wedding shit' before. It was nice just to have something low-key."

Garrett shakes his head. "Really? Has she been married before? Because I don't know a lot of women that would be okay with that."

"She's fine with it."

He glances toward the kitchen before turning his attention back to me. "Look, cut the shit. Kate seems like a great person. She makes a lasagna that could compete with Mom's and that rack—"

I stand up so quickly that my chair crashes into the wall. I grab Garrett by the collar of his button-down shirt, yanking him across the table toward me. "Do not finish that sentence."

I release him, and he sits back down, rubbing at his throat. "Jesus, Nate. Calm the fuck down. I was going to say that the rack in your oven was sparkling clean. Not a drop of lasagna was spilled. See? You freaked out for nothing."

I rub my hands on my pants, feeling like a prick. I'm usually an easy-going guy, for the most part. I don't know what it is about her that turns me into this. "Sorry, Gar—"

He cuts me off. "Apology accepted. And I just want you to know that, given the chance, I'd motorboat the shit out of your wife's tits."

He's out of his chair and in the kitchen with her before I can react.

I'm going to murder him.

Kate comes back in with a plate of lasagna and salad and a big grin on her face. "Is everything okay? You look upset. Did you have a bad day at work?"

I shake my head. "I'm fine. Just tired..." I trail off as Garrett strolls back in and drapes his arm around Kate, his fingers moving dangerously close to being snapped in half by me.

He's doing this because he's pissed that I got married behind his back. I get it. I do. It doesn't change how I'll react if his fingers slip any lower, though.

I tap my fingers against my leg. "Babe, come sit with me; tell me about your day."

She slides onto my lap and turns her face toward me. "It was great. Most of my patients want my advice, making me feel like I'm making a difference." She shifts to get comfortable, and I'm suddenly rethinking having her sit on me as her ass brushes against the front of my jeans.

Garrett sits down across from her. "Do you have some that don't want help? Why would they bother showing up?"

She leans forward. "Well, believe it or not, some people treat therapy as a dress rehearsal."

I take a bite of the lasagna and Garrett was right, Kate can cook. This might even be better than my mom's cooking—not that I would ever tell her that.

He wrinkles his brow. "What does that mean?"

She laughs. "It means that some people are sociopaths. They are incapable of feeling empathy for others. They learn how to react appropriately by mimicking the behavior of those around them. Some of my patients will use our time together as a confession—looking for my reaction. If I react in a way they deem appropriate, they'll probably use it on someone else. I also have patients who tell me nothing but lies."

Garrett shakes his head. "That's bizarre. God, what I wouldn't give to be a fly on the wall. I bet you've got some good stories."

I like observing Kate like this. I can see her passion for her job in how her face lights up as she discusses it. Without thinking, I press a light kiss against her shoulder. "What do you say, babe? Do you have any crazy stories you can share with us?"

She blushes and bites the corner of her lip as she mulls it over. "Okay. I've got this one patient. We'll call her Carmen. She became obsessed with her best friend's husband, stalking him to learn his habits. She used her friendship to gather intel, and then she drove a wedge between the two of them—"

Garrett chuckles and takes a sip from his water bottle. "God, that sounds like your ex, Nate."

It does sound like Jess. I'm disgusted by the thought that there might be more women like her.

Kate stands up and takes my plate. "I'm feeling a little sleepy. I think I'd better call it a night. I have another long day of unpacking ahead of me. Garrett, should we wake Daniel up?"

"Yeah. I need to get him home."

I feel like an ass.

Of course, Kate would be uncomfortable talking about Jess. I stand up and take the plate from her hands. "Let me clean up. Go ahead and go to bed."

She leaves me and Garrett standing in the dining room, staring at each other uncertainly.

"I think that went well."

I grab him into a headlock. "The fuck is wrong with you, dickhead? She doesn't want to hear about Jess. And keep your goddamn hands off of her."

He reaches around me and grabs hold of my ear, pulling me off of him.

"Daddy?" Daniel stands next to Kate, taking in the spectacle before him.

We immediately release each other and straighten our clothing.

Garrett scoops Daniel up, and the little boy immediately lays his head against his shoulder.

"C'mon, little guy. Let's get you home and into bed." He turns back to Kate. "Thank you for a wonderful dinner. Daniel and I had a great time."

She gives him a side hug, embracing Daniel in the process. "Anytime. It was great to meet you both."

I walk him out to the truck. "You can't say anything to Mom or Dad. Not yet. We're still trying to sort this out ourselves."

Garrett gets Daniel fastened into his car seat, and his little eyes drift shut almost immediately. He closes the back door and turns to me. "What do you mean you're trying to sort this out? You'd be a fucking toolbox to end things with her. She's shown more affection for you in the last few hours than Jess ever did."

I shake my head. "Things aren't that simple. Jess is sick."

Garrett claps his hands. "Good. Maybe she'll die, and whatever fucking spell she has over you will be broken."

I pop my neck to relieve the building tension. "Don't say that. Don't be an asshole. I'm not interested in getting back together with her. I'm just worried because she's all alone."

He shakes his head angrily. "She's alone because she chose to fuck half of Lubbock when she was married to you. It's karma, Nate. Open your fucking eyes. Look, I won't say anything to Mom about this, but don't screw this up."

* * *

I stand in the bathroom doorway, watching Kate shower. It's taking everything in me not to strip down and join her. We might have a piece of paper that says we're married, but this relationship is still in its infancy.

She hums, and I can see her body clearly in my mind. I'm having flashbacks to our first night together, and my resolve is slipping.

Fuck it.

I drop my jeans and kick them across the floor, adding my shirt and boxers to the pile less than a second later. I gently pull the glass shower door open, freezing when I see her hand between her legs.

She wasn't humming—she was moaning. I'm just debating whether to stay or go when her body goes taut, and she whispers my name.

My motherfucking name.

I'm a goner. Everything Garrett said is spot on. I'd be a fucking idiot to let her go. Her body shudders and stills, the water running like rivers over her skin.

I pull her back into my chest, and she exhales softly. "That was so fucking hot, babe."

She turns her head to the side and looks up at me. Her cheeks are tinged with pink, and I can't decide whether it's from her orgasm or embarrassment. "You weren't supposed to be in here."

I laugh softly. "Well, I'm sure as hell going to be in here from now on. You should know that the showerhead is detachable in case you need it for those hard-to-reach areas." My hands drop from her arms down to her stomach.

"Nate..."

I slide one hand lower, and she stops me. "Wait. You said we were going to take it slow."

I groan against her neck. "That was before I saw you doing that." She can't expect me to think rationally after that performance. All the blood is in my dick.

"So, ask me something." I move my hand lower, and her voice goes shaky. "Um, get to know me."

I nip at her earlobe. "Oh, I am getting to know you. Let's try this— you asked me for my favorite food earlier. What's yours?"

I slide one finger inside of her, and she moans again. "I—I like— um—"

I slow my movements. "C'mon, Katy girl. Don't keep me in suspense."

She nods, and I resume. "O-okay. I like chicken parmesan—god, I like it—but only if it's homemade."

I press a light kiss against her temple. "Good girl. See, that was easy." Then I press my thumb into her core, teasing her until she cries out.

Kate goes lax on me, and I have to use my right arm to keep her upright. I maneuver us out of the direct spray of the showerhead, and she looks up at me again, her voice hoarse. "What's your least favorite food? I feel like a wife should know this."

I smile. "See, this is more of a third-date conversation. Where were we on our third date?"

"Bent over my desk at work, I think."

I nod. Sounds about right. "Okay, right. Um, what was the question?"

She giggles. "Least favorite food."

"Right. I fucking hate cilantro, so anything that has cilantro in it is out. Everything else is fair game. What's yours?"

She thinks it over, and I wait until she opens her mouth to speak before sliding my finger back inside her body. "H-hey, that's cheating. I didn't mess with you."

"You could have. I wasn't stopping you."

I lick along her shoulder, loving the way she tastes. I hope like hell that she'll still be mine in fifty-eight days, but if not, I want to walk away having put my mouth on every square inch of her.

She leans back into me and closes her eyes.

"Katy girl... least favorite food. Go."

"Uh-huh. Food—okay. You can't laugh. Promise?"

I laugh. "No promises."

This is going to be good.

"I cannot stand mashed potatoes. I loathe them—"

I cut her off. "That's not funny or weird. A bit anticlimactic..."

She grabs my hand, slowing my movements. "If you just give me a second, I could tell you the rest. I hate mashed potatoes, but I love French fries. Isn't that strange?"

The water goes cold, and I shut it off before answering her. "What a freak."

"Jerk." She tries to swat at my arm, but I dodge it.

"I'm kidding. That's not all that odd. It's a texture thing for you. How do you do with oatmeal?"

"I love it."

I pop the door open and step out before replying, "That is fucking weird then." I laugh as I grab a couple of towels, stopping short when her hand connects with my still painfully hard dick.

She applies a little pressure and says sweetly, "Weird. Did I hear you correctly? Weird is what you said, right?"

She squeezes a little tighter, and I'm not sure whether I'm turned on or scared at this point. "I said adorable—adorable. So fucking adorable."

She loosens her grip but doesn't let go, and I want the sight of our reflections in the bathroom mirror permanently etched into my memory.

Her pale skin is perfection against my ink. I wonder what she'd look like with a tattoo—maybe a vine running the length of her spine.

She moves her hands up to rest against my hips. "Are we still getting to know each other?"

I nod at her reflection, incapable of using my voice.

"What made you decide to get all of your tattoos? Did you always know you wanted a lot of them?"

I clench my jaw. Her question is too personal because my ex-wife is the reason I have most of them. And that's sure as hell a conversation I don't want to have tonight. "Can we skip that one for now?"

She tucks her lower lip between her teeth and nods. I wonder how many men have fallen in love with that mouth—not that I'm in love with her—I just mean that surely someone has been before. She has a nice mouth.

"How many men have you been with before me?"

Excellent job, Nate. Way to steer around the sensitive topics.

Asshole.

Her eyes widen in surprise. She probably wasn't expecting that. To be honest, I wasn't expecting that shit to come out of my mouth either.

"Um, pass. Can I pass?"

I turn and pull her into my arms. "Sorry, babe. That was way too personal. Let's just get to bed."

She takes the extra towel from my hand and wraps it around herself before leaving the bathroom. I stand in front of the mirror, working to steady my breathing.

Why do I seem to fuck this up at every turn?

I roll my shoulders and run the towel through my hair before slinging it around my waist. She's already under the covers when I enter the bedroom, facing away from me.

I slip a pair of sweats on before joining her. "Um, I'm an adrenaline junkie."

She rolls over to face me. "Yeah?"

I nod. "Yeah. I always wanted to be a doctor but wasn't a big risk taker. Then, I met Jess."

Her eyes narrow, and I cup her chin in my hand. "You wanted to get to know me. This comes with the territory."

Kate sighs. "I know. It's just hard to hear about her."

"So, my life with Jess was stressful. Even if I hadn't been in med school, it would have been chaos. I guess I got conditioned by it, and I began to crave activities that fed that addiction. Surgery, snowboarding, skydiving, and even getting inked became a big part of my life. After the divorce, those activities became necessary."

She sits up and pulls me into a hug. "I don't know everything that happened to you, but I'm sorry. I'm sorry she put you through it."

I pull back and capture her mouth with mine. I don't do it to be romantic—I do it to avoid spilling my guts to her. I take risks every day, but I'm not willing to gamble if it means I might lose her.

The realization frightens me.

It's not rational. She's already been keeping things from me—it's taken everything not to bring up her dad or sister. I thought I'd broach the subject once Garrett left, but she distracted me with her shower activities.

Maybe she's just as scared to open up to me as I am with her. I did leave her in our hotel room after she dropped the bombshell about her sister being arrested—which, if Dakota is constantly going around posing as something she's not, then I'm not a damn bit surprised it landed her in jail.

I'm still trying to piece together how two sisters, who swore to me that they were open books, are so shrouded in mystery.

twenty-one

COMMANDMENT #22: THOU SHALT NOT INVITE THEM TO MEET THE FAMILY

Kate

"Did she say what this was about?" Nate asks me as we drive to Dakota's house.

I shake my head. "No. She just said to come for dinner. Maybe she wants to apologize for her behavior?"

He makes a noncommittal noise and focuses on the road again. I hadn't heard from Dakota in two weeks when she called me out of the blue.

She told me how much she missed me, and the ice around my heart thawed almost instantly. I'd missed her too. I'd even take hearing about comics every day if it meant things were good between us.

Nate and I have been making the best of our situation. He works all the time. I don't know if I knew how demanding his job was before when I thought he was a struggling tattoo artist.

Sometimes, he comes home and wants to know all about my day. We'll go back and forth with our twenty questions, tiptoeing around more sensitive subjects while trying to keep our clothes on. Other times, he comes home and wants nothing to do with me. He'll give one-word responses, seemingly upset at the world and me.

We move two steps forward only to take three steps back. He's always on call, and it seems they conveniently page him when we're starting to open up to one another.

Every day that passes leaves me with more questions than answers. In all fairness, I've still yet to tell him that my dad is alive or that Dakota is pregnant. It's still too much for me to wrap my mind around, much less a stranger.

Except for Jeremy, who was seemingly unbothered by all of it.

Jeremy.

I haven't yet found the courage to tell him about Benjamin or Jeremy. I'm going to... I just need more time, though.

"Hey, you okay?"

I realize we're parked in front of Dakota's house and push my thoughts aside. "Yeah, sorry. I got lost in thought."

He takes my hand and kisses it, and I forget my troubles. "Let's go face the firing squad, babe."

We walk hand in hand up to the front door and I pray that Zane won't be walking around shirtless this time. I don't want to get distracted by the wall of muscle. I'm here to make up with my sister, not ogle her superhero boyfriend.

Little Ricky answers the door. "*Hola*, Hail Mary. I see you brought *tu marido* this time."

He thrusts out a hand to Nate. "Hey, I'm Little Ricky. My mama was a fan of *I Love Lucy* and named me after Ricky Ricardo, Jr."

Nate's eyes widen, but he reaches out and shakes Little Ricky's hand. "Nate. Nice to meet you."

I pat Little Ricky lightly on the arm. "It's a lovely story, but you don't have to share it with everyone upon meeting them, do you?"

He laughs good-naturedly. "Hail Mary, I'm not ashamed of where I come from. You shouldn't be either. Come on inside. *Caparina's* just finishing up with dinner."

I wrinkle my nose. "She cooked?"

Zane comes around the corner and meets us.

Thankfully, he's found a button-up shirt to cover those muscles. He laughs at my question. "Cap cook? The smoke alarm would be going off. No, she used the grocery store caterer and is unpacking it all in the kitchen."

A caterer?

I push the bitterness back down.

Maybe Zane paid for it.

Maybe Zane should've been paying for it this entire time.

I take a deep breath to center myself, and Nate brushes my arm with his. "Are you okay?"

I nod. "Fine." I can't be upset. It's not like she's asked me for money since she got out of jail.

Zane looks back and forth between us. "Okay then. Welcome. Nate, good to see you. Kate, can I get you anything? Water? Tequila shots?"

Nate immediately cracks up and high-fives Zane. "That was great. Way to break the ice, man."

The mention of tequila turns my stomach, and I shake my head. "I think I'm okay. I'm going to go find Dakota."

Nate eyes the sling on Zane's arm. "So, law enforcement? I never would've guessed. How's the shoulder healing? Who was your surgeon?"

I leave the two of them talking and walk into the kitchen. Dakota is surrounded by containers, working feverishly to tear the plastic wrap off one.

"Hey. Can I help?"

She jumps and drops the container onto the counter. "Biscuits and gravy, Kate! You're like a ninja. Yeah, I can't get the damn—darn thing open."

I take it from her hands and find the seam. "You gave up on cursing? I thought that was your newest pastime—well, right up there with being the Punisher."

She rolls her eyes and takes the unwrapped container from my hand. "It's not good for the baby. How have you been? Are you still married?"

I nod. "Yep, still married. I left in kind of a rush the night I found out that you were pregnant. How are you feeling? Do you know how far along you are?"

Are you scared? Because I'm afraid for you.

She grabs another container and begins unwrapping it. "I'll be nine weeks next Friday."

We slip back into silence. I can honestly say there's never been a time when we didn't have something to say to each other.

Little Ricky comes in and breaks the silence. For what might be the first time, I'm thankful that he's in our lives. I'll never admit it to a soul, though.

"*Caparina*, toss me some napkins so I can set the table for this feast. The guys are talking some medical shit in there, and I got lost. Nate wants to know PT and OT and how much Thor can bench press."

I laugh. "He wants to know how much he can bench press?"

Little Ricky shrugs. "Just about. He's all, '*Which physical therapist did you get? Oh, that guy is awesome. Blah, blah. Bench press me, Thor.*' It's weird."

I'd pay good money to see Zane bench press Nate.

Strangely, I'm turned on...

Dakota hands him the napkins, her mouth in a hard line. "You brought him? I said you were invited for dinner—not him—"

"He's my husband. Of course, I brought him."

Little Ricky pauses with the napkins. "I like him. His tattoos are badass. I never would have pegged him as your type, though, Hail Mary. I always saw you with an attorney or some shit like that. Some guy that lived his life by the book, you know?"

An attorney?

Everyone must think I'm some rigid, unyielding shrew.

I open my mouth and manage to get out, "What the heck is that supposed—" as Dakota talks over me.

"He had me thrown out of the hospital while I was there trying to get paperwork from my new doctor. Did Doucheface tell you that?"

Little Ricky backs out of the kitchen, his hands raised in mock surrender. "Yeah, I forgot about that shit." He turns to me. "Good luck!"

I rub my temples, trying to ward off the migraine that I know will hit at any moment. "He did what? Why?"

"Yeah, had me thrown out for no reason! That's the man you married!" She places her hands on her hips defiantly.

Why would he do that to her?

Why doesn't life come with a reset button?

I would reset back to when my life made actual sense.

"I didn't know about any of that. I'm sorry."

Zane and Nate enter the kitchen, probably drawn by Dakota's yelling.

"You okay, babe?" Zane goes over to her immediately.

She shakes her head and begins brushing tears away. "I don't want him in my house, Big Guy. Not after what he did to me."

Nate looks at her and then over at me. "What the fuck is going on?"

Zane holds out a hand to silence him and pulls Dakota in closer. "Babe, I talked to Nate about that, and I'm not sure you told me the whole story. Does Dr. Quinn, Woman of Medicine, ring any bells?"

She shakes her head. "You believe him over me? I seriously was just trying to find my doctor's office, and he had me thrown out for no apparent reason. Sometimes, you must pose as a doctor to get correct information."

Nate's face turns red with anger. "That's—"

"Enough. That's enough out of both of you. Cap, we said we would have a nice dinner as a family. Let's table this discussion for now and enjoy our company." He leans down and presses a kiss to her cheek.

Dakota moves around him and leaves the room. The three of us stare uncertainly at each other while Little Ricky sets the table behind us—oblivious to anything happening.

Maybe I need to get high.

131

I'd like to be clueless right now.

Zane makes a noise in the back of his throat, and I look at him. "So, the pregnancy hormones aren't exactly helping things right now. Um, we had everyone over to announce that we're getting married."

I'm on the verge of tears, and Nate looks ready to rip someone's head off, so neither of us is quick to offer our congratulations.

Zane continues, "New Year's Eve—that's when it is. I, uh, just thought everyone might want to know that. Not like either one of you gives a fuck at the moment, but it's important to us that you're both there."

Nate snaps out of it and shakes his hand. "Congrats, man. She's... well, she's something." His sarcasm is hard to miss.

Little Ricky pipes up. "Hey, Hail Mary. There's something you need to know—"

"Why do you keep calling her that?" Nate doesn't appear to be amused by the nickname.

"Oh, well, her name's Mary Katherine—I dunno, man, look at her! Makes you feel like you need penance to atone for your sins and shit. Say ten *Hail Mary's,* and all will be forgiven."

We all stare blankly at him. This is more confusing than I previously thought. How could being around me make one feel that they needed atonement?

He continues, "She's a therapist, yeah? People confess everything to her on a daily basis. Fuck, it made a lot more sense in my head. *Pendejos.*"

He storms out, and the three of us resume our staring contest.

"This is going about as well as I expected," Nate offers, and I pinch the bridge of my nose. Yep, this migraine is going to appear at any moment now.

The old-fashioned doorbell chimes, and Zane leaves us to answer it. Nate comes over to me and cups my chin in his hand. "Do you wanna get out of here? We could hit up McDonald's, and then maybe if we're feeling crazy, we could get you a tattoo."

The smile on my face fades the minute I see the newest arrival to what I'm now lovingly going to refer to as *'The Party from Hell.'*

Jeremy.

Nate follows my gaze, and his jaw clenches. "You've got to be fucking kidding me. Is this normal with your family?"

I take a deep breath, but there is no centering myself this time.

Namaste... and kick Dakota's ass over this.

"Dakota Mae! Get out here now!" I scream at the top of my lungs, and everyone freezes.

"Holy shit, Hail Mary! You got some pipes on you." Little Ricky nods approvingly before sitting down in a nearby chair. All he's missing is a bucket of popcorn.

Dakota comes out of her bedroom with her arms crossed over her chest. Once she sees Jeremy, she smirks.

Do not hit a pregnant woman...

"Hey Jeremy, just in time! I think Nate was just leaving. Kate, did you say hello to Jeremy?"

Tears sting my eyes, but I refuse to cry right now. My hands are balled into fists at my side. I have never been so angry at my sister, including the time she drew superhero capes on every member of my N*SYNC poster to *make them happier.*

Jeremy takes in the situation. "I thought you said they broke up." He looks over at Nate, "I'm sorry, man."

Nate pulls his keys free from his jeans. His face is a mask, so I can't get a good read on him. "Kate, I'll be outside."

"Bye, Nate!" Dakota waves and Zane looks to me for advice. I give him a look as if to say, *She's your fiancée. You handle it,* but he just shrugs.

"Okay, I've had enough of this. Cut the crap."

Nate pauses in the doorway.

She widens her eyes. "I don't know what you mean. Is there a problem, Kate?"

I take a few steps forward, only to be stopped by Little Ricky. "Hold up, Hail Mary."

"Don't touch her," Nate warns, and I turn around to smile sweetly at my husband before kneeing Little Ricky in the balls. He drops to the floor with a groan. Yeah. What he said."

Zane takes a step forward with his hands held out. "Kate..."

"Move out of my way, you big tree, or you'll be next. This is between me and Dakota."

"What—are we supposed to fight like Captain America and Ironman now? Because you have me at a disadvantage."

I shake my head. "No, I'm not going to fight you, but I will give you a piece of my mind. And you're going to listen to me. I've taken care of you for far too long now. I have sacrificed everything for you!"

"No one asked you to do that, Kate."

My words are forced through clenched teeth. "What other choice did we have when Mama took off? Seriously, it fell on my shoulders. You watched me go through everything with Benjamin and claimed I deserved better. I find someone who makes me happy, and where are you? Oh, that's right. You're running behind my back, trying to sabotage everything. Just. Like. Nan!"

Dakota's mouth drops open in surprise. "I'm nothing like her!"

"You are exactly like her, carrying on with this ridiculous revenge plot and screwing with people's lives to get what you want. I've supported you as long as possible, but I can't be a part of this anymore. What you've done tonight is probably the cruelest thing anyone has ever done to me."

She puts her hands on her hips. "I have Zane and Little Ricky—I don't need you. So, anything else before you show yourself out?"

I take a stuttered breath, adrenaline coursing through my veins. No wonder Nate's addicted to this—it's better than being drunk. I feel invincible.

And I may not be able to hit my sister physically, but I can get her where it'll hurt the most. I smile. "Yeah, there is one more thing. I saw *Suicide Squad* and feel that *DC* has a much better lineup of superheroes."

She gasps and clutches her chest. "Y-y-you did not just say that. They're not even superheroes—they're villains! Get out!"

I wipe the tears that have begun to leak from my eyes and join Nate at the door. Little Ricky starts to stand and Nate gives him a look. "Don't even think about following us out right now."

* * *

Nate hands me a cup of hot tea and wraps a blanket around my shoulders. I can't stop shaking.

"I-I-is this what being an adrenaline j-junkie is like? I hate it." Gone is the feeling of invincibility. I now feel like I'm caught in a hurricane. So, it's basically like being hungover.

He chuckles softly. "Yeah, you just put your body into fight or flight and dumped a fuck ton of adrenaline into your bloodstream in the process."

My teeth clatter together. "H-how m-much longer w-will it last. I don't feel good."

He brushes the hair back off of my forehead. "I don't imagine you feel great at the moment. You're not in control of your body; it must be hard. Just inhale and exhale, slow and steady."

I lean into his hand and follow his instructions. "Thank you for not leaving me there."

He fidgets with his wedding ring. "Why'd you defend me against Dakota? You and I just met a couple of months ago."

"I didn't like the way she was treating you. We committed to this marriage for sixty days, so I'm going to do everything in my power to put you first."

His jaw tightens, and he stands up quickly. "Okay." His Adam's apple bobs slightly as he says it, and I wonder if his ex-wife ever put him first in anything.

I'm going to assume no since he questioned why I would.

I tap the table. "Sit. Did you have Dakota thrown out of the hospital?"

He sinks back down onto the coffee table and sighs. "Yeah. She posed as a doctor to get information on me. Things were going okay until she told me that you belonged with Jeremy. I lost my cool and had the nurses call security to escort her out."

I can't help myself, and I begin laughing. I wonder if this is fight-or-flight or if I'm just cracking up mentally. "Is that where Dr. Quinn, Woman of Medicine, came from?"

He tries and fails to hide a smile. "Yeah. I couldn't believe she'd never seen the show. That was a nice call with the DC reference at the end. I think you got under her skin."

I groan and put my head in my hands. "I'm an awful sister. I just wanted to hurt her as badly as she hurt me. Ever since she got arrested, our lives have been turned upside down. It would just be nice to have one thing go our way, you know?"

Nate looks down at the floor. "Is Jeremy? Were you two? God, what I'm trying to say is..."

Here goes nothing.

"Are you asking if we slept together?"

He nods, still looking down at the floor. "Yeah."

"We did, yes. A year ago, I went to a chamber social event—"

He moves to stand up again. "You don't owe me an explanation—"

I put my hand on his thigh, pushing him back down. "Please let me finish. I kind of need to start at the beginning, though. I dated a man for a year, Benjamin. On our anniversary last year, I went over to his house to surprise him. I guess I was successful—I walked in on him and his boyfriend."

Nate's head pops up in surprise, and I continue. "I went to the chamber social a few months later, where I met Jeremy. I was feeling reckless then and ended up going home with him. I had a one-night stand and lost my virginity. I didn't see him again until right before I met you."

He holds his hand up. "Wait, what did you just say?"

"I didn't see him again until right before I met you?"

He shakes his head. "Before that."

"I had a one-night stand?"

He shakes his head again, his voice almost a whisper. "After that."

I swallow past the lump in my throat. "I lost my virginity to him?"

He nods. "That was just last year. How many guys have you been with?"

"Including you? Two."

He leans closer to me, his forearms resting on my thighs. "You were with him one time and then me? No one else?"

I nod, rendered speechless by his line of questioning.

Is this a big deal to guys?

"Fuck. I'm going to assume that you and Benjamin weren't experimenting. How'd you manage?"

"I have an arsenal of battery-powered gadgets," I slap a hand against my mouth in horror.

I did not just say that. That's got to be the adrenaline, rendering my internal filter useless.

His eyes sparkle with amusement. "Show me?"

twenty-two

COMMANDMENT #23: THOU SHALT ASK FOR SEXUAL HISTORY UP FRONT

Nate

Kate immediately begins shaking her head. "Pass."

I hide a smile. I never would've guessed that she'd only had one sexual encounter before me. She was so confident. "Okay, we'll pass. Anything you want to ask me?"

She mulls it over. "How many women have you been with?"

I chew at my lip. "Including you?"

She nods.

"Two."

She chokes on her sip of tea and ends up spitting most of it onto my shirt. "That can't be right! That would mean you've only been with me and your ex-wife. You divorced three years ago, though. How?"

I wipe at my shirt with a shrug. "I went out some, but my job has kept me pretty busy. I just needed a break from women after the divorce—a chance to clear my head."

"I'm sorry about your shirt. It just... surprised me. She really did a number on you, didn't she?"

I get up to grab a dish towel from the kitchen, intentionally ignoring her question. Honestly, I'm not sure how to answer.

Did Jess fuck me over? Absolutely. There's no denying it, but being with Kate these past few weeks has lessened the blow. I remember less and less from my first marriage the more I'm with her.

Kate softly taps me on the shoulder, and I turn around. "Who was your first celebrity crush?"

Ah... she's going back to safer topics.

I think back to the late eighties/early nineties. "Hmm...first would probably have been Kelly Kapowski. I watched a lot of *Saved by the Bell* back in the day. What about you?"

She nods. "Kelly Kapowski is a good choice. Who's your second pick?"

"Nice try, Katy girl, but you still owe me your answer."

She focuses on the cabinet behind me, avoiding eye contact. "Oh, um, it was Tommy Franks—the green Power Ranger."

She's embarrassed by it.

God, why does she have to look so adorable?

"Go go, Power Rangers," I sing with a laugh. "Lucy Lawless was my second choice. I dug *Xena: Warrior Princess*, and don't get me started on her battle cry. Hot."

Her cheeks are still tinged with pink, but she grins at me. "My second choice was Duncan MacLeod from *Highlander*. Pops loved that show and always thought it was nice that I'd watch it with him when we visited. I didn't dare to tell him exactly why I enjoyed watching it with him."

I picture Little Kate sitting with her grandfather, repeating along with the television, *"In the end, there can be only one."*

Oh, fuck me.

I'm going to fall in love with this woman.

* * *

"So, her family's nuts?" Garrett takes a swig of his beer.

I haven't seen him since the night he unexpectedly showed up at the house. Between work and getting to know Kate, I haven't found the time. When Garrett asked me to grab a beer, Kate stepped in and offered to watch Daniel.

I nod. "Pretty much."

"Okay... but you're still into her?"

"Fucking crazy about her. This is why I've got you to tell me why it won't work."

He shakes his head. "No, you know what? I think this is exactly what you need. You let Jess turn you into a workaholic. It's nice to see you relaxed like this. Speaking of Jess, I think she followed me the other night."

I sit up straighter and look around the bar, taking in the various patrons. "Where? When?"

He takes another drink. "Well, Mom picked up Daniel at school last Friday, so I decided to grab a quick drink with Clayton after work. We'd only been there for maybe twenty minutes when a woman caught my eye. She was wearing a wig and trench coat, but I swear it was Jess. It was like some low-budget spy movie. When she noticed me staring at her, she took off."

This doesn't make any sense.

When I saw her a couple of weeks ago, she was on her deathbed, and now I'm supposed to believe that she's running around in disguises.

"Garrett, there's got to be a mistake. Jess has been really sick, and I don't see any way that the woman you saw was her."

He shakes his head. "No, it was her. She was much thinner than I remember, but it was definitely her. I think she was following me."

Our food arrives, and we eat in silence. My head is swimming in confusion right now. I know Jess cheated and then lied to cover it up for a while, but this just seems so far beyond that. I can't see how she'd be capable of stalking or even what her endgame would be by doing it.

"So, you think McKenna will be back to play next week? Because it's obvious that Kody needs him out there. We're down by a touchdown when we should be ahead by at least two. Fuck, I hate the Flyers." Garrett gestures toward one of the many television screens around the bar.

I read the ticker at the bottom of the screen, grateful for the distraction. "I didn't see it. What's he out with?"

"Foot injury in week seven. They've got Holt in his position, but it's obvious he doesn't have a fucking clue."

I search my phone for any information on *The Bad Boy from Dallas*. "I forgot that he fractured that same foot late last year. This report says he had it repaired during the off-season, so I'm not sure what's happening."

Garrett rolls his eyes. "Aren't you a doctor? Anyone can look that shit up. I expected better from you, Nate."

I cuff him on the side of his head. "If I haven't examined the guy, and they're not releasing specifics of his injury, then how in the hell am I supposed to diagnose him?"

His phone vibrates, and Garrett loses interest in the conversation, distracted by something shiny. "Hey, Mitch wants to know if there's room for one more next month. I said it's up to you."

"I think we can make it work. He may have to sleep on the couch, but I'm cool with him joining us." I don't know how I forgot, but I scheduled a weekend snowboarding trip up in Snowcliff, Colorado. I've gone with these guys for the past three years.

I didn't exactly plan on having a wife to think about when I booked everything and got our lift tickets.

Garrett replies to Mitch, and everyone in the bar starts shouting. We look up to see the Steel score. They managed to tie it up with three minutes left in the game.

Kody throws it to Rodgers to clench the win, and we pay our tabs before heading out, still high on the last-minute victory.

"Does Kate snowboard? Maybe she could come with us." Garrett climbs into the passenger seat.

"I don't know, Garrett. I can't picture her on a snowboard."

A runway? Sure.

Sports Illustrated: Swimsuit edition? Absolutely.

Zipping down a mountainside? Not so much.

He fixes me with his stare. "Well, what does she like to do?"

I focus on the road, not meeting his gaze. "How the hell should I know?"

He throws his head back and laughs at my response. "Are you kidding me right now? You're the one who's married to her. You should know what she likes. Does she have any hobbies?"

I try and think back over the last couple of weeks. "She cooks and cleans. She likes to read case studies and psych books before bed."

The streetlights illuminate Garrett's frown. "God, that sounds boring as hell. So, are you saying that she has no hobbies or just that you haven't taken the time to figure them out?"

I pull into the garage. "I don't know."

I married a woman who quite possibly has no interests outside of work. I wouldn't expect her to share all of mine, but how can I expect us to last if she and I have nothing in common?

I've already been married to a woman who had zero interest in anything I did, and look at how well that turned out. The doubts begin to creep in, and by the time he and I walk inside, I've convinced myself that Kate and I are doomed to fail.

It's after eleven, and the house is dark. I don't know what I expected Kate to be doing—maybe sitting up and reading. Instead, she's fast asleep on the couch with Daniel wrapped up in her arms. His little head lays against her chest, mouth slightly open.

Garrett pulls out his cell phone and snaps a picture, whispering, "That's too damn cute not to document. Lucky kid."

I debate whether or not to hit him.

If we make it, this could be us.

The thought comes out of nowhere, but my mind runs with it once it's out there. I can see her asleep on the couch with our oldest in her arms, her belly round with our second baby.

She'd look amazing carrying my children.

I know it without a doubt.

With Jess, I had impending fatherhood thrust upon me at the worst possible time. I'd experienced a lot of guilt over the relief I'd felt when she miscarried not long after we were married.

This is different.

I don't know how much we have in common, but I know with absolute certainty that I don't want her to leave once this trial period ends. I want everything I just imagined.

I've got to be losing my grip on reality.

I want a family with her.

twenty-three

COMMANDMENT #24: THOU SHALT NOT SLEEPOVER

Kate

"You missed our last session. How have things been for you over the last week?"

Carla can't keep the grin off her face, which is surprising because she usually looks like she's swallowed something bitter. "I've been taking better care of myself. I even joined a gym."

I consult my notebook, looking over our past visits. "That's a very positive change. Have you been in contact with your ex?"

The problem is that she'll do something positive for herself, only to forget about it when Jackie returns to the picture. Their relationship sounds very co-dependent. No matter what she's done to him, he just can't seem to stay away from her.

She nods, but her smile falters just a little. I might not have noticed it had I not been studying her face. "We are—things are just a little complicated right now. I took an opportunity; now we just wait and see."

She returns to smiling at me as though I'm supposed to know what she's talking about. I flip through my notes again but come up empty-handed.

My office phone rings, and I silence it before asking my next question. "Sorry about that. So, last time we met, you said your doctors were still trying to evaluate lesions on your brain."

She waves her hand dismissively. "Oh, they misdiagnosed me. It turns out that it was just shadows on the scan. They're lucky I'm not suing them for faulty equipment. I think that the headaches might've been related to a new medication. I stopped taking it, and it seems to be helping."

My phone starts ringing again before I can process the newest development. "If you'll just excuse me for one second."

"Hello?"

"Kate, I need you to come up to the hospital." The male voice sounds completely distraught.

"Who is this?"

"It's Zane. Dakota started spotting...we don't know anything yet, but she's really sick. Please hurry." His voice cracks, and my heart is in my throat.

I barely register that Carla is still here as I gather my things. "I'm so sorry to cut things short, but I've had a family emergency come up."

She gives me a strange look. "I hope everything's okay. Is there anything I can do?"

I shake my head and usher her out of my office. "No, I'll call you once things are settled to reschedule. I'm so sorry."

I need Nate.

No, I can't call him. He's probably in the middle of surgery, and Dakota isn't exactly his favorite person right now.

* * *

My office is downtown, so it only takes a few minutes to get to the hospital. They direct me to a blue curtain with a black number four painted on it, where Dakota is hooked up to an IV with her eyes closed.

Zane's body engulfs the small plastic chair beside her, making it seem like he's sitting on a toddler's chair.

Big Guy in a little chair.

He looks up at me. "Hey, Kate."

I force my mouth into a straight line to keep from crying. "Is the— is she going to be okay?"

He rubs his eyes. "We're waiting for an ultrasound. They started an IV to get some fluids in her; I think they put something in there for the nausea as well, so she's been sleeping on and off."

As if sensing that we're talking about her, Dakota opens her eyes and gives me a weak smile. "Hey, Katydid."

I can't fight the tears off anymore, and they fall freely down my face. "Hey, kid. Are you okay?"

She shakes her head and starts crying. "No."

Zane is on his feet and leaning over her before she can say more. "What do you need? Should I get a nurse? Tell me what you want me to do, babe?"

She reaches up and rubs his arm. "Big Guy, relax. Just sit down and hold my hand so I can get through this. Please?"

He presses a soft kiss to her lips and sits back down with her hand in his.

I sit down on the end of the bed. "What happened?"

She swallows and grimaces. "Ugh. Swallowing even hurts right now. I went to the gym this morning, just like every morning. I always get the strawberry smoothie from the juice bar, and I don't know if it was that or something I ate last night, but within twenty minutes of drinking it, I felt awful. It was like food poisoning—I couldn't keep anything in."

She stops talking and wipes the tears under her eyes with her free hand. "My stomach was cramping to the point that it hurt to stand, and I realized then that I was bleeding. I was so scared that I was going to pass out alone in the women's locker room, so I forced myself to go get help."

I take her in my arms, rocking her gently on the bed. "Dakota, I'm so sorry. I'm sorry about our fight and that you had to go through that all alone. I haven't been a good—"

She stops me. "No, it's my fault. I know how much you've sacrificed for me, and I just didn't want you to get hurt again. I was wrong, Katydid. So wrong."

I cry harder. "But I said *DC* was better."

She starts laughing. "That was pretty terrible. I accept your apology for that part."

The curtain opens, and a woman in a white coat comes in, pushing a large white cart with a screen on top. "Hey, Dakota, I'm Dr. Harper. I'm the OB-GYN on call today. You were severely dehydrated when you were brought in and presented with some spotting. I'd like to perform a transvaginal ultrasound to see what's going on."

Dakota nods shakily, and I move to leave. "Please stay, Kate."

I stand near Zane, allowing the doctor to work. He's still holding her hand tightly in his. Dakota's legs shake slightly as she places them in the stirrups at the foot of the bed.

The black and white screen remains empty for what feels like an eternity, and I don't realize I'm squeezing Zane's arm until he moves it to wrap around my shoulder.

The doctor maneuvers the wand, and suddenly, the screen changes. There's a lot of movement. I look at the doctor's face to determine if it's good or bad.

Dr. Harper smiles. "There's your baby, just moving and shaking like nothing's wrong. Heartbeat is strong, too."

I exhale the breath I didn't know I was holding as she takes some measurements and prints pictures.

Zane is shaking slightly, and I look up to see that he's crying. Something about seeing Thor cry unleashes the waterfall of tears within me. His voice is shaky. "So, she's going to be okay? And the baby's good?"

He releases me to sit beside her, looking expectantly up at the doctor. Dakota wipes at her streaming eyes while giving him such an adoring look that it makes me feel like an intruder.

Dr. Harper pulls up Dakota's chart on the main computer. "Yes, I think you'll make a full recovery. Take it easy the next few days; rest and elevate your feet. I would hold off on going to the gym for a few weeks, and once you go back, stick to less strenuous exercises."

Dakota nods as Dr. Harper gives her more instructions and a prescription for nausea. Once the doctor's gone, she turns to Zane. "I can't go to the gym for weeks? We're getting married in sixty-one days. What am I supposed to do?"

He takes her face in his massive hands. "I don't know if I've mentioned it before, but I think you need to hear it. The thigh gap is bullshit, babe. I love your curves."

I fan my face, trying to dry my tears. "Wow, my eyes are watering. I'm just going to step out—"

Dakota holds up her hand. "Don't. I still need to talk to you." Then she whispers something in Zane's ear, causing his smile to widen.

"You got it, Cap." He gets up and steps around me to leave.

"Where'd you send him?"

She smiles. "For cupcakes. Now, sit. I need to talk to you about Nate."

I drop onto the hard plastic chair, dreading what she's about to say. "Look, I know you don't like—"

Her hand covers my mouth. "No, no, no. None of that. Listen to me. How familiar are you with *Captain America & Bucky #624*?"

I force my lips into a straight line. "I think it's safe to say I am completely unfamiliar with it."

She nods. "I thought that might be the case. Well, I'll give you a brief version. It covers Bucky's years as the Winter Soldier and how that's affected him. Nate is your Bucky."

I nod, still unsure of where she's going with this. "Okay... and I'm Captain America?"

She shakes her head. "No, Kate. You are not Captain America. God of thunder, that's almost laughable. Anyway, a line from the comic has always stood out to me. In it, Bucky says, *'I might have put a bullet in my brain to quiet the ghosts... if not for Natasha...'* You, my dear sister, are Natasha."

"That's Black Widow, right?"

Dakota sighs. "Yes. Seriously, Kate, it's like you haven't been paying attention all these years."

I pick at the sheet on the bed. "So, you don't hate him anymore?"

She shakes her head, and her lips turn up in a slight smile. "No, not even a little bit. He loves my sister, and that's all I could ever want."

"Whoa! Pump the brakes on the love bit. We're still getting to know each other."

Dakota reaches for my hand. "Trust me, he loves you. I think you love him, too."

I squeeze her hand. "That's sweet of you, but it's still too soon to tell. We're trying to take things slowly right now."

She smiles like she's got a secret, so I give her my best stern look. "Spill it. What do you know that I don't?"

Her smile grows wider. "Who do you think brought me to the hospital, Katydid? Nate was at the gym. I grabbed the first person I saw; it turned out to be him. I'd been so hateful, but he didn't even hesitate. I told him my symptoms, and he rushed me out to his car and brought me here."

As if confirming Dakota's words, my heart starts beating faster.

My god, am I in love with him?

"Love?" My voice cracks.

I'm super protective of his feelings and want him to know how much I care about him.

But love?

It's scary and messy. Love is what brings people to my office in tears. It's what causes mothers to abandon their daughters...

"It's what makes life worth living."

I tuck my hair behind my ear and reluctantly look over at her.

She continues, "I know that you're scared. It's written all over your face, but when it's real, it's incredible. It makes what we had with Jackson and Benjamin seem ridiculous. You know what I'm talking about. Now, we can sit here and keep crying, or my maid of honor can help me plan this wedding."

I run my thumbs under both eyes. "Is this your way of asking me?"

She smiles and pulls me into another hug. "I can't do it without you, sister. Little Ricky is just hopeless at this kind of stuff. And, let's be real. There's no way he could pull off the dress."

* * *

I glance over at the clock—two in the morning.

Halloween is officially over, and after the day's events, I want nothing more than to crawl into bed. My head drops onto my chest, and I doze off before immediately jerking awake again. I've been doing this for hours, but I refuse to fall asleep until I see him.

Right on cue, the garage door rises, and I hastily rub the sleep from my eyes before standing up. The door opens softly, and I can hear the slight jingle of his keys as he hangs them up.

"Hey," I whisper as he rounds the corner and jumps back into the wall.

"Jesus, Kate!"

I wrap my arms around him and lay my head on his chest, his heart pounding steadily against my cheek. "Sorry... sorry. I didn't mean to scare you."

He brings his arms around behind me. "I thought you'd be asleep. Why are you sitting up in the dark?"

"I wanted to thank you for what you did for Dakota today. I don't want to think about what would've happened had you not taken her to the hospital when you did." My eyes fill with tears just thinking about it.

He releases me to turn on a light, and I can see that he's dead on his feet. He stumbles over to collapse on the couch. "Anyone would have done it, babe."

I shake my head. "No, Nate. They wouldn't—especially not for someone who'd said half of what she did. I just want to thank you for stepping up like that. It meant a lot to me," My voice cracks with emotion, "I was so scared for her."

He pats the empty spot on the couch, and I curl up next to him. "I checked on her before she was discharged, and all the tests came back normal. She's going to be okay, Katy girl. You don't owe me anything—you could have gotten some sleep instead of camping out in the dark." He kisses my forehead lightly while massaging the back of my neck.

"I bought some Halloween candy, but it wasn't near enough for all the kids in the neighborhood. I tried turning off the porch light, but that didn't fool anyone. So, I dug through the pantry—you're going to need more energy bars, by the way. When I ran out of those, I just turned off all the lights and pretended not to be home."

He starts chuckling. "That's got to be the cutest damn thing I've heard all day. I hate that I missed seeing you, moving around the house in stealth mode. Come on, babe. Let's go lay down. We've both had a long day. I just want to lay in bed and hold you."

We slip into bed, completely drained, and I trace my fingers lightly across his ink. His voice startles me. "You asked me a few weeks ago about my tattoos. I know that I never gave you a straight answer."

I continue moving my fingers over his chest, silently urging him to keep talking.

He clears his throat. "I didn't consider getting a tattoo until I got married. She pushed me to get one—was constantly bringing it up in conversation—and one day, I broke down. I thought I'd get one, and that'd be the end of it. It wasn't, though. You know people who have marriage problems and decide that a baby will fix everything? Well, it was like that. I got the tattoos to keep her happy. I tried to turn myself into what she wanted, convinced it would solve our problems. When we divorced, I spent every free minute covering up anything she chose. Strangely, the feel of the needle on my skin was cathartic."

Nate's voice is like the perfect cup of coffee in bed on a rainy day when you know you have nowhere to be. The rich timbre of his voice vibrates against my head as I lay on his chest.

I never knew that a voice could be deep yet soothing at the same time.

I pick my head up until our faces are mere inches apart. "That explains why you're a doctor."

He smiles. "Okay, counselor. I'll bite. Why am I a doctor?"

I move my hands to rest under my chin. "You probably feel like there's nothing you can't fix—most doctors have a god complex to some degree. For example, do you ever approach a case and think you might be unable to save that person?"

His eyes look thoughtful as he mulls over my words. "I guess I don't even consider it. I assume my training has prepared me to deal with anything I encounter."

"Well, that's part of what makes you a good doctor. You refuse to fail. If I were to guess, though, I'd say that trauma was not what you envisioned for yourself when you started med school. You've mentioned that the drama conditioned you until you began to crave it, and I think that also holds true for your profession. As chaotic as your career is, it still gave you more control than your marriage."

"I always knew I wanted to help people in some capacity, but being in the emergency department was a high for me—well, it still is. There's no time to worry about anything other than what's coming through the door. That's probably why I don't mind working on-call shifts."

He trails off, and I ask the question that's been on my mind since day one. "What exactly—I mean, I know she cheated, but why did you get divorced?"

"Pass," he groans. "It's late—or early, at this point."

I nod and lay my head back down on his chest. His hands lazily move up and down my spine, and I feel a shift. It's no longer a game of twenty questions—I want to know what makes him tick. I like hearing his thoughts on things—it can be as minor as the orange juice he prefers.

If I didn't know better, I'd say that I was falling in love with him. It's still too soon, but maybe someday.

twenty-four

COMMANDMENT #25: THOU SHALT NOT BE OPPOSED TO ENDING SINGLE GIRL LIFE FOR THE RIGHT PERSON

Kate

"What about this one?" I hold up an ivory dress, and Dakota shrugs.

"It's okay, I guess. I'm just not feeling any of these. God of thunder, I've been stuck on bedrest for two weeks, and this is how I spend my first day of freedom?"

I look around the sea of white, cream, and ivory. This is the second bridal shop we've been to, and I'm starting to worry that we won't have time for alterations at the rate we're going.

Dakota holds up a cream off-the-shoulder gown. "What about this?"

"It's gorgeous."

She gives me a mischievous smile. "Try it on."

I manage to sputter, "Me?"

"Yeah. You never got a chance to wear one of these. Humor me and try it on." I give her a strained look, and she rubs her belly and mouths the words *'bedrest.'*

The assistant grabs the dress in my size and helps me slip into it in the fitting room. I step up onto the carpeted pedestal to take in my reflection.

It's the most beautiful dress I've ever seen.

I feel like a princess. When I spin around, the A-line skirt flares out slightly. This is why people get so emotional on that TLC show. I desperately want to say yes to this dress.

Maybe I'll never have the wedding of my dreams, but I could probably wear this to clean the house—wait, what if Nate wants to renew our vows at some point? Wouldn't it be helpful if I already had the dress?

Dakota snaps a photo on her phone and begins tapping away.

"What are you doing over there? You're not posting that online, are you?"

Dakota shakes her head and continues typing.

"Dakota Mae, do not make me chase you around this store in a wedding gown. Tell me what you're doing."

She hands me her phone. She's been texting Nate.

After what he did for Dakota, he revealed his true character to me, and something changed between us. Our conversations no longer felt like interviews. He'd come home a few nights after the hospital incident and ask over dinner, "Tell me something I don't know—what do you do when you're not working?"

I'd thought about it and answered, "Well, I take spinning and yoga classes."

He'd smiled at the mention of yoga, and I knew exactly where his mind had gone. He tried to recover with, "What about outdoor sports? Have you ever gone skydiving?"

I'd snorted from laughing so hard. "Skydiving? Do I look like someone who would jump out of a perfectly good airplane?"

He'd persisted with, "Snowboarding? Skiing?"

I'd tried to keep a straight face as I answered, "I don't like the cold, but I'd go with you and drink hot chocolate in the lodge."

So maybe he thinks I have no hobbies—given the opportunity, I can learn to like what he does.

I glance down at Dakota's text messages.

> Dakota: Doesn't your bride look gorgeous?

> Dakota: Oops, I think she's on to me.

> Dakota: Welp, gotta go. Pray for my soul.

I smile and hand the phone back. "You're off the hook—only because you were being sweet."

She rolls her eyes. "Geez, thanks. Alright, it's crunch time. *Operation: Find Cap a Dress.* Surely there's something in here that doesn't suck." She looks at the assistant. "No offense."

I tap my finger against my cheek as I survey the room from my carpeted perch. None of these dresses fit her personality—she needs a dress worthy of a superhero.

That's it!

"Dakota, I've got it. Follow me." We make our way to the back corner of the store, and there it is—the perfect dress.

The cap-sleeve gown hangs alone in the corner. It's covered in vintage black lace, with hints of white peeking through from underneath. Its plunging neckline and fitted style make it a dress fit for a superhero.

Dakota's eyes light up as she reverently runs her hands over the material. "Kate, it's exactly what I pictured."

I clap my hands together. "You wanted a unique wedding. What if we do a masquerade ceremony? It ties in with your superhero theme with the masks, but it's elegant at the same time."

She nods, not breaking eye contact with the dress.

I turn back to the assistant. "We'll need that in her size, and would you mind helping me out of this one?"

My work here is done.

twenty-five

COMMANDMENT #26: THOU SHALT NOT USE THE L-WORD

Kate

"Hello, Kate. Welcome to our home. I'm Beverly, but everyone calls me Bev. Or if you're comfortable with it, call me Mom." Nate's mother pulls me into a crushing hug.

I give him a questioning glance, and he shakes his head. He hasn't told his family we're married yet, but his mother hugged me like she already knew.

"Mom, let her breathe."

She releases me and grabs hold of him. "Nathaniel, you smart ass. She's fine."

She glances at me and then lowers her voice into a mock whisper. "And she's gorgeous. You failed to mention that."

He turns and looks at me. "Is she? I hadn't noticed."

She pops him on the arm, and I smile. I think I'm going to get along with her just fine.

"Aunt Katy! Aunt Katy!" Daniel runs in, holding a piece of paper in his little hands.

I kneel down to his level. "What do you have here?"

It looks like two aliens floating beside a house.

He proudly points to it. "See! It's you and me. And that's the table with basketti on it. Just like how you made it for me."

I smooth his unruly hair. "It looks just like us. Where's that crazy dad of yours?"

He pulls back and turns serious. "He's on the phone with my mama. She keeps taking off to god-knows-where, and there's not a damn thing he can do about it."

I instinctively cover his mouth, and he giggles. "Oh, we shouldn't say that word. Um..."

Beverly leans down. "Daniel? What did Grams say about grown-up words?"

He looks down at his shoes. "We shouldn't say them until we're in college and ignore Daddy and Uncle Nate because they're bad influences."

She kisses his head. "That's right. Now run on and tell Poppa that you need a snack before we have Thanksgiving dinner. Nathaniel, are you going to show Kate the property? There's a lot to see, and we've got a little bit of time before dinner."

Nate rubs at the scruff on his face. "Yeah. Can we take the Gator?"

She tosses him the keys. "Just promise you'll wear the helmets."

He laughs easily. "Mother, I'm a doctor. I know how important helmets are."

My boots crunch over the fallen leaves as we make our way out to the barn. His parents live on an enormous section of land with mature trees surrounding the house. It's only about a half-hour outside Lubbock, but it doesn't feel like a desert out here.

Nate pulls the helmets from the back of the little vehicle. "You ready for a ride, Katy girl?"

I lick my dry lips and nod.

I do want a ride... desperately.

Has it been sixty days yet?

He brushes my hair back off my face and helps me put the helmet on, even taking the time to fasten the strap under my chin.

The cool breeze catches his cologne, and I fight the urge to clench my thighs together.

Keep it together, Kate.

We climb in and buckle before Nate takes off down a narrow path near the barn. The little vehicle easily navigates the steep drops and shifts in the terrain.

It's exhilarating.

I am less aware of the landscape and more focused on the man operating the vehicle. He navigates the rocky path like he was born to do it.

Nate drives until I can no longer see the house. We pull up to another large barn surrounded by nothing but fields, and he kills the engine. I pull my helmet off and look around. "What do you keep out here?"

He takes his helmet off and runs his hand through his hair. "It's mostly farm equipment. It was my favorite place as a kid, though. Come on."

I take his hand, and we walk inside. It doesn't look like there's much to see, but he walks with purpose to the back of the barn. Then, I see the wooden ladder leading up to a loft.

"I used to climb up here as a kid. It was quiet, and I could read without anyone bothering me."

"Did you read medical textbooks and dream of being a doctor?" I tease.

He gives me a guilty grin. "Nah. Mostly, my dad's *Playboy* magazines. Do you want to see it? The loft, not the magazines."

I swat his arm and climb up the rickety ladder. He follows close behind. There's an old hay bale positioned to block the view of anyone walking in below and an old quilt covering the plywood floor.

"I like it. It's warm up here, too." I take off my jacket and set it aside before sitting on the quilt.

He nods. "Yeah, my dad has an office below this that he keeps heated during winter. In the summer, it's not nearly as enjoyable."

I watch Nate as he describes everything, his hands becoming more animated. I don't know that I've ever observed him in his element. As he talks, I notice the cassette player in the corner, and he grins.

"You want to hear it, don't you?"

I smirk. "Well, obviously. I need to get the full loft experience, don't you think?"

He plugs the tape player in and hits play. The song is familiar, but I couldn't tell you the band's name. "Is it KISS?"

Nate's mouth drops open in shock. "Please tell me you're joking? This is Foreigner, one of the greatest bands of our time. How do you not know this song? Urgent? Come on, Katy girl." He sings a few bars.

"Well, I am pretty young. So, tell me something I don't know about you. This loft was made for secrets—give me one of yours."

He cocks his head to the side, suddenly serious again. "What do you want to know?"

I settle in against the warm floor. "Everything. I want it all."

"Okay. Even the parts about Jess?"

My smile fades, but I nod. "Especially those parts because they made you who you are."

"Okay, Katy girl, it's time you heard the whole story. I met Jess in a bar when I was twenty-two. I went home with her under the guise of losing my virginity, but I didn't have any serious plans for a relationship. I was supposed to graduate and move to Seattle in a few short months. Well, I graduated, and Jess got pregnant.

"She tried pushing me to go to Seattle, but I stayed. I stayed and married her. I was young and naïve; I just didn't see any other options. A few months after we got married, she lost the baby. My life was chaotic at that point, though, as it was my first year of med school. I was more relieved than anything. I wanted to quit so many times along the way. I just felt like I was disappointing her at every turn by not being home much—hence, why I most likely have a god complex." He pauses to stare into the dim barn, the ghosts from his past very much visible to him.

I place my hand on his arm. "If this is too hard, we don't have to—"

He shakes his head. "No. I want to tell you. I did my residency in

Dallas, so we rarely saw each other. I'd beg her to spend a weekend with me, but she always seemed to have something come up.

"I made the mistake of coming home a week early and caught her. The guy she brought home was just one of many. After our divorce, she even went after her best friend's husband. That was the guy you met at the gym."

The story pricks my memory, and I interrupt him. "Was this story ever on the news?"

Nate looks puzzled. "I don't think so. I mean, our divorce was listed in the court section of the paper, but nothing that would have made headlines."

I try to organize my thoughts into a sentence. "I have this patient, Carla, who went through something almost completely identical. It just doesn't make any sense. Would Jess have told people about it?"

"Anything's possible. Maybe Carla gets her hair cut by Jess? People have done stranger things for attention."

I nod, still feeling like I'm missing something.

He takes my hand. "So, your turn. Tell me something I don't know about you."

"I, um, I don't have a lot of hobbies because most hobbies cost money. That's something we didn't have growing up. I wanted to try out for basketball in junior high, but my mama couldn't come up with the money, so I was a yearbook editor instead."

He rubs my arm. "I'm sorry if I made you feel bad about that. Yoga and spinning are great hobbies. I never played sports in school—that was Garrett. I was usually reading."

I smile at the thought of Nate ever being a nerd. I just can't picture it.

He just told me the most painful thing he went through. I need to be brave enough to tell him my own experience. I take a deep breath. "My dad died when I was six, I think. Our mother struggled to keep the power on and food on the table. There was a man who would stop by from time to time. He never came inside, and it was always late when he showed up, so I never got a good look at him. He'd give my mother money, but it never lasted long.

"She began gambling. One day she took Dakota and me to our grandparent's house, and she never came back. I became Dakota's mother that day, trying to take care of everything so that we didn't burden our grandparents. I was so afraid that if we caused any trouble, they'd find somewhere else to drop us. When Dakota was arrested in the fall, I had to call my mom for bail money." I brush away a stray tear, and he jumps in.

"So, your mom gave you the money. If it's a loan, I can pay it off for you. You shouldn't have to work yourself to death trying to fix someone else's mess."

I laugh despite everything. "Then how will you ever prove to your dad that you don't need to run the vineyard, Nate? You keep the tattoo money for your dreams."

He cracks a small smile at my joke but waits for me to answer his question.

"It wasn't a loan. She just paid it and told us where she'd been for the past decade. I guess her gambling got her into some trouble, and the mystery man had to bail her out. Oh, side note: The mystery man runs a motorcycle club... and is apparently my father."

Nate whistles through his teeth. "That is some heavy shit, babe. So, he was never dead?"

I sigh. "Nope. I guess the whole time my mother was gone, she was sending money for Dakota and me to live on. Our grandparents pocketed that money, though. There was enough to cover clothing, vehicles, and college. We never saw a dime of it, though. Maybe it's just as well knowing where it came from. So, there you have it."

He pulls me into his strong arms. "Have you talked to your grandparents about the money? I can't believe you've been trying to handle this alone. I know your sister had all the charges dropped against her, but I had no idea you were facing all this. Has your dad tried to contact you?"

I shake my head. "I haven't spoken to any of them. I think I'm still trying to make sense of it all. You can only handle so much news before it becomes too much."

Nate's lips brush against my forehead. "I'm here now. Let me shoulder this burden with you. You don't have to take on everyone else's problems anymore."

Tears drop down onto the quilt beneath me. "I'm in love with you, Nate."

I hadn't meant to say it, but the minute the words are out there, it's as if a weight has been lifted off my chest.

His hands stop making circles on my back. "You're in love with me or you love me?"

I frown. "Are they not the same?"

He turns me until I'm facing him. "Well, there are—"

I place my fingers against his lips. "I'm going to go ahead and stop you right there. I love you. I have for a while now. I don't need sixty days to try it out. I want you for as long as you'll have me."

I'm just a girl standing before a heavily tattooed man with my heart in my hand.

No big deal.

He grins. "I love you too, Katy girl. I've known since the moment you went down on me in my car while you were drunk on tequila shots."

I slap his arm playfully. "Why do you have to ruin a perfectly romantic moment?"

He pushes me back against the old quilt, rolling his hips to pin me in place. "Did you say romantic? Because I saved Dakota's photo of you in a wedding gown. You're so fucking perfect, babe."

I tip my head back to look up at him, knowing that all that scruff and roughness is just a façade. It's there in his eyes—the same fear that I have.

It's as if they're pleading with me.

Please don't leave me.

Don't hurt me.

I nod, answering both his spoken and unspoken questions.

I'm not going anywhere.

He leans down and nips at my lips with his teeth, even as his hand snakes its way up under my sweater. His fingers are like ice, and my skin prickles almost instantly. Nate pulls back just enough to lift my sweater over my head before his mouth moves down.

He licks lazily along my stomach as if we've got all the time in the world. I groan in frustration, and he pauses to look up at me. "Everything okay, babe?" His lip turns up slightly, and it's apparent that he's well aware of the torture he's inflicting.

I shake my head. "More... I need more."

Nate rests on his knees and grabs my left leg, taking his sweet time unzipping my boot before moving to the other leg.

More.

My body has reverted to the most primal instincts, and all rational thought ceases. I'm beyond caring that we're inside a barn where anyone can see us. I need my husband inside of me.

He unbuttons my jeans, deftly sliding them down my body like it's an art form. My breasts rise and fall with each ragged breath I take, and he stares at me almost reverently.

His gaze is so intense that I have to look away, but he hooks his hand under my chin and draws my eyes back to his. "You're beautiful."

I nod shakily, silently urging him to keep going while patting myself on the back for wearing matching lingerie. When he doesn't appear to be on the verge of making a move anytime soon, I take matters into my own hands.

I take my time unlacing his boots while looking up at him from under my eyelashes. It's my turn to torture him. He brings his fist to his mouth and exhales slowly as I unfasten his jeans and slide them down.

I can see the outline of his cock through his dark grey boxer briefs as it strains to break free from its polyester prison. I run my hand along the front, and his head drops back with a loud groan.

Taking the sound as an encouragement to continue, I slip my fingers beneath the waistband, gripping him in my hands. The tip of his head is already slick, and I use the lubrication to slide my hand up and down his shaft.

I wonder what he tastes like.

Before I can change my mind, my tongue darts out to lick along the tip, and Nate's hands fist in my hair.

"Fuck. My turn, Katy girl." He whispers before his hands drop down my back to unfasten my bra. His hands are on my breasts before the bra has even hit the floor. His palm squeezes one while his mouth teases the other until it's stiff.

My brain is being overrun with dopamine, oxytocin, and serotonin in a chemical reaction that leaves me aching with need.

I briefly register that Nate still has his shirt on, and I reach for it, needing to see his ink. His mouth moves off of my breast with a pop, and he obliges before grabbing my panties in his fist and yanking them down.

His hips shift to hold me in place again. There's nothing between us but skin. His lips catch mine, kissing me like he'll never get another opportunity. His tongue thrusts against my lips, and I open up, ushering him inside.

He doesn't break contact with my mouth as the head of his cock aligns with my body, pushing gently against me as if asking for permission.

I reach my hand between our bodies, guiding him. He moves slowly as my body works feverishly to accommodate all of him. Growing impatient, his hands reach up to grip my shoulders, and he pushes into me until he bottoms out.

I cry out against his mouth and push back against him, needing him to move... needing the friction.

He growls against my lips and thrusts harder inside of me. We fit together perfectly—his hard muscles against my soft flesh. He grabs one of my hands in his, forcing it over my head and keeping my body where he wants it.

He pulls all the way out only to force himself back in, and I pant heavily. His thrusts increase, each pump of his hips punishing yet bringing me intense pleasure.

"I'm close... I'm so close..." I murmur the words to no one in particular, but Nate takes it as a challenge. His mouth moves back down, and he latches onto my breast, sucking hard enough to leave marks. Just when I think I can't take another moment, he bites down, and I moan his name as I come.

Wave after wave of pleasure pummels me until I can't even tell where I end, and he begins. He continues thrusting, each grunt becoming more pronounced, and I hold onto his hand as another orgasm hits me.

"Come inside of me, Nate. Come inside of me... please. I want to feel you." It doesn't sound like my voice.

His eyes fly open in surprise, and his thrusts become unsteady. I'm drunk off of the power, and I use my free hand to grab onto his hip.

"Come with me, babe." His words are hoarse, and with a final thrust, he surges inside of me with a groan, filling me entirely. Watching his face is enough to send me over the edge, and I bite down on my lip until I taste blood as he crushes his body against mine.

The barn is silent except for the sounds of our heavy breathing as we try to return to earth.

He props himself up on his forearms and looks down at me, still out of breath. "That was incredible."

I push the hair back off his forehead and smile before noticing the sky growing dark. "Um, Nate? What time did your mom say that dinner was?"

He checks his watch. "Fuck. Okay, so we're a little late."

* * *

It's completely dark outside when we pull up in front of the house. I pull my helmet off and leave it on the seat before rushing toward the front door.

Nate grabs my hand, pulling me back toward his body. "You trust me?"

I nod, confused. "Yes, what's going on?"

He only smiles and leads me into the house. Everyone but Daniel is gathered around the table, waiting to eat.

"Hey guys, sorry we're late. I have a little announcement to make. Kate and I got married."

Bev's eyes widen in surprise and she starts shrieking. "What! Like just now? Is that where you've been?"

Nate is still standing behind me, his hands resting on my hips, and I hate that I can't see the look on his face. He laughs softly. "No, Mom. Not just now...a while ago."

"October 14th, to be exact," I add helpfully, and his hands squeeze me. I feel a slight tremor of pleasure at his touch and wonder if a body is capable of orgasm aftershocks.

His dad stands up. "Well, I've heard of waiting a few months to announce a pregnancy but never a marriage. Congratulations."

He pulls both of us into a hug as Bev dances around. "Married? I can't believe it. This is amazing."

Daniel runs in with a crayon and begins dancing with her. "Why are we dancing, Grams?"

She picks him up and swings him around. "Because Uncle Nate and Aunt Katy got married!" Then she lowers her voice to mock whisper, "And Grams is gonna get more grandbabies."

My cheeks flood with heat at the thought just as Garrett decides to speak up.

"Were y'all up in the loft?"

Nate nods. "Yeah, why?"

Garrett taps a spoonful of mashed potatoes against his plate with a knowing grin. "Because Kate still has some hay in her hair. Mom, you might get your wish sooner than you think."

twenty-six

COMMANDMENT #27: THOU SHALT NOT ALLOW ANYONE TO MAKE THEM A FOOL

Kate

"So, you spent the entire weekend in bed?" Nicole raises her eyebrows, and I nod happily.

"Once we told his family, every secret was out there. I can't even put into words how perfect it was; the sex was different too— better."

She tucks a strand of blonde hair behind one ear. "So, what about the ex? Did he ever explain what happened between them?"

I recount everything he told me and her mouth falls open. She gets up from her chair and starts pacing. "Okay... okay. Surely millions of people deal with this..."

"What's wrong?"

She shakes her head. "I counseled a woman a few years ago. She'd been in a car accident and lost her memory." She sinks back down onto the chair. "Through our sessions, she recovered enough of her memory to realize her husband was having an affair with her best friend."

I stand up and walk over to the window, holding the ledge in a death grip. "What was the best friend's name?"

Nicole's voice is quiet. "It was Jess, Kate."

"Let me guess, David was the husband?"

She nods, and I lean over to clutch my knees. "Carla... Carla is Jess."

Nicole runs over to me. "Deep breath. What?"

I don't know how I didn't see it before. The answer was staring me in the face the entire time. She was gauging my reactions in every session we had.

"I stayed the night with my ex-husband."

I try to recall that conversation and realize it was right before I found the underwear and perfume in his house. She was trying to get a rise out of me.

But why did he lie and say no one had been there but me?

Why did she stay the night?

"Carla, Nic. Carla is Jess... and I'm supposed to counsel her in fifteen minutes!"

She taps her index finger against her mouth. "You've got a log of every session the two of you have had, right?" When I nod, she continues, "Dr. Nicole White is about to become your fairy godmother."

* * *

"Aren't you going to ask me how my week was?" Jess asks, shifting uncomfortably in her chair.

I rest my hands on the arms of my chair, channeling all of my rage into focused energy. "Are you familiar with chess?"

She shakes her head and laughs. "No, not at all."

"In chess, the queen can become the strongest piece on the board through a series of exchanges and attacks. Many people mistakenly believe it's due to the queen's ability to move all over the board, but that's not what makes her so destructive."

She leans forward in her chair, taking the bait. "So, what makes her so destructive?"

I smile. "It's her willingness to make sacrifices to save the king. In this folder, I've documented every visit we've had, Jess."

Her eyes widen in understanding when she realizes I know exactly who she is.

"I hold more than enough information to qualify you for involuntary admission to a mental health facility. So, you see, we have quite a dilemma here. Either you disappear and never contact me or my husband again, or I will use every tool at my disposal to ensure that you never see anything outside the walls of a psychiatric facility ever again. The queen protects her king... at all costs. It's a lesson you failed to grasp when he was yours."

She shakes her head vehemently. "You don't understand what he and I have! You could never understand our bond. You're just jealous!"

I stand up and calmly walk over to the door. "That's where you're wrong. Jealousy would imply that you have something I want, when in reality, it's the other way around. I know his heart belongs to me, and unlike you, I will guard it at all costs."

Jess jumps up from the chair and stalks over to me. "He's going to come back to me... all the signs pointed to it. He could never see in you what he sees in me! You wear second-hand clothing and tape your shoes together—you're nothing but a basic bitch—"

I cut her off. "And you're nothing more than a psychotic bitch who relies on palm readers and tarot cards to live your life. We're done here. I've given you my warning—that's all you'll get. I will turn everything over to the court if you even think about going near him. Are we clear?"

She glares at me. "Crystal."

"Good." I slam the door shut behind her and sink down onto the soft carpet, working to control my breathing.

My god, did that feel good.

twenty-seven

COMMANDMENT #28: THOU SHALT KNOW WHEN IT'S TIME TO CALL IT

Kate

I take in the beautifully set table and debate whether or not to light candles. A quick glance around the house reveals that Nate apparently doesn't own any candles, so we'll have to do without.

I feel like jumping up and down and screaming in victory. Nate is free from the demons of his past. She'll never mess with him again. I still have questions about how Jess was able to leave things here, but we'll get to that when he's ready.

I also may have gone overboard on dinner. I had to watch a few YouTube videos on how to cook lobster tail, but this is day one of the rest of our lives together. I splurged and bought champagne—even though I'm a bit wary of drinking more than a glass.

Nicole was kind enough to give me some good book recommendations on how to heal after divorce and infidelity. *"His ego was bruised from the infidelity of three years ago. Knowing the lengths Jess went to to get close to him again—well, it might trigger a relapse for him. You need to be there to boost his self-esteem."*

I rather enjoy boosting his self-esteem.

I hear the garage door rise and smooth down my dress. I left work early and went to a department store to purchase it. I'd initially balked at the price, but it was a special occasion, and he was worth every penny.

I turn with a smile as he walks in, and my heart drops. He isn't smiling—in fact, he looks downright angry. I swallow down the feelings of uncertainty. "Hey, babe. How was your day?"

Nate doesn't say a word before disappearing into the bedroom. I follow him and stand awkwardly in the doorway. "I made dinner for us —I even got champagne if I'm brave enough to give drinking another try." I laugh weakly.

You're rambling, Kate.

He loosens his tie and finally makes eye contact with me. "Did you see Jess today?"

I knew that she couldn't be trusted to stay away from him. "I did— I gave her a nice warning, too."

Which she ignored completely, it seems.

"I see."

I can see that he's hurting, so I cross the room and wrap my arms around his waist. His arms remain stiffly at his side, and my heart beats faster in panic. "I should have consulted with you first before handling it myself. I'm sorry."

His hands move up to grip my upper arms, and I briefly relax before he pushes me away. "Get out."

Wait... what?

"I get that you're mad because I confronted her without you there, but please don't push me away right now. You need me."

He laughs bitterly, and my blood runs cold. "I need you? That's fucking cute, Kate. You're just some chick I enjoyed fucking—I never meant for it to go this far. Now, get the fuck out."

"No. You told me you loved me. You don't mean that!" My voice is small. Weak.

He shakes his head and sighs. "God, you really aren't that bright for a therapist. Men will say anything to get laid."

My chest tightens in agony. "Don't say that. I don't know what she told you, but don't push me away."

He runs his hands through his hair. "What she told me? Well, let's see. Her jaw is wired shut right now, so talking is an issue for her. They were initially worried that she might have a brain bleed. What else? Oh right. She'd been raped repeatedly. She was still brave enough to turn over your emails to the police. Did you learn to give warnings from your biker club daddy? Is he the one who carried this shit out?"

My eyes fill with tears, and I shake my head. "I didn't do any of that to her. I did—"

He crosses his arms over his chest. "Did you not just proudly state that you gave her a warning? And now you're saying you didn't. Jesus, Kate! You're so full of shit. You wanted to pretend that you were so fucking different, but what you've done is worse than anything she ever did. You knew I was a doctor the entire time—using me for my money. Unbelievable."

"I didn't do any of this! I didn't know who you were!" I sob, my chest heaving with each labored breath.

Why won't he listen?

"She's pressing charges, so get ready for prison orange. Who knows, maybe Dakota will fuck up again, and you two can share a cell. And when I find out who you recruited, so help me, god, they will pay."

I'm choking now—it's like trying to breathe through a straw. I clutch my chest to force more air in and out.

He walks toward the door leading out to the garage. "Have you been like this your whole life—a fucking psychopath? No wonder your mother left you. I meant what I said. I want you and your shit gone from my life by the time I get back."

The door slams shut behind him, and I drop to my knees on the carpet, completely eviscerated. I used to pride myself on my ability to let praise and criticism roll off my back, never allowing them to change who I was.

Until him.

I wrap my arms around my body and rock on the floor.

I need a lawyer.

But right now, I need my sister.

* * *

"Is that everything?" Zane asks from the doorway, and I nod before breaking down again.

Dakota, Zane, and Little Ricky arrived to help me pack up within minutes. Not that there was much of mine to take.

Little Ricky pulls me into a hug. "I just don't get it, Hail Mary. It seemed like things were going so well."

"I'm gonna cut his balls off and then force them down his throat," Dakota states to no one in particular.

Zane clears his throat. "Babe? Violence?"

She shakes her head. "I'm sorry, Big Guy. I meant to say that I'm going to cut his balls off and then bury them. Better?"

My eyes are almost swollen shut, and I haven't been able to breathe out of my nose for hours now, but I manage to smile a little at her threats. "I just don't know what happened between the time she left my office and her ending up in the hospital. Zane, have you heard anything?"

He rechecks his phone. "I reached out to Detective Sullivan. He said he'd let me know once he had more information. Now, we wait."

Little Ricky releases me long enough to start bagging the food on the table.

"What are you doing?"

He looks up. "What? We can't leave all this here to go to waste. We'll take it back to Caparina's and have ourselves a proper feast."

Once the food is packed, he offers to drive my car back to Dakota's, and we ride in silence for a few minutes. "Hail Mary, I'm gonna need you to start at the beginning."

I shake my head. "I can't talk about it right now."

He nods. "Well, I could sing then. I can't stand the quiet—it's no good for my brain." He flips through the stations, finally settling on a song he likes. "*No me queda mas...*"

I grimace. "You're right. Let's talk."

He shuts off the music with a pleased smirk. "Awesome, *dígame que pasó.*"

I sigh and tell him everything, including my sessions with Jess. I'm probably going to jail already—what's a HIPAA violation going to matter at this point?

Little Ricky pulls the car over on a side street near Dakota's house. "*Ay de mí.* Carla Snyder? Let me guess; she delivered a stillborn in prison and named her Nora."

I pause and stare at him in shock. "How could you know that?"

He slams a fist into the steering wheel. "*La puta* was playing you this entire time. Carla Snyder is the main character in *The World Will Still Go On.*"

In light of the situation, I start giggling uncontrollably. "And how would you know this, Little Ricky?"

He shrugs. "I'm home a lot during the day. I like the drama. Plus, *CarJack* is my couple." His phone rings. "Yeah? Okay, ten four." He shifts my Tahoe back into drive.

"Who was that?"

He glances over at me before pulling back onto the street. "That was Zane. Mikey's at the house, waiting."

"Who's Mikey?"

He laughs. "Sorry, Hail Mary. I forget sometimes. Detective Sullivan is waiting on us."

I swallow the bile that rises in my throat. "Is he—am I going to be arrested?"

I start shaking, and Little Ricky reaches across the console. "Hold my hand. It's going to be fine. You are not going to jail, Kate. I'll call Grey myself to ensure it."

We pull up in front of Dakota's house, and there he is—the detective who looks like everything I asked the universe for. It seems like a lifetime ago.

I unbuckle and reluctantly climb out.

What if he throws handcuffs on me, and I end up in jail for days like Dakota did? What if my alibi isn't strong enough, and I go to prison? I'd tell them I was innocent, but they would just laugh and tell me that's what everyone says before feeding me bread and water.

"Hey, Kate." Mike nods at me as I get out.

My teeth are chattering together loudly. "Am I under arrest?"

He frowns. "No, I just need you to come with me down to the station. I need to get your statement."

Dakota starts crying and wraps me up in a hug while Zane storms inside to make a pot of coffee because "Fuck it. We're not going to bed tonight."

I refuse to look Mike in the eyes, instead focusing on the simple gold band on his ring finger. A wedding band isn't very big, but it sure has the power to destroy lives, doesn't it?

"Should I ride in the back?" I point to his truck.

"No, I already said you're not under arrest. You can ride up front."

"Please call whoever you have to so I don't have to stay there. I'm not like you," I whisper to Dakota.

She shakes her head. "Stop, you're the strongest person I know. I'll call Dad... he can fix this—"

Mike cuts in. "I've already contacted Grey. I'm going to use every resource I have to keep you out of jail, Kate. Please trust me."

Reluctantly, I get into Mike's truck, my entire body quaking at the thought that this might be the last time I see my sister without a plate of plexiglass between us.

twenty-eight

COMMANDMENT #29: THOU SHALT EMBRACE THE INDEPENDENCE AND FREEDOM OF BEING SINGLE AGAIN

Kate

"Kate, we're looking into Jess Davis's claims against you. The emails are going to be difficult to dispute. Mike pulls a sheaf of papers from a manila folder and hands them to me. We're sitting in a small interrogation room at the station. All that's missing is the two-way mirror like what you see on television.

I keep expecting him to go from good cop to bad cop as I take them from him.

From: marykatherine.quinn@gmail.com
To: jessdavis12@live.com
Subject: Nate

I warned you to stay away. I don't know how many messages I've sent now saying that exact thing. Good luck today—remember as your screaming and begging for your life that I gave you every opportunity to walk away. He wants nothing to do with you're lies. I'm taking out the trash. He'll thank me for it.

The rest contain similar variations of the same threat.

"I didn't send this. This is my email address, but I didn't send any of these." I point to the third sentence. "This person used 'your' and 'you're' incorrectly. I would have never made a mistake like that. Surely, this proves that I didn't write it."

Mike nods. "Yeah, it could be said that you did it to throw off suspicion, though. I don't think you wrote this, but we now have to figure out who did, or you'll be facing forcible rape, assault, and stalking charges."

Another officer comes in and hands me a cup of black coffee before leaving us alone again. I take a sip and immediately recoil at the bitterness. "Have you checked the IP address on these? Surely there's a way to prove they didn't come from my computer."

"Yeah, it's pinging all over the place, which is super helpful right now." He rubs at his face, and I wonder if this is all in a day's work for him because I feel like I'm in *The Twilight Zone*. He lowers his voice. "I've got Jeremy working on it."

My brain tries to condense everything I've learned into a believable story. "Jeremy, as in Realtor Jeremy?"

Mike nods. "Yeah, I called him. He said he could hack the server and pinpoint the location. We're going to need everyone working on this. I'm trying to keep you out of a jail cell."

I peer down into the half-empty Styrofoam cup of coffee. "Is there alcohol in this?"

He gets up to pace. "No. Do you need some?"

"No. I'm just confused by everything right now.... I thought I might be drunk."

Hoped for it, actually.

There's a light knock on the door, and Mike pulls a gun from the back of his jeans before checking to see who it is. He throws the door open and ushers Zane in.

Who was he expecting to pop up in the middle of the police station? ISIS?

Zane grabs an empty chair before firing up his laptop. "Jeremy said your pizza is in the oven as we speak."

Pizza?

Incapable of reprieve, my brain immediately switches gears to something equally painful.

Men will say anything to get laid.

I walk over to the window, pressing my hand to my mouth to stifle the sound of my sobs.

"Hey. Kate, it's going to be okay."

"I'm fine," I lie. "Jeremy's making pizza?"

Mike scratches at his beard. "He didn't tell you?"

My mouth opens and closes in confusion. "I—I'm sorry? What are you talking about? Oh my god."

I grab a pen and write:

Jeremy's a hacker?

He nods. "I thought you knew. Shit. Well, no taking it back now. God, I'm fucking starving—that pizza better be done soon."

Zane rolls his eyes and continues typing.

I sigh. "So, what? He works in real estate and bakes pizzas in his spare time. How does 'the pizzeria' fit into all of that?"

"Getting this sorted sometime tonight would be wonderful. I've got a wife I'd like to get home to," Mike complains while peering over Zane's shoulder. "Please tell me Jarvis has something,"

Zane looks up long enough to flip him off. "You're not the only one who'd rather be at home, asshole. The pizza wasn't baking as fast as Jeremy wanted, so he scratched the order and started over."

I clear my throat. "Again, how does 'the pizzeria' factor into this?"

Mike texts someone from his phone, not bothering to look up to answer. "The owner likes buying property—kinda like your sister's house."

"He owns Dakota's house?" I exclaim before nodding. "That makes more sense than anything I've heard over the last month. Okay, go. Bake the pizza or whatever."

I lean forward in my chair and rest my head on my arms. I'll just close my eyes for a minute and try to sort this out in my head.

"Pizza's been delivered—eat up, boys."

That sounds like Jeremy.

I blearily rub my eyes and pick my face up off the table. I'm probably the only person ever to fall asleep during an interrogation. I don't even know how long I've been out.

Mike and Zane study the computer screen as if it holds the answers to all of life's mysteries.

"That's fucking perfect, Jarvis—pepperoni and everything. Trace it." Mike points at something on the screen, and Zane nods.

"Did you find out where it came from?" I ask sleepily.

Jeremy's voice comes through Mike's phone. "Look at that. How'd we miss that? Kate, you're going to want to see this."

I stand up and stretch before coming around behind them. Once Jeremy points it out, I don't see how I missed it either.

My email address is mary.katherine.quinn@gmail.com, while the dupe is marykatherine.quinn@gmail.com.

"Who sent the messages?"

Jeremy answers, "Jess. And Mike? I think the police department will be very interested in her Google searches. She was studying brain tumors, getting away with a hit-and-run, and even masking the taste of castor oil in smoothies."

My jaw drops, and I look over at Zane. His eyes are wide with shock. "When was that search done?"

Mike looks at the screen as Jeremy navigates through the phone. "This was done the week before Halloween. Why? Does this correspond with something?"

Zane's jaw is clenched. "Yeah, my fiancée just happened to end up severely ill and in the hospital on Halloween after drinking a smoothie from the gym."

Little Ricky's voice speaks up from the phone, and I jump in surprise. I had no idea he was with Jeremy. "Mikey, you wanna give her to your old man? Cause I'd be down to help with that. Comedian could put a big smile on her face. Oh, wait—shit. I mean, do you want to turn her into a fucking pizza?"

Mike shakes his head. "No, man. We're going to keep this on the up and up here. She belongs in prison, and with her priors, she won't be getting out. Jarvis, wipe surveillance when you're done."

"What will they charge her with?" I ask him.

"Falsely reporting a crime, for starters. I might be able to get her on perjury... forgery... grand theft. I think we can get her on attempted murder charges with what she did to Dakota. I'll have someone at the gym review the tapes and see what we come up with. On top of that, she's violating her parole, so she won't be going anywhere anytime soon."

I lean down and hug him. "Thank you."

He nods and squeezes me tightly in his arms. "Happy to help."

"I'm going to go home and go to bed; try to forget this happened. Wait, can I leave?"

Zane stands up and stretches. "I'll drive you back to your car. We're not charging her, right?"

Mike looks down at his watch. "No. I've got someone up at the hospital right now with Jess. I'll need a search warrant to get her computer. Just lay low until we arrest her. Do not talk to anyone."

Zane grips Mike's shoulder on the way out. "You make sure what you've got on her is enough to keep her locked away forever. You don't want me getting my hands on her."

Mike nods. "I'll take care of it. Kate, stay home until this blows over."

I agree and drag myself to Zane's truck, blasting the heat on high until I stop shaking. I feel like I'm coming down with something—maybe the flu.

He looks over at me. "You gonna be okay over there?"

I shake my head. "I feel awful. When did you start working with Grey?"

Zane keeps his eyes on the road as he answers, "I'm not. I'm just trying to keep you out of jail—the same as Sullivan."

Once I reach Dakota's, I wearily climb into my Tahoe and drive back to my apartment, feeling like I'm returning to another life—a life without Nate.

Grief hits me like a sucker punch, and I lay my face against the steering wheel, sobbing until I'm incapable of producing any more tears.

He slipped past my defenses and burrowed under my armor. And six hours ago, he left me standing in our bedroom alone, holding the battered remains of my heart.

Fairy tale over.

* * *

A soft tap on the glass jolts me awake. Jeremy stares at me from the other side. Sunlight streams into the car as I move my stiff body away from the steering wheel.

"Hey. Are you okay?"

I try to nod and wince in pain. I definitely have the flu. My whole body aches. He helps me out of the car and upstairs to my apartment.

It smells musty like I've been gone for years, not five weeks.

I flip on the kitchen light and grab a bottle of water from the fridge. "So, you and Grey?"

"Yeah, I work for him. I kind of wish Mike would have let me tell you when I was ready. Grey wanted someone to keep an eye on you, so I followed you to that chamber event. I was only supposed to watch you—I never thought that—"

"I'd lose my virginity to you?" I supply helpfully, and his face goes white.

"Oh, fuck. I didn't realize that. Okay, you should never mention any of that to your dad. Please."

I press the cold bottle against my neck. "Why are you here, Jeremy? Sent to check up on me again? Because I'm going to be real honest with you. I'm not in the mood for sex. I'm in the mood to sleep until I'm dead."

He touches my forehead and exclaims, "You're burning up, Kate. Let's get you into bed."

"I'm fine." I take a couple of steps, and my legs give out. Thankfully, Jeremy is on the ball and quickly scoops me into his arms.

I lay my face against his shirt. It feels cool against my cheek. "Um, Jeremy? Do men say anything just to get laid?"

He pulls back the covers and lays me down on the sheets. "What do you mean? Do you think that's what I did?"

I tuck my hands inside my sweatshirt and roll onto my side, alternating between hot and cold. "No. Nate said that he only told me he loved me as a way to get laid. I just wondered if all men are really like that."

He pulls the comforter up around my head and sits beside me. "I think Nate was misinformed, and he's probably about to regret everything he said to you. He'd be a fucking idiot to let you leave."

I nod. "I think that too, Jeremy. I'm a nice girl. I'm just going to rest my eyes now because they're burning."

He pats my back. "I'll be in the living room. Your dad said I should stay with you until everything's clear."

'Why don't you wear a leather vest if you work for a motorcycle club? I thought all you guys did that."

He chuckles, "Well, we don't want to advertise or draw attention to ourselves. We try to blend in, so I typically save it for the clubhouse."

I struggle to lift my head off the pillow, but it feels like it's made of cement. "Dakota? Is someone with her?"

"She's got Zane and Little Ricky. Try and get some sleep. I'll run and get you some meds soon." He cups my face, and I turn away. "Sorry. I'm just—I'm sorry. For all of it."

The bed shifts as he gets up and walks out. I still have a lot of questions, but my eyes drift closed, and I slip into fever dreams.

twenty-nine

COMMANDMENT #30: THOU SHALT NOT MAKE THE SAME MISTAKE TWICE

Nate

I can't believe I ever trusted her.

I was sick when the police showed me the emails. They dated back to August. Days after we met, she emailed Jess cryptic messages and veiled threats. Jess was no peach to be married to, but having her beaten and raped?

That's beyond anything I would ever wish upon another human being, regardless of what that person did to me.

And then she stood there and lied to my fucking face, acting like she was completely innocent of wrongdoing. God, the worst part is that I almost believed her.

She was so damn convincing that I considered staying.

What does that say about me?

"I didn't think you were on the schedule for today."

I look up from my lukewarm cup of coffee to find my surgical nurse coordinator frowning at me. "I was on call last night and didn't have anything better to do, so I just stayed here."

Truthfully, I have no idea how long I've been sitting in the physician's lounge. The days are all blurring together. I've been sleeping in my car or here. I keep telling myself I'm doing it to avoid an awkward run-in with Kate, but the reality is that I'm not ready to go home to an empty house.

Eventually, I'll have to, but not today.

"Are you feeling okay?" Monica asks, peering into my eyes. "Flu's going around right now."

I shake my head. "I'm fine. Why?"

"Because you look like shit," she says bluntly before taking the chair across from me. "I'm guessing you witnessed the drama downstairs firsthand since you were here all night."

"What drama?" I ask before taking another drink of coffee, praying the caffeine will snap me out of this fog.

Monica leans forward conspiratorially. "Remember the female that was brought in Monday afternoon? The one that seemed to point to a 'for-hire' attack?"

"Jessica Davis?"

Her eyes widen. "Yeah, I'm surprised you remember. Then how do you not know—"

"That a woman named Mary Katherine Quinn set the whole thing up?"

Monica's brows furrow. "What? The police obtained a warrant to search Jessica's house. They haven't said specifically what was found, but it must have been incriminating enough for them to arrest her. I'm just upset that I wasn't downstairs when it happened. I always miss the good stuff and had to hear all about it from one of the residents."

My heart sinks even as my mind races through the last seventy-two hours. "That's impossible. She was beaten and raped—no one in their right mind would do that to themselves."

"No one in their right mind would, but from everything I heard, I'm not so sure she is," she says, circling a finger near her temple.

Jess is a lot of things, but crazy is not one of them.

Right?

* * *

"Yeah, I'm here to see an inmate—Jessica Davis," I say, tapping my fingers impatiently against the laminate counter.

"Nate?"

My shoulders drop at the sound of the voice. Of all the fucking people to be here right now, it had to be him.

I turn around and paste a fake smile on my face. "Detective Do-Right, what a surprise."

His eyes narrow at the nickname. "What are you doing here? We released Kate yesterday morning."

I knew they would arrest her, but hearing it from Mike is like a knife to my heart. If anyone's crazy, out of the three of us, it's bound to be me.

"I'm here to see Jess. I think you've got the wrong girl."

Mike waves his hand at the woman behind the counter. "Hey, Sierra, I'll take it from here. Come on, Nate. Let's talk."

I should tell him to go fuck himself, but I'm desperate for answers. So, with my head held high, I follow the son-of-a-bitch into his office.

He gestures toward a chair and shuts the door behind me. "You want coffee or water?"

"Yeah, I'd like a latte and maybe a scone to go with it," I mutter dryly. "Is this the police station or a fucking *Starbucks*?"

He lowers himself into his chair with a murderous glare. "Still defending her after all this time, I see. Were the bitch not fucking up the lives of nearly everyone I know and care about, I might find it adorable."

"I don't have time for this shit—"

"Sit the fuck down!" Mike barks, slamming his hand down on his desk. "You don't know shit about fuck—"

"Really? I saw the emails. They came from Kate."

He shakes his head. "Only, they didn't. We obtained a search warrant for Jess's apartment. It's standard procedure—we were looking for any evidence that could help us locate the suspects. All those emails originated from her laptop, and upon taking a closer look at the address, he points to the discrepancy, and I don't know how I didn't catch it before. "That's not your wife's email address, correct?"

"No," I'm forced to admit. "It's not. The grammatical errors are consistent with Jess's writing, too."

Mike continues, "Kate pointed that out as well. There were photographs of her and several of you on Jess's computer. I don't know how far back they go, but I think it's safe to say she's been stalking you both for a while."

My head drops down, and I brace my arms on my thighs. "So, Jess is responsible—not Kate? How? She admitted she gave her a warning."

"We videotaped Kate's statement of her interaction with Jessica Davis on Monday, along with her whereabouts during the time Jessica claims she was assaulted," he says, turning his laptop toward me. "As part of this investigation concerns you, I think it's only fair that you see it."

Seeing a pale-faced, trembling Kate is enough to pull my breath from my lungs, but hearing the way she defended me to my ex-wife is like a battering ram to my heart.

I told her that the queen protects the king.

My brain decides that now is an excellent time to remind me of everything I said to Kate in anger and the look of devastation on her face.

"Jess violated the terms of her parole. She's being charged with damn near everything: perjury, forgery, making a false report, attempted murder—"

"Attempted murder? Who did she try to kill?"

"She poisoned Dakota Quinn," he says, his lips flattening into a thin line.

My pulse picks up. "What—when?"

He taps several keys, and there it is, in grainy black and white: my ex-wife at a gym she doesn't belong to, slipping something into Dakota's smoothie.

"October thirty-first. The gym released this to us after we found some disturbing searches on Jess's laptop."

Halloween.

The same fucking day that Dakota came stumbling out of the locker room, collapsing in my arms. The thought of her losing the baby leaves me feeling sick.

Mike taps the screen with his knuckle. "You know, if we hadn't had a hunch that something was off with Jess's story, Kate would be going to prison. We'd have nothing right now if she'd wiped the hard drive. Side note: you might be interested in researching the soap opera character Carla Snyder."

My brows lift. "Soap opera character? How is that related to this?"

"It's ridiculous, but we had an anonymous tip, and it checks out. Fake pregnancies, drugging men and telling them they slept with her, brain lesions—you name it, and the character's done it. So has Jess, for that matter, if the evidence is any indicator."

I stumble out of the station in a daze, feeling like I've been hit by a semi-truck. Kate's only crime was falling in love with me, and I was too much of an asshole to hear her out when she tried to tell me the truth.

She must have been so scared.

The only woman who's ever truly loved me for me, and I pushed her away, telling her she meant nothing.

My phone rings. Garrett, of course. His timing is impeccable.

"Hey, it's not—"

"Ding dong, the witch is dead," he crows. "What did I tell you about karma, huh? I knew something was off with that girl, and I was right. Are you and Kate celebrating?"

"Garrett—" I swallow hard. "I fucked it all up."

"Fucking hell, Nate! No, Dad, they're not celebrating. Why? Because Nate did what Nate does—he *Nates* everything up. Yeah, I just might," he mutters with a chuckle that raises the hair on my neck.

"What? What did he say, Garrett?"

"Our father thinks it might be time for Kate to get herself a real man, like myself. So, can I get her number?"

"Not if my fucking life depends on it," I force out through clenched teeth.

He laughs like everything's one big joke. "Oh, look, Dad. Right here. Kate Quinn-Davis. You bet your ass I'm going to call her. She won't even have to change her last name when I go and marry the shit out of her."

"Garrett," I warn.

"I'm going to have to let you go. I've got a hot date later." He ends the call before I can say another word.

I'm going to kick his ass.

I have to find her. I'll get down on my knees if I need to, but I can't accept losing her.

I can fix this, can't I?

thirty

COMMANDMENT #31: THOU SHALT NOT OVERSTAY YOUR WELCOME

Kate

"What do you mean we don't qualify for an annulment? Neither one of us had any business making that kind of commitment while intoxicated." My voice is barely above a whisper as I'm still fighting off some sort of plague.

My lawyer looks over some paperwork on her desk. "You got married October fourteenth. It's now December second. To qualify for an annulment, you would've needed to file immediately after the marriage took place."

I clutch my heavy head in my hands. "No...that can't be right. Intoxication was listed as legal grounds for nullifying a marriage."

"You admitted that you voluntarily cohabitated with Nathaniel Davis until just a few days ago. The court won't consider an annulment when both parties voluntarily stay together after sobering up."

My head hurts so badly, and this only makes it worse. I've been tested for flu, strep, mono—you name it. Everything has come back negative, though.

Little Ricky said I'm suffering from a broken heart, but last I checked, that doesn't cause flu-like symptoms and laryngitis.

I croak out, "What about fraud? Nate grossly misrepresented himself."

The lawyer fights a smile, and I want to punch her in her smug face. "And how exactly did he misrepresent himself?"

I start stumbling over my words in anger. "He—well, he said—he's still in love with his ex-wife, okay?"

Her eyebrows rise until they disappear under her hair. Someone should have talked her out of the bangs because they only make her face more punchable.

"So, you were unaware that he was in love with his ex when you married him?"

I sigh. "No, I knew—wait, if I said that I didn't know, could I get the annulment?"

She takes a stack of papers and begins tapping them on the desk to straighten them. "Mrs. Davis, your best option is to file for divorce. I can get the papers drawn up immediately, and either you can give Nathaniel his copy, or we can have him served."

I sit, stunned. There's no way to make this go away. I'm going to be a divorcee.

Wait, if I file, am I the divorcer?

"Mrs. Davis? What would you like to do?"

I hesitate until I remember the hate that was in his eyes. "I want him served. Preferably at work. In front of a large crowd. Maybe his family could be invited beforehand?"

Lawyer Lara rolls her eyes. "Okay, we'll see what we can do."

I roll my eyes back at her, adopting the same tone. "Well, that's what I'm paying you for."

* * *

"Nate!"

I wake up tangled in the sheets, my body dripping cold sweat. My fever spiked when I left the lawyer's office, and I was so foggy-headed that I couldn't even see straight.

It would be nice if I didn't dream of him every time I fell asleep. Instead, my brain insists on conjuring up images of a life we'll never have.

The grief hits me the minute I open my eyes and stays with me until I lie down at night. I never realized how powerful of an emotion it was until now. I don't need food or water. Grief is my only sustenance, and my tears quench my thirst.

I'm starting to sound like Sylvia Plath—one crisis away from sticking my head in the oven.

"Is she sick? I'm not trying to cause a problem; I just want to know she's okay."

Nate?

Great, now I'm hearing things because it isn't enough to just dream of him anymore.

He is consuming me.

I kick the sheets off and stand up, swaying heavily. I use the wall for support and approach the living room, feeling like I'm on a boat, being tossed around on the ocean.

"Nate?" My voice is nothing more than a hoarse whisper.

There's a giant standing near the front door, talking to someone on the other side. Maybe not a real giant, but this guy has got to be as tall as Zane—and that guy's like a redwood.

Redwood...

I giggle weakly and continue moving at a snail's pace.

The giant turns around. He's a handsome giant—not at all like I expected. "Katydid, let's get you back to bed."

I point to the door. "No... it's Nate."

The door is pushed open, and I'm not crazy. It's Nate—and he looks awful.

"Katy girl, can we talk?" He tries to enter, but the giant stops him with his arm.

"Sweetheart, you're not well. You need to be resting."

197

What an odd thing to say to another man.

Oh, he's talking to me.

I shake my head. "Jolly Giant, I'm fine. See?" I take a step and immediately fall into the back of the couch.

Nate pushes past the giant and kneels beside me. "You're burning up. Let me stay. Please. Let me take care of you."

Before I can reply, he dissolves into the carpet.

"Come back!" I hoarsely scream, frantically digging at the carpet.

He'll die if I don't get him out.

The giant comes over and quickly lifts me into his arms. When he brushes the damp hair off my forehead, all thoughts of Nate disappear. It's his eyes—a striking electric blue I've only ever seen on the detective and my sister.

"Grey?" I croak. "Is it you?"

"I've got you, sweetheart." After swiping a tear from the corner of my eye, he presses a light kiss against my hair and carries me back to bed.

I should be afraid, but as he lays me back against the pillows and tucks the blankets around my shoulders, I feel like a little kid again— safe, protected, and most of all, loved.

Fat tears spill onto my cheeks as I consider Nate was the last person to make me feel that.

"Nate. Where did Nate go?" I cry, drowning in a sea of grief.

"Nobody's been here but me."

I shake my head firmly. "I saw him. Nate. He was here, and he wanted to take care of me."

"I think you're hallucinatin', darlin'." His jaw tightens, and he climbs into bed, drawing me up against his chest

I'm going mad.

My shoulders shake as I release another anguished sob against his shirt, and his hold tightens. "Which one heard voices? Was that Sylvia Plath or Virginia Woolf?"

He laughs easily. "Well, I think it was Virginia Woolf. In your case, though, I'd blame it on the pneumonia and not any mental break on your end."

"So, Nate hasn't been here at all?"

He still thinks I'm a psychopath.

Someone dropped by earlier," he admits, toeing off his boots before settling against the pillows. "Dressed like a cowboy? You were sleepin', and I didn't want to wake you."

I sigh. "That would be Nate's brother, Garrett. He must not have heard how insane I am yet."

"You know, when you were a little girl, you would refuse to go to bed until you'd had a bedtime story. Your mama would offer to read it, and you'd throw a fit—it had to be me. You loved for me to read comics to you—"

"I think you're mixing me up with Dakota," I mumble.

"No, it was you. Dakota wasn't even around then. You were picky about them, too. You always requested the same comics. They had to be Spider-Man, or they were no good. I once asked you why, and do you know what you told me?"

"Not a clue," I rasp before going into a coughing fit.

Grey lightly rubs my back until it passes before continuing. "You told me you liked him because he wasn't perfect. He lost his uncle and the love of his life, but you said somethin' that day that's always stuck with me: 'he's been through so much, but he just keeps tryin' to do the right thing —even when it would be easier to give up.' You've always had a soft spot for broken things, Katydid. I can't imagine that Nate is much different. You were drawn to Peter Parker's story because it's your story, too."

"No, I'm uptight. Rigid. Unyielding—nothing like your friendly neighborhood Spiderman. Just Not So Fun Kate. What a terrible superhero I'd make."

Grey makes a noise that sounds like disapproval. "No matter what life has thrown at you, you've taken it all in stride, knowing that with great power comes great responsibility. You were Dakota's keeper when your mama left, but you don't need to do that anymore. You've shouldered that burden for too long—if I had known things were that bad, I would have stepped in a long time ago."

My eyes grow heavy. "What are you going to do? Shower me in money? Break anyone who crosses me? Because I've got quite the list, starting with my grandparents. And then Nate... obviously."

My head bounces against his chest as it rises and falls with laughter. "I don't think you're cut out for this lifestyle, kiddo. Hell, there are days that I don't think I'm cut out for it. Sleep, Katydid. I'm gonna get you some more medicine."

I cough until my eyes stream, rasping out, "You know, I'd argue with you, but I feel like dying. I can't handle one more thing. I'm so tired, Grey. I'm tired of feeling guilty... tired of constantly being pulled in fifteen different directions. If I'm being honest, I'm tired of living this life."

"Daddy's here now," he murmurs, gently rocking me. "Ain't got much of a plan yet, but I'm gonna get us out of this, Katydid. You just rest and let me take over for a while."

He leans down to press a kiss against my head, and little drops of water fall onto my face.

It's raining in my bedroom.

That's what's happening here.

Bikers don't cry, do they?

thirty-one

COMMANDMENT #32: THOU SHALT NOT SURPRISE HER WITH OVER-THE-TOP ROMANTIC GESTURES

Nate

"Hey asshole, a lot of guys go to college for a decade." Brad takes a bite of steak.

Yep. They're doctors, Brad.

Garrett drops his fork onto his plate. "You're still in college? Please tell me you're at least working on your doctorate by now?"

Mitch and Clayton join in, and Brad sulks into his beer. I look forward to this trip every year, but I just can't get my mind into it right now.

Kate dominates my every thought.

I miss her like crazy.

What's that song lyric?

'You don't know what you got 'til it's gone.'

Who the fuck sings that song?

"Earth to Nate. Do you want to get in on this? Brad's only been your best friend since high school." Garrett taps my shoulder, and I blurt out the first thing that pops into my head.

"Is it Cinderella? Big eighties hair? Is that right?"

Brad gives me a puzzled look. "What the fuck are you talking about, man?"

Garrett sighs. "Here we go. Nate's pissed because I'm going to marry his wife as soon as his annulment goes through."

Mitch nods. He's been high since we got here. "Dude, congratulations on the marriage. Many blessings."

He's even starting to sound like a stoner when he talks.

"You're not marrying her because I'm not getting an annulment. And I won't be held responsible for what I do if you bring that shit up again."

Clayton raises his hand until Garrett and I shout, "What?"

"You're married? Since when?"

Garrett pulls out his cell phone. "He married her in Vegas. You've got to see her. She's gorgeous and smart as hell. A therapist. Look at this. She and Daniel fell asleep on the couch. Is that not the cutest fucking thing ever?"

He might as well run me through it with his steak knife.

She's perfect.

I went to her apartment last week just to see her face. The guy who answered the door looked like he could break me in half, so I correctly guessed that it was her dad.

"She's sick and resting right now."

I'd tried to get around him when I heard that. *"I'm her husband. Just let me check on her—I'm a doctor."*

His hand in the center of my chest had me backtracking right out the front door.

"Nate, can I call you Nate? I don't wanna be that guy, but that's my baby girl in there. Ya feel me?"

I nodded, instantly regretting crossing the man.

"Now, I believe that fair is fair, so I'm going to give you a warnin'. Stay the fuck away from her—if she wants you, she'll come find you. Disregard that, and you'll find out just how bad Kate's 'biker daddy' is. Alright?"

A younger me would've mouthed off and told the old man to go to hell, but the look in his eyes? I didn't doubt that he'd kill me slowly and somehow make it look like an accident.

"Jesus Christ, Nate. You're shaking. I didn't hold a gun to your head... yet." He'd thrown his arm around my shoulder and walked me back down the stairs, laughing like we were old friends.

I snap out of it and take a long drink of beer. Garrett is enlightening everyone at our table and several surrounding ones about what happened with Kate.

"And now he's pouting in his beer because he had a fantastic woman, and he fucked it up."

I down the rest of my beer. "Thanks, Garrett. Super helpful of you to let everyone know."

Mitch suddenly turns to me, and I jump. "You need a grand gesture. That's what they do in the movies."

Clayton nods. "He's right. You fucked up epically."

Garrett slams his pint glass down on the table, earning us some curious looks. "Mitch, you're a goddamn genius. Nate, what was your plan for this weekend?"

I point to the window. "Snowboard—"

Garrett shakes his head. "No. You're just going to bring the group down with your sadness. And I can't have you killing my good snow vibes. You need to go home."

I roll my eyes and answer with as much sarcasm as possible. "Okay, sure. I just paid for the fucking trip; let me catch a flight home before I've even gotten the chance to step foot on the slopes."

Mitch holds his fork in his hand like a microphone. "Hey, Nate. You should go home."

I nod slowly. "Okay, Mitch. Good talk."

Garrett stands up. "Patrons of *Snowcliff Brewing Co.*, should my asshole brother go back to Texas so that he can grovel at the feet of one Mary Katherine Quinn in a grand gesture made for the big screen?"

Several people raise their drinks while the grand majority ignore him. I bury my face in my hands. "Are you finished?"

He continues, "No. Her Christmas party is tomorrow night. If you quit dicking around here, you might make it back in time."

I frown. "And you know this how?"

"Nate, I had coffee with her last week. What Kate and I have is something special, and I'm not going to throw that away because you had confusing feelings toward a woman who thought she was a soap opera character."

I kick my chair back and stand up, fists clenched.

I'm going to beat the shit out of him.

* * *

Eleven hours and four Red Bulls later, I pulled into town. No available flights would get me back to Lubbock in time, so I took my car and left Garrett to find another ride back.

Driving has got to be one of the most monotonous things ever; I found myself drifting off several times. Don't get me wrong, I've pulled plenty of all-nighters, but the adrenaline kept me going strong. Most of the drive was spent with the windows down and Rage Against the Machine blaring through the speakers.

I made it home just after noon, and as much as I wanted a few hours of sleep, I needed a tux. The invitation said coat and tie, but I was going for a grand gesture—not the bare minimum. So, I spent more than I should have, but it was do or die at this point.

I manage a quick nap before jumping in the shower. My beard has gotten a little unruly after being up in the mountains, so I take my time cleaning it up with the razor.

I've got hair gel holding my hair in place.

I'm wearing a black tux.

Fuck, I even went as far as *manscaping*—it doesn't get any grander than that.

The doorbell rings just as I'm adjusting my bowtie. I open it to some college kid I've never seen before.

"Nathaniel Davis?"

"I'm Nate—"

He hands me an envelope. "You've been served."

I stare down in shock at the papers in my hand. I've never been on the receiving end of one of these before, and I sure as fuck don't like the feeling.

Okay, grand gesture time.

Think, Nate.

Something that will win her over and get her to rethink our marriage.

My phone chimes.

> Garrett: Did you come up with a plan yet?

> Nate: You know me. I'm more of an off-the-cuff kind of guy. I'll think of something.

> Nate: Also, she may have had me served.

> Garrett: Shit. You better come up with something spectacular then; otherwise, you missed out on snowboarding for nothing.

I clench my teeth. The fucker seems to have forgotten that this whole thing was his idea.

> Nate: Thanks for the tip, dickhead.

I throw the envelope on the kitchen island and stalk to my car. Kate's Christmas party is at an upscale hotel near campus. I arrive within five minutes, and I still have no idea how to get her back.

I leave my car with the valet and slip on my tuxedo jacket. The lobby is littered with people, but I don't see her anywhere.

A hotel employee directs me into a crowded ballroom and I find the inspiration I need. The DJ booth is set up on a small stage near the front of the room.

My pulse picks up, and I start grinning.
I've got just the plan to win her back.
But first, whiskey... lots and lots of whiskey.

thirty-two

COMMANDMENT #33: THOU SHALT READ THE ROOM

Kate

I'm not sure who decided that cramming a bunch of therapists into one room was a good idea. We specialize in psychoanalyzing—it's a recipe for disaster.

Hit the bar too often, and you're using unhealthy coping mechanisms.

Bring an obnoxious date, and you're rebelling against your parents due to unresolved conflict from your childhood.

Hit on another co-worker, and you're probably sexually repressed.

Thank god for Nicole, or I would have already made up an excuse to sneak out.

"So, did I miss anything?"

I turn to her. "Nothing. I was actually thinking of grabbing a glass of champagne just to cause some drama and liven this evening up."

The music cuts off only to be replaced by—

"Is that Foreigner? It is, isn't it?" Nicole's brow wrinkles in confusion.

"Well, it's official. This Christmas party is going down as the worst in company history."

"I gotta take a little time. A little time to think things over..." A male voice croons.

I turn toward the stage and feel the breath leave my lungs in a pained gasp.

It's not Foreigner, and I have officially crossed the threshold into Hell.

Nicole is standing, open-mouthed, and transfixed by the man on stage. I tap her on the arm. "Are you seeing the same thing I'm seeing? Is that Nate?"

She doesn't even look at me. "Yes, that would be your husband belting out an eighties love ballad in front of everyone you work with."

I laugh weakly. "Good. I was afraid that I was hallucinating again."

Nate hits the chorus, and to my surprise, several people begin cheering. He's good—like he took voice lessons. And he looks amazing in that tuxedo—I'm suddenly having trouble remembering why I decided to file for divorce.

Damn you, Nate Davis.

"Did you know that he could sing like that?" Nicole fans herself with her hand before grabbing a glass of champagne from a passing tray.

I shake my head, feeling feverish again for the first time in days. This time, it has nothing to do with pneumonia and everything to do with him.

Why is he here?

Several women in the crowd begin echoing his words—as if they're an actual cover band.

"Kate, I think we have a little problem—he's three sheets to the wind." Nicole points to where Nate is beginning to sway unsteadily on his feet.

We move toward the stage as he belts the song's last few words. Once he spots me in the crowd, he gives me a lopsided grin, and my heart turns over.

"Ladies and gentlemen, give it up for my wife, Tequila Shot Katy."
He points down at me, and several colleagues gasp in surprise. I can
hear the whispers starting from somewhere behind me.

My face floods with heat, and I shake my head. "Stop."

Please stop talking and get off that stage.

His tongue slips out and licks along his lower lip. "Katy, Katy, Katy
—this is so us." He sways into a speaker, nearly knocking it off the
stage.

Nicole steps around me and up onto the stage. "Why don't we get
you two somewhere to talk privately." She tries to pry the microphone
from his hands, but he brings it back to his mouth.

"I'd like to talk privately if you know what I mean. Mic drop." Nate
lowers his eyebrows suggestively before letting the microphone hit the
stage.

People begin clapping, and one yells, "You can do it!"

Nicole leads him down the stairs toward me just as my date
returns.

"Jesus Christ, I just stepped outside to take a call. When did he get
here?"

I cringe. "He showed up about the time that you left."

Jeremy places a hand on my arm, and Nate narrows his eyes. "Who
invited the leprechaun?"

Nicole closes her eyes and purses her lips, trying to keep from
laughing.

"He's my date. I can't do this right now."

Nate stops me with his arm. "You agreed to talk to me."

I shake my head. "I did not. Nicole suggested it, and I said nothing
in return. Why are you here right now?" My voice cracks, and I have to
channel my frustration to avoid crying.

His eyes, like the color of his favorite whiskey, narrow in concern.
"Katy, if you'd just come with me—I can't talk to you with Lucky
Charms here looking over your shoulder."

Jeremy puts a hand on my shoulder. "You're drunk, Nate. Why
don't you leave before you embarrass her any further?"

Nate shakes his head like a belligerent child. "You embarrass her—"

I grab Jeremy and walk toward the exit. "Let's go."

Nate follows closely behind. "You're my wife...just talk to me."

I turn around, and he slams right into me. His cologne hits my nostrils, and I fight to regain my balance. It's because he just ran into me, not because his cologne brings back memories or anything.

It's not like I'm picturing the face he would make before pushing into me, the way his eyes would fixate on mine as if he were spellbound. I'm not thinking of the secrets we shared while lying in bed at night.

I shake my head and try to regain focus. "Now you want to talk. What about a few weeks ago when I tried to explain myself to you?"

He tries to touch me, and I take a step back. "Don't—you threw me out. You don't get to pick up like nothing happened. If you'll excuse me, Jeremy and I are going home together—and we're going to have sex."

Jeremy immediately jumps in. "Jesus. That is absolutely not true. At all. I haven't touched her."

He glances around wildly before shooting me a death glare.

Oh, right, Grey has ears everywhere. Almost forgot about that.

"We've had sex before, though—we might do it again. Just sex... all night long."

"Fucking hell," Jeremy hisses. "Are you trying to get me killed?"

Nate starts laughing to the point that he has tears in his eyes. "Did you just use sex as a verb? Now I know you're lying." He sways again and has to brace himself on a pillar. Once he's steady, he pulls his car keys from his pocket. "Guess I'll just drive myself home then. I hope I make it in one piece."

* * *

"How much did you have to drink?" I change lanes to avoid a car before glancing over at him.

He rubs his temple. "Not enough—I'm running on two hours of sleep here. Whiskey just added insult to injury."

"Did you work last night?"

Nate shakes his head and shifts closer to me. "Nope. I was in Colorado. I needed to see you, so I drove back."

Don't you do it, heart. You stay right there and keep beating as though this means nothing.

"Oh...so you came back yesterday?"

You've got this, Kate.

Nate's hand reaches across the console and rests on my thigh. "I drove all night. So, why'd you lie about Jeremy?"

His hand finds the hem of my dress and begins inching the material upward.

"I—I don't know. Can you not do that while I'm driving? It makes it hard to focus."

He ignores me and begins stroking the front of my panties. "Have you let him touch you like this?"

I fight the urge to throw my head back and moan, instead focusing on street signs.

22nd Street...

23rd Street...

He pulls my underwear to the side and pushes a finger inside of me.

24567th Street...

Eleventy Hundred Million Avenue...

A Trillion Bazillion Court...

"Come for me, Katy girl."

I moan loudly even as I curb-check the tires of his car. I come with a small cry, but the high is gone almost immediately, and I'm sick over what I just allowed him to do.

"I said not to touch me—I'm trying to get you home safely."

He pulls his hand back and sucks his finger clean, and I almost drive up onto the sidewalk again. "Now you know how it feels. I'd say we're even. Are you going to talk to me now?"

Miraculously, I find his house and park his car straight in the driveway.

"You're here." I unbuckle and get out.

"Stay with me." He gestures toward the house, and I want to say yes. I'm going to need an emergency session with Nicole about this one.

"No. This doesn't change anything between us. I'm still just a girl you enjoy having sex with. That's not enough to make a marriage work."

He slams the car door and walks over to me. "I'm sorry, Katy girl. I'm drunk, and I'm screwing it all up, but I want to take care of you. I was worried sick when I found out you had pneumonia, and it killed me that I wasn't there for you. I never want to experience that again— let me fix this."

I shake my head. "Oh no, your god complex can't get you out of this. Some things are just beyond fixing. What happens the next time Jess snaps her fingers? You know you'll go running to help her."

He exhales and leans back against his car. "Jess is gone. I can't believe I believed her over you. I'm sorry and I'll do everything I can to make it up to you. You've seen the real side of me—that's not something I share with just anyone. What we have is special. You said you loved me once; give me another chance."

Jeremy pulls up in my Tahoe, and I look at Nate sadly. "Girls will say anything to get laid, Nate."

Then I turn my back on him and get into my car, tears hitting my cheeks before the door closes.

Jeremy touches my arm. "You okay?"

I just shake my head and press my lips together as if doing so will keep the flood of tears inside.

There's nothing sadder in the world than driving away from a man who has your heart wrapped around his finger and knowing that you're leaving it with him permanently.

I'd waited my whole life to be loved fiercely, and for a brief moment, it was everything I had imagined it to be, but crashing back to earth left me broken.

I can't imagine ever voluntarily putting myself through that again.

thirty-three

COMMANDMENT #34: THOU SHALT NOT BE ANNOYED IF THEY DON'T REPLY TO YOUR TEXTS

Kate

"So, we'll take it from the top. Just do what you did before." The wedding coordinator kneels and marks the tile floor with tape before ushering us all outside again.

I shiver and jump up and down to warm up my limbs. My sister would pick the coldest time of year to get married. Little Ricky stands a few feet away, fidgeting in his dress shirt and checking out Dakota's best friend, Ava.

She's pretending not to notice, but the slight smile on her face gives her away. I can't imagine that ever working out—he's so rough, and Ava, well, she's not.

Kind of like me and Nate...

Nope, I'm not going there today.

I made a commitment to Dakota, and this weekend is all about her. I even left my cell phone at home since Nate seems to think that 'I never want to speak to you again' is the same as 'Please call and text me constantly.'

If he thinks he'll wear me down, he's wrong. We were nothing more than star-crossed lovers, doomed from the start. As if Nate shared the same wavelength as me, I woke up to a Shakespeare text message this morning.

> Nate: Madam, you have bereft me of all words.
> Only my blood speaks to you in my veins.

I had to Google it to discover that it was from Shakespeare's *The Merchant of Venice*. The male character, Bassanio, tells his lover, Portia, that the day he takes his ring off will be the day he dies.

Smooth, Nate. Real subliminal.

"Do you need anything?"

I look up to Dakota standing right in front of me. I've got to quit letting my thoughts take over.

"Shouldn't I be asking you that? It's your big weekend."

She waves her hand dismissively. "I should probably be more concerned with how things are going, but I've got him, so I don't even care what happens from here on out." She looks over at Zane and smiles. He's deep in conversation with Jeremy over something and doesn't even look up.

What if Dakota's feelings are stronger than Zane's?

What if he hurts her?

I pull her into a hug, squeezing her as tightly as I can. I just want to keep her safe from everything—it's all I've ever wanted. "Are you sure you're ready for this? It's a big commitment."

She narrows her eyes. "It is? Because I heard you could just catch a flight to Vegas and do it. You don't even have to remember it. Of course, I'm ready, Kate. I love him."

I gesture toward the building. "Let's find a room and talk. I won't be long."

She agrees, and we sneak past the wedding coordinator as she works to get the music keyed up again.

I find a small room and close the door behind us. "Look, I know you think you're in love. I get it. Sometimes, lust is confusing, and you get caught up in the moment. I just don't want you to make a mistake because you're pregnant and feel you have no other options."

Dakota gives me a strained smile. "Wow, okay. I don't even know where to begin with this. You realize that Zane asked me to marry him before he knew I was pregnant, right? And as for this being nothing more than lust, we're not all you, Kate. You fell in love, and it didn't work out—you don't have to shit all over my happiness in the process, though."

Zane asked her to marry him before he knew.

That can't be right.

I try to hug her again, but her jaw is set in a hard line, and I'm a little afraid that she'll hit me. "I'm not trying to cause a fight, Dakota. And, for the record, I was never in love with Nate. It was just sex. I need you to evaluate what you and Zane have in common besides the physical stuff. Don't rely on a man to make your dreams come true."

She brings a hand up to rub at her forehead. "The night before the wedding is when you decide to drop this on me? And I thought Jackson was the world's biggest asshole; you might just take the cake on this, though. I have more than enough money to make it alone, and so do you, for that matter."

I shake my head. "How do you figure that?"

"Because our father made sure of that. He wanted to make up for all the money we lost to Nan and Pops. Oh, and I'm supposed to tell you to quit reporting it as an error to your bank. I forgot about that. Pregnancy brain, am I right?"

The money was mine the entire time?

I can't accept money from Grey, can I?

It's dirty.

It would also make my life so much easier.

I cross my arms over my chest while taking a deep breath. "Dakota, don't end up like our mother. Don't be so eager to have a family that you end up losing them. Just think about it, okay?"

She stalks away from me and out of the darkened room, slamming the door shut behind her.

I scrape a hand roughly over my face, trying to erase any traces of tears. When I rejoin the rehearsal, everyone is waiting in their correct places.

"Okay, we've got sister here. Let's run through this, and then it'll be time for the rehearsal dinner."

Zane gives me a questioning look while Dakota incinerates me with her eyes.

I think it's safe to assume that the rest of the night will be miserable.

thirty-four

COMMANDMENT #35: THOU SHALT NOT MEDDLE IN THE AFFAIRS OF OTHERS

Kate

O ut of all the things I expected on my sister's wedding day, being locked out of the dressing room was not one of them. Ava came out and apologetically informed me I would need to get ready elsewhere.

Running into my grandparents as they tried to sneak in a back door at the event center wasn't high on my list of possibilities, either.

"Mary Katherine, there you are," Nan crows. "Where have you been? I've been calling you for months now."

Her hair still has a faint purple tint, and I suppress a smile, knowing who was responsible. The coldness reflected in her eyes, though, tells me everything I need to know.

She doesn't feel a shred of remorse for stealing from us.

"Nan. Pops," I say, my tone indifferent. "I didn't think you got an invitation."

Pops takes in the decorated tables. "We didn't. Will you just tell us what's going on? Your Nan and I have done just about everything, trying to get in touch with you girls. When I saw the announcement in the paper, I told her we had to try at least. So, I'm here to say we're sorry for whatever we've done to upset the both of you."

I blink rapidly, fighting against the lump in my throat. It's been there for so long that I'm beginning to think it's a tumor. "Pops, you know why Dakota and I are so upset. Mama told us everything."

My grandmother's eyes bulge. "Your mother? What lies did she feed you this time? She's always tried to turn you away from us!"

Little Ricky rounds the corner, only to retreat immediately upon seeing the commotion.

Some help he is.

My fingernails dig into my palms, and I take a deep breath. "My mother sent money from the moment we moved in with you. Money to cover clothing, college, and cars. We never saw a cent, though. Oh, and my father is alive. Which part is a lie?"

Pops shakes his head adamantly. "We never received money from your mother and had to dip into our retirement savings to keep you two as comfortable as possible. As for your father, he isn't exactly an upstanding citizen, and your mother felt it best for you to believe he was dead. If we're guilty of anything, it's honoring her wishes."

I narrow my eyes at Nan, giving her the sweeping once-over she often used on me and Dakota growing up. "Really?" I ask with a bitter laugh, jerking my thumb toward my grandmother. "Care to explain how she's afforded all her little surgeries and that expensive Cadillac?"

His face darkens, and a vein bulges in his forehead. "Mary Katherine, what your grandmother does is none of your damn concern! That money was an inheritance from a relative of hers that passed a few years back! Young lady, I ought to—"

"Ought to *what?*" a voice growls from behind me, raising the hairs on my neck. "Choose your words carefully, old man. That's my baby girl you're speaking to."

Grey steps in between us, and Nan's face drains of color. Even Pops stumbles back in fear.

"Which relative was it, Norma? Last I checked, not a single one of 'em had a pot to piss in."

"J-J-Jamie, we don't want any trouble," Pops stammers. "Mary Katherine was mistaken."

Jamie?

I thought his name was Grey and had long assumed his parents were hippies who had a thing for the names of colors.

My father stands in a wide-legged stance, effectively blocking me from getting around him to defend myself.

"Dick," he says, keeping his voice low. "Kate ain't mistaken, and I never for a minute thought you knew jack shit about what went on under your roof. But I'm out a fuck ton of money—money that was meant for my girls. Norma knows all about it, though, and she's gonna come clean, ain't she?"

Nan nods shakily, lowering her head as she admits, "I—I did it. I took the money."

Pops gasps. "Jesus, Norma! How much did you take? We can fix this. Please, let me make this right."

"The time for fixin' it is long gone—"

"I still have some of it left!" Nan interjects. "There was a lot—I put it in savings. I thought if I let it earn some interest, it'd be like it never happened. Please..."

My stomach churns, watching my grandparents beg for their lives. "Don't."

He jerks his head back and looks down at me in surprise. "Katy, after what they put you and Dakota through?"

"It's over now. Let it go." I take a deep breath. "Daddy... please."

I try not to think about how long it's been since I last said his name —try not to think of the years we've lost because of his lifestyle.

He freezes at the term, nostrils flaring as he stares down at me. I see the war raging in his eyes—the battle between ruthless biker and the man who had been my safe place for the first six years of my life.

"They're about to start," Little Ricky announces, popping his head around the corner.

I squeeze my father's arm, praying he makes a decision he can live with.

221

Little Ricky escorts me back to the event center, practically bouncing with excitement. "You ready for this, Hail Mary?"

I force a smile. "Sure. Let's just hope it lasts."

He stops in his tracks. "Why would you say that? Escúchame—what Caparina and Big Guy have is the real thing. He'd do anything for her and vice versa. For all your education, you don't know a lot about love. It makes me sad for you."

"And what would you know about love?" I snap. "Please enlighten me."

His eyes go dark with pain, and I regret asking. "I was in love before. What's with the face? Are you surprised?"

I nod dumbly.

"You think you're an expert on love because you got burned, but you're not. When it's the real deal, nothing can stand in the way of it. Now, let's go. I ain't about to get my ass chewed out by Caparina because you're late."

I tighten my grip on his bicep. "I'm sorry."

He squeezes me back. "Apology accepted. You and Nate will figure things out—you just need to stop gettin' in the way of it first. Love can't be neat and tidy—"

"Well, it wasn't love," I quickly interject. "It was just—"

He presses a finger to my lips. "Shhh... you're not the love expert, remember? So, you know nada. Okay, good talk."

When the music starts, I can't help but smile. It isn't traditional, making it perfect for my sister.

Zane stands like a statue, his hands clasped in front of his body, watching the back of the room with an expectant smile. Maybe Little Ricky's right—maybe they are perfect for each other, and I couldn't see it because of my own broken heart.

After the ceremony, I'll apologize to both of them.

The doors open, and my smile fades when I realize it isn't my sister coming down the aisle but Little Ricky. People begin murmuring when he reaches Zane's side.

Zane leans down to hear him before stiffening in response. Then he turns to me and growls, "What the fuck did you do, Kate?"

A collective gasp works through the room, and my cheeks heat.

"Nothing!" I turn to Ava. "Was she fine when you left?"

The bridesmaid frowns. "She just said she needed a few minutes alone. What's going on?"

"She's gone," Zane says, almost too quietly to hear.

"Did she mention anything to you that would help us figure out where she is?" Little Ricky directs the question at me.

"No." I sink down onto a nearby step, recalling what I said to her during the rehearsal the night before. Why did I take it upon myself to warn her not to go through with the marriage just because she was pregnant?

Maybe she didn't run—perhaps she's still in the building.

"Wait, is Jeremy here? He can track her phone, right?"

Zane pulls me up and propels me toward the exit, telling the confused guests, "Hey, we're having a slight technical difficulty. Excuse us for a moment."

"We're gonna find her, and everything will be good. It will be—"

"What. Did. You. Say. To. Her?" he demands. "She wasn't right after your little chat last night."

I swallow nervously. "Um... I just wanted to ensure she was getting married for the right reasons and not because she's pregnant—"

Zane's fist collides with the brick wall above me. I yelp and try to squirm out of reach.

"Found her," Jeremy announces, holding up his laptop. I wonder if he takes it everywhere. I can't recall ever seeing him without it. "Her phone's pinging near the gym."

"I'll do it," I declare when they begin bickering over who should go.

Zane snorts. "Sure, so you can convince her to leave town and change her name? You ruined what was supposed to be the best day of our lives."

I place a hand on his arm, pleading, "Let me fix this, please!"

"Fine. Thirty minutes, and then I'm coming after her on my own."

"I won't let you down," I promise.

thirty-five

COMMANDMENT #36: THOU SHALT APPROACH YOUR PARTNER WITH CONFIDENCE

On the way to the gym, I try to come up with a list of reasons Dakota needs to marry Zane. Most lead back to the fact that he looks like Thor. One is because I don't want him to kill me.

Dakota stands near a leg press machine in full wedding attire.

"It took you long enough to get here," she says when she sees me, her lips curving into a wide grin.

I ignore the sinking feeling in my gut at seeing her so happy, knowing there's a good chance she won't be coming back with me.

"Why aren't you at the event center?" I ask tentatively. "You know, getting married?"

"I've got plenty of time to kill," she says with a careless shrug. "Thought I'd round up all the guests who hadn't RSVP-ed yet. You know how rude that is."

It's a Friday night and New Year's Eve, so the gym is deserted. Most people are probably out partying.

I open my mouth and then immediately close it, unsure if it's even worth asking.

Her satin skirt swishes as she walks over. "Remember when I told you Nate was your Bucky?"

I nod, more than a little thrown off by the change in topic. "Yeah, and you said I was Black Widow. But then Grey said I was Spider-Man, which just confused everything. You might have to reiterate your point."

"Spider-Man?" she blurts, her nose crinkling in disgust. You aren't even a good climber! No, you're definitely Black Widow. So, Bucky and Natasha trained as assassins but were then brainwashed and used as weapons for years."

She pauses to acknowledge my raised hand. "Uh, I've never been used to kill people, so..."

"Maybe not," she agrees with a grin. "But you're pretty dang uptight. I think it's because you're afraid—afraid to fall in love and lose control. I get it. I do. But what is it you always say? Fear is just a blanket—"

"Don't you dare psychoanalyze me, Dakota Mae," I bite out, ignoring the tears pooling in my eyes. "It was never going to work out between me and Nate. We're just too different."

"Why won't you let yourself be happy?" she sobs. "What's wrong with someone wanting to take care of you?"

"Because when you love someone, they leave," I blurt, the words like poison on my tongue. I'm not thinking of Nate but of my parents. It seems everyone I love leaves me eventually. And even though they reappeared years later, it doesn't make it hurt any less.

"I'm not Black Widow, and Nate's not Bucky. We're two messed-up individuals who will never make it work. He left the first time because he trusted his ex-wife's word over mine. And maybe it makes me a coward, but I know I won't survive losing him a second time."

Dakota takes my hands in hers. "You've both been used by people, Kate. Nate's ex-wife was a psycho-crazy person, and he still tried to stay loyal to the vows he made—even when she used him and left his heart broken. You—you've had to take care of everybody since we were kids, and I'm sorry for that. I'm sorry for the ways I used you—"

"Don't," I warn, the tears now flowing freely down my face. "Don't apologize—not to me."

"You want to know why I love comics so much? It's because of all the broken heroes—the ones who redeem themselves in the end. Bucky and Natasha are at the top of the list because, despite all the bad they lived through, they continued to fight for the good."

I blink to clear my vision. "That—That's a lot to process—"

"He still loves you," she interjects. "Despite everything you two have gone through, he loves you. That's why he is, and will always be, your Bucky."

I glance around as if the gym might magically alleviate my confusion. "How could you possibly know that?"

Dakota steps back with a triumphant smile. "Who do you think I've been talking to this whole time?"

"But you left your own wedding... no one knew where you were. You came here? For him?"

"I left a note," she insists before her eyes suddenly widen in horror. "Biscuits and gravy, I didn't leave a note! Zane must think I—"

"Pulled a runaway bride," I helpfully finish for her. She gathers up her skirt and hurries toward the exit. "Wait—where's Nate?"

"Locker room," she mutters distractedly. "Said he needed to shower."

After urging her to get to the event center, I rush toward the locker room, my heart beating double time. I don't know where to begin and wish I'd written something down. Dakota's speech was eloquent and moving. I have nothing.

A man with gray hair steps out of the sauna, and I bypass him, searching for the showers.

He tightens his grip on the towel slung around his waist. "Miss, you're in the—"

"Men's locker room. I know. I'm trying to find my husband."

Nate is right where Dakota promised he would be. He shuts off the water and steps out of the shower to grab a towel.

Speech time. I'm going to say something great—*just as soon as I finish shamelessly ogling his naked body.*

"You know this is the men's locker room, yeah?" he asks when he catches my stare.

I shrug. "Turns out I don't even need alcohol to make poor decisions anymore."

He wraps the towel around his waist and raises a brow. "Did you come all the way down here to tell me that?"

I sigh and try again. "Is it true?"

"Is what true, Katy?" Instead of coming closer, he turns away.

A strand of hair slips from my updo, and I nervously tuck it behind my ear before asking, "Do you still love me?"

He gives me his profile, his jaw tight with tension. "Does it matter at this point?"

"Answer the damn question," I demand, refusing to give in to the sob in my throat.

"Yes!" he bellows. "You fucking happy now? You run so deep in my veins that there's not a chance in hell I could ever get rid of you!"

I close the gap between us, wrapping my arms around his warm body. "Then don't. Don't get rid of me. Stay."

He pulls back with a frown. "I got the divorce papers, babe. What's changed in the last two weeks? What—I'm supposed to just believe you want to stay now? You seemed pretty cozy with Jeremy last I checked."

I resist the urge to walk out and hold my head high as I tell him, "Jeremy's nothing more than a friend—well, minus the one time before I met you. Look, maybe nothing's changed, and we're still too damaged to make it work. Maybe this whole idea—"

"Let's do it right, then."

"What—what do you mean?" I ask, my head swimming in confusion.

His mouth splits into a wide grin. "Let's get married, Katy girl. A real wedding—one we'll hopefully remember this time around. What do you say?"

I say I need this man. *Badly*.

I kick off my heels and launch myself into his arms. His hands come up to grip my ass, holding me steady as I wrap my legs around his waist.

"I say yes," I breathe against his lips. "And also, what is the gym's policy on sex?"

He laughs and his mouth slides over with mine before he whispers, "Anything for you, babe."

Keeping his arms locked around me, he backs me against the wall. I shiver against the cold tiles on my back and the feel of his fingers brushing against my core. He tugs my panties to the side with a barely repressed growl.

"Tonight, when you're back in our bed, I'll go slow. I'm going to take my fucking time worshiping every inch of this body." His lips move down the column of my throat. "But right now, I need to feel you around me."

"Please," I beg.

I missed everything about him. His voice, his smell, the way he touches me, just like—

I bite down on his shoulder with a moan, the edges of my vision already blurring. His hand moves between us, stimulating me—encouraging my body to open up for him.

"I'm close," I hiss, feeling my inner muscles flutter around his length.

Taking it as a challenge, he rolls his hips forward, forcing me to take more—to take all of him. I gasp as his thumb and forefinger squeeze my clit before coming apart with a loud cry.

Nate's mouth finds mine, silencing my cries while he continues to push my body to the brink of another orgasm. I suck his lip into my mouth to keep from screaming, and he groans, his thrusts becoming shallow.

The room fades away, and I see stars. Well, and the old man from the sauna. But I'm beyond caring at this point. Nate holds himself deep, releasing a low growl as he chases his own release.

"I—I love you, babe," he pants, crushing me against the wall with his body.

I drop my head onto his shoulder with a content sigh. "I love you too, Nate. I don't want to navigate this life with anyone but you."

The older man clears his throat. "And I'm happy for the two of you, but I'd really like a shower before the new year. Do you mind?"

"Guy, do you mind?" Nate barks. "We're trying to have a moment here."

He threatens to call gym security before stalking toward the exit, grumbling about public fornication.

I dissolve into giggles. "We may have to find a new gym."

Nate curses when he sees the time. "Let's go, Katy girl. We missed the wedding, but if we hurry, we might still make the reception."

thirty-six

SUPERHERO RULE #64: ALWAYS MAKE A
DRAMATIC ENTRANCE

Dakota

I burst through the side door of the event center with my shoes tucked under my arm. Several employees jump back in fright, but I don't slow down. I'm late enough as it is.

"Do not be alarmed," I murmur with a breathless wave and a British accent. "'Tis only me."

"Holy shit, you came back!" Little Ricky intercepts me as I round a corner, spinning me in a small circle. Then he sets me back on my feet with a stern expression. "Why the hell did you run away?"

"I had some unfinished business," I pant, still out of breath from running. "And I forgot to leave a note explaining where I was. Speaking of, where is Zane—is he still here?"

"Right here, Dakota."

My mouth goes dry as I turn to face him. Even without a cape, he is the sexiest superhero, with his slate gray three-piece suit and golden hair waves cascading down his shoulders.

And he's all mine as soon as I clear up some confusion.

"I meant to leave a note—"

He jerks his chin in a brisk nod. "You had second thoughts. Maybe we rushed this."

I run a hand over his chest, stopping to pat his rock-hard abdominal muscles. "Look at me, Big Guy. Do I look like a woman who's having second thoughts?"

He cups my cheek in his hand and studies my eyes as if trying to read my thoughts. "Babe, you look incredible. But you left, and I—"

"I know," I interject, resting my chin on his chest with a sigh. "This is the happiest day of my life, and call me crazy—I wanted to share it with my sister. So I may have gone out to get the happily ever after she deserves—superhero style."

Zane rolls his eyes with a chuckle, eyes sparkling with amusement. "Jesus, babe. You're insane, but I love you." His hands move down to cup my rounded belly. "You're feeling okay, though? Baby's good?"

"Big Guy," I begin, feeling as if my heart might burst. "If you haven't broken me yet, I doubt running around will, either. When you're carrying a superhero's baby, you're pretty much invincible."

"Babe, you're killing me over here," he says in a low voice, nostrils flaring. "Get your ass down that aisle so I can make an honest woman out of you."

I narrow my eyes. "Language."

He smirks. "Sorry. Get that fine ass of yours down the aisle."

"Shouldn't we wait for Kate?" I argue as he helps slip my masquerade mask over my eyes.

"Oh no, I'm not waiting a minute more. See, I need to be inside you in the next half-hour—we can't stall this wedding any longer."

I couldn't agree more. "I mean, Kate's done this before, so surely she knows how it goes. Right?"

thirty-seven

COMMANDMENT #38: THOU SHALT BE OPEN TO LOVE WHEN IT FINDS YOU

Nate

I sit back in the chair with a plastic cup of punch in my hand. I'm on call, and New Year's Eve is always a mess. For once, though, all is right with the world. I don't know how Dakota knew where to find me, but I'm glad she did.

I'd convinced myself that maybe I was the only one in misery. I thought maybe Kate was better off without me—I had no idea how much she was struggling.

Little Ricky staggers over and falls into the chair next to mine, his eye mask only covering one eye. I had to hand it to them. The Quinn sisters were geniuses.

With everyone wearing masks, no one noticed the blond-haired biker walking Dakota down the aisle. If they did, well, no one would say anything about it.

The entire affair is so unapologetically Dakota—instead of the typical bride and groom's side, there's just a large picture in the lobby of Zane and Dakota in a face-off. The caption reads, 'Everyone must choose a side.' The only thing missing is that she isn't dressed as Captain America, and he isn't dressed as Ironman.

Each table is labeled with a different superhero and random facts about each one. I look down at the marker on my table.

Captain Marvel

Captain Marvel is the alias of Carol Danvers.
Fun Fact: Dakota drove a little red car that she fondly referred to as Carol Danvers. That car was nothing more than scrap metal and nothing like a superhero, regardless of what Dakota would tell you.

I smile and take another drink.

"I gotta be real honest with you." Little Ricky leans awkwardly across the table toward me.

"Okay."

He continues, "You asked me where Hail Mary came from. I think maybe I came up with it because she has a body that makes you want to sin. So, you better ask for forgiveness first, yeah?"

I narrow my eyes. "I'm going to pretend you didn't just say that. Because I just got my wife back and don't feel like fighting tonight."

He looks back at her on the dance floor with Dakota and then at me again. "But you see it, right?"

I sigh and watch Kate move to the beat of the music. "Yeah, I do see it. I'd prefer I'm the only one who sees it if you know what I mean."

Little Ricky nods thoughtfully, his eyes never leaving Kate. "*Sí*, I know. You're a lucky man. Don't take it for granted. She's stubborn as an ass, but women like her? Once in a lifetime, man."

I'm surprised to find that the kid runs deep.

"I won't take it for granted."

He smiles and pats the table between us. "That's good. If you fuck it up, I'll slit your throat." Then he stands up and comes over to hug me. "I love you, Dr. Nate. You're my boy!"

I slap him awkwardly on the back before excusing myself to grab my wife on the dance floor. Zane must have the same idea because he grabs Dakota almost simultaneously. He threads her arms around his neck as they dance, her feet barely touching the floor.

Kate giggles as I spin her toward me. "You drinking tonight, darlin'?"

She shakes her head immediately. "No way. God knows where we'd end up if I did."

I glance over to where Little Ricky is chatting up one of the bridesmaids. "So, Rick's drunk and completely fucked in the head."

She tilts her face up and grins. "You're just now finding this out? Are you going to run out on me?"

I shrug. "Well, I can't. He said he'd slit my throat if I screwed this up."

Kate pats me on the cheek and shakes her head. "Little Ricky doesn't have that kind of authority." My shoulders relax slightly before she adds, "I do, though."

I grin. "There are some things I didn't get a chance to say in the locker room—what, with the interruption and all."

She chuckles. "You mean the recommendation that we not show our faces there for a while?"

"Right, there was that. What I'm trying to say is that I'm just so damn glad that you came back. I know we'll have to work harder because we don't have much in common. You're always reading those case studies at night; maybe I could start doing that, too."

Kate bites her lip and looks down at the floor, shoulders shaking. When her head pops back up, she's got tears running down her cheeks. "I'm sorry, it's not funny. It's just that I was never reading case studies. I just used a psych textbook to hide my phone."

I narrow my gaze as we take another turn around the dance floor. "What were you really doing on your phone?"

She giggles again. "Um, I like to read romance novels. So, I download books on my phone and read them at night and between patients during the day."

"Like *Pride and Prejudice*?" I ask.

Kate shakes her head. "Think *Fifty Shades* meets *Pride and Prejudice.*"

She looks up with a self-conscious smile, and my mouth goes dry. "Um, I could be into that. What kind of husband would I be if I didn't try it?"

The song ends, but we don't let go of each other.

I move my hand up to cup her chin. "So, I'm your Bucky?"

She runs her tongue against her top teeth, giving me a sly smile. "Yeah, and apparently, I'm your Natasha."

"I'm not much of a comic guy, but I know the movies. Shouldn't you be in a skintight black suit?"

Kate clicks her tongue against her teeth, our bodies swaying in time to the song. "Keep it up, and you'll need a metal arm, buddy."

She playfully swats me on the ass before her eyes widen. "Oh! I almost forgot to tell you! I did something a little risky while we were apart. I went to the Christmas Festival of Lights, and guess what? I rode the Ferris wheel! I'm trying to be an adrenaline junkie, just like you."

I almost crack up, but the smile on her face is so earnest, and it's pretty damn obvious she's proud of herself. "You know what, babe? It's a start."

Then, without another thought, I lean down and press my lips lightly against hers. Our relationship began under less-than-ideal circumstances, but I don't regret a second of it.

We're two people with a lot of baggage, but marrying her in Vegas was the best decision of my life. The odds were stacked against us initially, but we're still here—still fighting.

I know we're both still afraid of being hurt and that there will be times when either one or both of us wants to call it quits. But I'll cling to the memory of tonight, holding her in my arms and feeling as if all is right in the world.

And if that doesn't work?

Well, I guess I'll just have to break out the tequila shots.

epilogue

THE NIGHT OF DAKOTA'S WEDDING

Grey

Goblin paced the sidewalk just outside the event center, nostrils flaring wildly.

"Did we get somethin'?"

He loosened his collar and rolled up his sleeves before shaking his head. "Jarvis texted, said he hacked our mole's computer and was going through his messages. *El cabrón* never came tonight. Someone tipped him off we were gonna be lookin' for him."

"Fuck," I growled, catching the kid as he stumbled forward. "You drunk, kid?"

He held his thumb and forefinger a few inches apart with a nod. "*Sí*, because I'm so happy for *Caparina*."

I made sure he stayed on his feet before taking off toward the parking lot. He bounced along behind me, making small talk about Dakota's wedding. I grinned at the appropriate times and responded as if nothing was wrong, but my head was spinning.

The mole had known not to show up because someone in my clubhouse had gotten to him first. I glanced back at Goblin as he patted at the air in front of him like it was a dog. He was out, for obvious reasons.

No, the guy who'd rolled over was someone with a motive.

I'd taken the club back from Bear after Celia's attack, but never once gotten the impression he held it against me. Plus, he'd been a patch longer than I had. If anyone knew what our colors meant, it was him. He might have had the motive, but wouldn't have destroyed the club from within to take it back.

If love was a motive, then Jarvis should've been a suspect, but turning on the club wouldn't guarantee him Kate. Not only that, he'd been giving me solid intel and stood to lose his entire career if the club went down.

It had to be someone who would benefit if Silent Phoenix fell.

I quickly ruled out Angel and Wolverine. The two had been riding since God was a boy and had made more than enough money for several lifetimes. One by one, I went down the roster, ruling out members.

When I got to Mikey, I paused. He'd been forced into club life by a man who'd lied about being his father. His motive for taking down the club was stronger than anybody else's. And if my club disappeared, so did the crimes of his youth.

It wasn't him, though.

I didn't know how I knew it. But I did.

Convinced I'd gone through every member, I stumbled when it hit me.

The one man with the motive and means. I knew who my rat was. It had been right in front of my face all along. The biker who should've been a brother but had always been an enemy.

Comedian.

I'd been going about it the wrong way—trying to figure out who would have the most to gain financially.

It was never about money, though.

It was about revenge.

I'd just opened my mouth to tell Goblin when something shifted.

The air around us felt as if it was suddenly charged with electricity. I glanced up, expecting to see lightning, but there wasn't a cloud in the sky. Still, the hair on my arms stood on end, warning me I was in danger.

A black suburban turned into the parking lot, engine revving and tires slapping against the pavement as it barreled toward us. Time seemed to slow down, drowning out anything other than the steady thumping from my chest and the sounds of my heavy breathing.

Goblin's mouth fell open, and his hand dropped to his hip as the tinted glass on the vehicle rolled down with a hum. A rifle moved through the open window, a ring on the shooter's hand glinting from the streetlight overhead as he shifted into position.

Only one of us was wearing a vest.

I didn't hesitate, knocking Goblin off his feet as a deafening crack of thunder pierced the surrounding silence, echoing around us until I was convinced they surrounded us on all sides. My back ignited, the flames bursting through the front of my chest like a fireball, dropping me to my knees against the asphalt.

The scent of gunpowder and burning flesh filled my nostrils as I collapsed onto Goblin with a sharp exhale, knowing the next explosion would be the one that sent me to the Reaper.

Only, it never came.

Tires screeched against the pavement, and smoke from the rubber coated my lungs, choking me with the knowledge that I was a dead man. The vehicle roared out of the parking lot and sped off; the sounds growing fainter until the air fell silent again. I'd prepared for everything but a slow death. I should have known a monster like me would be forced to suffer before being sent to hell.

Goblin moved me onto my back, and I looked up at the stars with a grin, consumed by a memory that hadn't taken place in this lifetime.

Maybe that was what the Reaper did.

Showed you how things could have been had you made different choices. It was like something out of a Dickens novel, only I wouldn't wake on Christmas morning to right my wrongs.

"You see those, Mikey? They're called constellations."

"Daddy," he said with a grin, displaying a mouth full of missing teeth. "Those are stars."

I squeezed his little body and pulled him onto my lap. "The stars create a picture when you put them together. See that one?" I traced the sky with my fingertip, his blue eyes tracking my every movement. "That's Perseus. If you look hard enough, you can see the head of Medusa in one hand, and a jeweled sword in the other."

His eyebrows drew together. "I see it, Daddy!"

"That's my boy. He was a warrior who went up against the monsters and married the princess."

Mikey stuck his tongue out. "Ew, I don't want to have to marry a princess. Kissing a girl would be worse than fighting monsters!"

I tickled along his ribs until he was squirming. "Is that so? You gonna tell your mama that when she tucks you in tonight?"

He pulled his chin onto his chest and hunched his shoulders with a giggle. "Daddy, Mama doesn't count as a girl. She's just a mom!"

"Is that so? And what about your sisters?"

He scrunched his nose. "Katy and Dakota? No way! I'll fight the monsters and keep them safe, but I'm not kissing them. They have to find a prince for that."

"Boys, time to wash up for dinner," Celia called through the open kitchen window.

"What if I wanna kiss your mama?"

He hopped off my lap with a shrug. "I guess, but don't do it in front of me. That's gross."

"Mikey, someday you'll realize that killin' the monsters and fallin' in love with a princess ain't a bad gig. Maybe that's all Perseus wanted... maybe that's all any of us could want."

"Sure." He grinned. "When I'm a hundred."

The vision faded, leaving me in darkness. If the Reaper wanted to torment me, he'd failed. I'd made a million mistakes, but even while dying, I knew the things I hadn't accomplished didn't matter.

They never had, because I'd had the love of a woman I didn't deserve and three kids who had turned out better than I ever could have imagined.

Even if we'd never been under the same roof.

* * *

"Hail Mary, full of grace, the Lord is with thee. Blessed art thou among women, and blessed is the fruit of thy womb, Jesus sanctifying. Holy Mary, Mother of God, pray for us sinners, now and at the hour of our death. Amen."

I knew the voice, but the sound was muffled, like talking to someone underwater. A clock ticked loudly from somewhere above my head, and my heart raced, steadily pumping blood through the wound in my chest. I was no longer lying in a parking lot but was being thrown around in a cage.

Had it just been one bullet?

I didn't remember.

My only instinct had been to keep the bullets away from Rick. I didn't even know if I'd been successful.

The truck swerved, and I gasped in pain at the movement. Staying awake was agony, but my body refused to let me pass out. Fire burned its way through my chest, every breath like the stab of a hot poker.

A sheen of cold sweat bathed my forehead—the blistered skin on my chest felt as if it had been ripped away from the muscle and bone beneath.

It was as if the goddamn sun itself had taken a baseball bat to my body.

I kept waiting for the numbness to set in, but it never came, leaving me painfully aware of every bump and jerk of the steering wheel.

So, this was what dying felt like.

"Jamie? Jamie, look at me!"

I tilted my face up toward the sound and forced my eyes open.

My girl.

"You can't be here," I forced out. "It's too late for me, princess."

She shook her head and pressed down on the wound. "No, I won't let you. You promised me, Jamie. You swore to keep us safe!"

I took a shallow breath and struggled to reach her hands. The pressure made it impossible to breathe.

"Gotta stop now. It's done."

Someone continued praying in the background, and I closed my eyes again. I didn't want to see the love of my life kneeling over me, frantically trying to stop the bleeding.

"You were supposed to wear the vest! You told me you would!" Her tears hit my face, and I mashed my lips together to keep from joining her.

I had worn the goddamn vest, just like Mikey had asked me to, and the motherfuckers had used armor-piercing bullets. I took at least one to the back, and it had gone all the way through.

"Our baby girl," I gasped, forcing my eyes open again. "She looked so good, didn't she?"

"I'm here, Daddy. I'm right here. Do you feel my hand?" Dakota squeezed, and I nodded, my own tears sliding down my cheeks.

"I feel you. Is—is anyone else—"

Mikey answered. "We're all here, Grey. We'll stay with you until it's over."

"I've got you, Dad." Katydid's fingers brushed the tears from my face. I was grateful to be surrounded by family, but they didn't need to see me like this.

This wasn't how I wanted to be remembered.

"I know—I know who's responsible," I whispered.

I should have seen it from the beginning, but I didn't want to believe that my sins could ever catch up with me.

"None of that matters now."

I didn't recognize the voice and briefly wondered if I was already dead. The stinging in my chest was my only reminder that I was still clinging to life.

Barely.

They weren't here; I knew that. It was a dream I didn't want to wake up from, though. The ticking slowed, ready to stop at any moment.

This was it.

No second chances—no time to make amends.

"Listen to me," I whispered as a firm hand gripped mine. "The girls —you have to tell the girls everything."

The sacrifices we'd made for them.

The threats we'd kept hidden.

Instead of words of wisdom, I was leaving my family in no man's land, forced to fight a war they never started for a man they never really knew.

I panted, each shallow breath pulling me away from the pain. If I had to do it over again, I never would have deserted them.

Wolverine had given me the name Grey, but Jean hadn't just become more powerful as the Phoenix. She'd been corrupted; turned into something else. Something that made her a danger to the ones around her.

The power I'd held within the club was second to none. I'd thought nothing else would ever come close. Until Celia. My actions had almost destroyed her, but maybe me giving my life now would set things right.

Jean Grey was most known for her suicidal sacrifice and not how she'd failed the ones who loved her. Instead of living as a god, she'd chosen to die as a human.

I was no hero, but if they knew the truth, they could be different.

Better.

Maybe my pathetic existence would serve as their origin story. The best I could hope for at this point was that once all the cards were on the table, they would better understand the enemy we were up against.

* * *

Thank you for reading OPERATION ANNULMENT! I hope you loved Nate and Kate.

The story continues with Grey and Celia in THE DESERTER!

I grew up in the dark.

Right and wrong?

In my world, it was kill or be killed.

I spend my time in the shadows, doing what I want when I want. I refuse to follow anyone's rules—I own this town.

They might not see me, but my club controls everything... including her. I took Daddy's little princess and defiled her to send a message. Now, I want to keep her down here in the dirt forever.

She's crazy not to run.

Around here, there's no right or wrong. I'm the judge, jury, and executioner, and god help any fool who tries to lay a hand on what's mine.

If you're looking for a hero, you're in the wrong place.

One-click THE DESERTER now!

* * *

If you loved Operation Annulment and want more of Jess's villain origin story, you can find it all in the From This Day Forward duet.

And if you enjoyed Nate and Kate's story, please consider leaving a review on Amazon. I appreciate your help in spreading the word, even by telling a friend. Reviews help readers find new books to fall in love with.

In the mood for something sweet? Check out this modern retelling of The Little Mermaid now!

Want to be the first to know when I have a new book? Sign up for my newsletter. You can also join my Facebook group, Shannon Myers's Fan Group, for exclusive giveaways and sneak peeks at future books. Follow me on BookBub!

Turn the page for an excerpt from Wait For It...

wait for it

"Burdens are for shoulders strong enough to carry them."

-Margaret Mitchell, *Gone with the Wind*

The screen door slammed shut behind me with a reverberating bang, but I kept running. I couldn't take another second inside that house.

It had been my turn to sit and read to Mama.

Usually, she stared blankly at the wall with a thin line of drool running down her cheek. Every now and then, her eyes would seemingly dance around the room, focusing on my face for a brief second before bouncing off to something else. Grandmother once told me that they were just filled with the joy of God's love, but Mama never seemed happy when her eyes were like that.

She would cry out and speak to people who weren't there. It used to frighten me until I discovered she was sick.

I wasn't supposed to have heard, but I was really good at hiding and just as quiet as a little church mouse. Most of the time, people didn't even realize I was in the room.

Papa had told Mama she was sick with sin and begged her to

repent, but she'd just laid there, moaning loudly. I wasn't sure how the sin had gotten to her when she never left her bed, but if Papa saw it in her, then it must have been true.

Once he left, she'd cried until the pillowcase beneath her head was soaked with tears before calling out for me and my sisters. Her voice was soft like mine, though, so no one ever came.

The July air was thick with humidity, and without even a hint of a breeze to cool things down, it was like running straight into an oven. My gray linen dress clung to my skin, and each inhale felt like I was trying to breathe underwater.

I ran until I reached the hedges lining the perimeter of our small gated community before dropping to my knees with a wince. Sharp leaves and twigs scraped along the exposed skin on my arms and legs, compressing the old and new bruises lining my sides. Still, I took a deep breath and pushed forward until I was completely hidden from view.

It was the only place I knew I wouldn't be found. At times, the house felt like a living, breathing thing peering over my shoulder. Like it was studying my every move in anticipation.

Out here, it was silent.

A sanctuary.

And right now, I wanted to stay hidden forever.

Mama hadn't stayed quiet today.

I hadn't even gotten through the first chapter before she reached out and grabbed my arm, knocking the book to the hardwood floor. Her grip had been surprisingly firm as she'd yanked me off the chair and into the bed beside her. The sheets were damp with sweat and stunk of sick. Mama's room always smelled different than the others in the house.

She tucked my back to her chest and wrapped her heated body around mine. While I lay stiffly in her arms, I tried to recall whether she'd ever held me before.

Perhaps when I was a baby, but if so, those memories had faded long ago. As far as I could remember, she'd always been like this.

Sick.

"Ari, my little dove," she'd whispered, her breath warm against my ear. "I've been so naïve...about all of it."

I'd tilted my head up and watched as she licked her chapped lips, surprised to find that her eyes were bright and focused for the first time in ages. "M-m-mama?"

"Shhhh... I've got you now. You're safe." The soft cadence of her voice had a mesmerizing effect, lulling my body into a relaxed state.

I'd settled against her with a sigh, feeling her mouth curve up into what might have been a smile against my cheek. That was what had made her next words all the more shocking.

I hadn't been prepared for them.

"He's going to kill me," she'd stated simply. "I'm getting in the way of his dreams. I think... I think that maybe I've always been in the way because I know the truth. There's nothing beyond the wall that doesn't exist here."

I'd sucked in a breath but hadn't said a word. My heart had thumped steadily while my curiosity wrestled with Papa's teachings.

"And I love him... maybe that's my biggest sin," Mama had said, her voice remaining steady and calm. "I'll always love him, Ari. He was so charismatic—I thought we were gonna change the world together."

"Y-y-you—you s-still c-can—"

I hadn't meant to say the words aloud.

"Do you remember when that man came to the gate seeking help? I think you were five—maybe six? He came right in the middle of a tropical storm. The streets were starting to flood, and then, there he was, under one of the lights. You could smell the booze on him from a mile away as he hollered to see Pastor James..." Mama's words had tapered off, and I'd rolled over, expecting to find her asleep again.

Instead, she was mashing her trembling lips together as if to keep from crying. "The man needed help—at the very least, he needed a place to dry out and sober up. Your daddy turned him away and went back inside.

"I waited until everyone disappeared before slipping out to find him. I handed him an old coat and a sack of—goodness, I don't even remember what was in it. I just grabbed whatever I could from the fridge and pantry. Do you know what he said to me?"

"W-w-what?" I'd whispered, far too invested to not hear every last detail. Thoughts of life outside our community made the hair on my arms and neck stand tall, yet sparked my curiosity in ways that no other topic could.

Mama's lips had stretched into a thin smile as she'd brushed the hair back off my forehead. "Told me about how all he wanted to do was get back home to his boy and be a good man. Said he must have prayed the right way to be sent an angel. Do you see what's wrong with that?"

I'd shaken my head, completely puzzled.

"I'm no angel, Ari. But that man mistook my kindness for something otherworldly. And that was when I knew that your daddy didn't want to help people... not really. He wants to lock himself away behind the walls, turning a blind eye to their suffering. No matter what he tells you, we're no better than they are, little dove. We're all the same."

I'd scooted toward the edge of the bed when Mama closed her eyes, only to be tugged right back. She'd crushed my small body to her chest, making it hard to draw a breath. As I didn't know the next time she'd be lucid, I let her hold me just as tightly as she wanted.

"Need you to promise me something, Ari," Mama had whispered urgently before cupping my cheek with her palm. "Promise me that when you're old enough, you'll get out. You and your sisters will run and never come back here."

Whatever hold she had on reality loosened, and she began mumbling nonsense about the house listening in on our conversation before slipping back into a state of silence. Her mouth had gone slack, and the tears she'd cried clung to her lashes as she stared unseeingly toward the wall.

It was as if she were dead. I knew better, but my mind dredged up a ghost story my sister, Ashlynn, had once told me. Behaving like the entirely rational child I was, I'd scooped up my book and bolted from the room faster than a prairie fire with a tailwind.

Perhaps it wasn't how Mama had wanted, but I'd run... right to my hiding spot in the hedges where I was determined to stay until her desperate warning made a lick of sense.

My skin was hot and sticky, and my bladder had suddenly become uncomfortably full. Still, I wasn't stepping one foot inside that house until Papa and my sisters got back.

As the youngest of six girls, I had a tendency to get stuck with the most tedious of tasks. Sister Sarai oversaw the community library but had fallen ill over the past year. When I wasn't reading to Mama, I helped out, sorting through the book donations for appropriate additions.

Papa preferred that we only keep books that reinforced our faith in some way. Otherwise, it was as if we were giving our brains junk food.

Trash in, trash out.

Instead of burning the rejects, as was customary, I hid them in the folds of my dress and smuggled them back to my room. I'd always been a voracious reader, and these books were no exception. I kept them hidden in the wooden slats of the box spring beneath my mattress, devouring the words by the soft glow of my nightlight while the rest of the house slept.

I fell in love with Mr. Darcy alongside Elizabeth, wept with Jane over Mr. Rochester's deceitfulness, and learned about courage and compassion through the eyes of Scout Finch. The one constant in every book was that the world was a flawed, but ultimately beautiful place in which to live.

There's nothing beyond the wall that doesn't exist here.

I freed a particularly worn copy from the bodice of my dress and lay back against the earth with a shake of my head. Grandmother had warned us that we weren't to trust anything Mama said while she was sick, yet here I was, doing just that.

Mama also thinks the house is alive... just like you.

"J-j-just a c-c-coincidence," I said under my breath. "A s-silly little c-c-coincidence."

"Ariana!"

At the sound of Brother Bradley's voice, my shoulders rolled forward, and I dropped my book before tucking myself into a tight ball. Beads of sweat ran down my arms, stinging the cuts left behind from the thick bushes, but I didn't dare move.

For the most part, the church followers left me alone. Not Brother Bradley. It was as though the man had a radar that alerted him to my presence. He always needed me to hug him or sit on his lap, things I'd grown too big for years ago.

I would have preferred to sit with Mama while she stared blankly over being alone in the house with Brother Bradley. He made my skin feel prickly, but he and Papa had been friends since they were children, so I was forced to be polite.

"Come on, sweetheart. Your mama is wondering where you ran off to."

I hurriedly tucked the book back into my dress. Keeping my body close to the wall, I crawled away from the sound of his voice. Had I stayed put, I would never have known the hole existed.

It had clearly been used by animals as they made their way in and out of the neighborhood, yet had somehow remained undiscovered by the security guards.

Grandmother liked to tease me because I was small, but it just meant the hole was the perfect size for me. As I squeezed through, the sleeve of my dress got caught, tearing a small hole in the fabric I'd be forced to explain later.

I stared down at it, my stomach already churning in anticipation. I belched softly, fighting to keep my lunch from coming up onto the sidewalk. "I-I-it was just a l-l-little accident."

My hands began to tremble as Brother Bradley called for me again. I tucked them across my chest and took in my surroundings.

There were several cars parked along the sides of the street, but otherwise, it was deserted. Brother Caleb sat in the guard booth, reading a magazine. His head was down and his feet propped up against the glass, completely unaware I was nearby.

"I-I-it's not as if you're r-run—running away," I muttered. "Y-you're j-just looking, so c-c-c—calm down."

I managed to get the shaking under control after several deep breaths, enough for me to venture away from the wall. Doing my best not to trample across the flower beds, I slipped around the corner.

There was laughter coming from behind a nearby copse of trees. After checking for people, I jogged across a grassy field and crouched beside a chaste tree.

This was a test, plain and simple.

Papa believed it wasn't safe for us to be out in the world. It was the entire reason he'd developed our little gated community.

The walls are in place to keep us safe.

Either he was lying, or Mama and the books were, and I was not going back in until I knew the truth.

I made it to the tree line, confident in my decision, only to freeze in my tracks at the sharp snap of a twig.

Coming out here had been a mistake.

A heat-induced madness.

Papa had warned us the world was full of evil people— people who wouldn't think twice about hurting us to get to him.

And I'd stupidly left behind the safety of the wall to run right into their waiting arms.

I jerked my head wildly to the left and right, hoping to spot the danger before it managed to find me. I could explain away a torn dress, but not a kidnapping. My eyes came to rest on the broken twig beneath my shoe, and I exhaled a shaky breath.

"S-s-see—see? It was you the whole t-t-time. Now, don't you f-feel s-s-silly?"

"N-no... n-not really," I responded with a snort before clapping a hand over my mouth.

Well, if my loud stomping hadn't frightened the evildoers away, the fact I was carrying on a conversation with myself should do the trick.

Another giggle broke free, and I mashed the heel of my hand against my lips, thoroughly amused at the thought of anyone being scared of me.

This time, before taking my next step, I carefully checked for stray twigs and branches. And perhaps I kept a firm grip on the silver cross around my neck until it left indentions on the palm of my hand.

Just in case...

Sweat trailed down my spine, leaving me irritated I couldn't wear loose-fitting clothing like the boys did during the summer months. Each damp trickle set my teeth on edge. Still, I'd come too far to turn back, so I pushed through the low-hanging branches until a large body of water came into view.

Karankawas Lake.

It wasn't as if I hadn't known it was there. The library in the main house overlooked the water, and I'd spent many an afternoon idly watching the colorful blur of boats as they zipped past. Seeing the rippling waves left in their wake wasn't the same as hearing the whir from the motors or breathing in the faint smell of fuel.

Sunlight reflected off the surface of the lake at just the right angle, making it appear as if the water was glowing. Along the shore, young children ran back and forth, shrieking as they splashed lake water at one another. I smiled and resisted the urge to join them before settling back against a large tree trunk with my book. It was the perfect spot.

I could see everything, but no one could see me.

The sun moved across the sky as the hours passed, but I was lost in a world of cotton plantations and southern belles, completely oblivious. Perhaps if I'd been paying more attention, I would have remained ignorant to the ugliness lurking just out of sight.

I initially mistook the sounds of raised voices as my own imagination. Most of the boats were now nothing more than tiny dots of color on the horizon, and the beach—almost deserted.

Almost.

Even from where I sat, it was clear the three boys hadn't come to enjoy the water.

"She was my girlfriend, you son-of-a-bitch!"

I sucked in a breath and flattened my spine against the bark of the tree. The boy who'd spoken turned and glared in my direction. I brought my hand over my mouth, pleading with my body to be silent. An eternity later, he returned his attention to his companions.

A boy with dark hair, who I assumed was the target, stepped forward until his toes were almost even with the angry boy's. He let out a rough bark of laughter as if seeing someone upset amused him. "You want me to believe that Blair was your girlfriend? How much crack did you smoke before you called me down here?"

My nostrils flared from the exertion of keeping my breathing steady, but no one spared a second glance in my direction.

Then, without so much as a warning, the angry boy clenched his hands into fists and punched the smug one square in the jaw. The two began to pummel each other while the third boy stood off to the side, clearly not willing to get involved. He was obviously the intelligent one of the group.

Those who spare the rod of discipline hate their children...

I'd heard Papa say the words more times than I cared to admit, but it was apparent that no one had ever told the dark-haired boy. Rather than making a scene, he needed to take his correction and choose to do better in the future.

Then again, it seemed they enjoyed being hurt.

After landing a particularly rough hit, the boy stepped back and ran a hand through his dark hair. He flashed a triumphant grin, seemingly ignoring the river of blood running from his own nose.

The mistake was in not checking behind him. His heel got caught up in a pile of rope someone had left behind, propelling him backward. As he fell, his head caught the edge of an abandoned metal cooler, and he landed against the dock with a sickening thud.

My lips parted in a silent scream when the boy didn't get back up. He lay motionless, arms splayed out at his sides. The other two looked at each other in question, but it was clear the fight was over.

"H-help him," I urged with a whisper, sighing in relief when the angry boy bent to lift his body. Instead of going for help, he dragged him farther onto the dock before unceremoniously dropping him into the water when he reached the end.

My book fell from my lap, forgotten, as I mashed my fist against my lips to keep from screaming.

The smart boy seemed to share my horror. "What the hell, Chris? I said I'd help you fight him, not kill him. Shit, I can't be a part of this!"

Get him out of the water.

It was now close to dusk, and the sunset cast an eerie orange glow over everything, but there was no longer beauty in this place. The two boys took off across the beach in a dead sprint while I watched the end of the dock, hoping the boy would resurface.

"H-h-he's not y-your problem," I reminded myself, the words bitter on my tongue. The theology I'd cut my teeth on had collided with a new reality. If I held fast to my beliefs, I was condemning someone to death. But if I acted on his behalf, then I was betraying my family and my church.

Fear paralyzed my limbs, keeping me pinned up against the tree. I stayed there until the two disappeared from view before making my decision.

"Y-you are S-Scar—Scarlett O'Hara," I hissed. "B-br-bravely f-facing down the Y-Yankees on your way home to T-T-Tara."

And then, with no regard to the teachings or even my own safety, I ran toward the danger. The water cooled my sweat-drenched skin, yet pushed my small body back to shore. I fought my way past the waves before diving under with a growl. The water was murky, and every blue-green shadow looked like a body until I was right on top of it.

Just as I began to lose hope, I saw him, caught under the dock. I looped an arm around his chest and tried tugging him toward the shallows. Instead, his dead weight pushed us toward the bottom, and it took all of my strength to propel us in the right direction. My lungs burned something fierce, urging me to let him go and swim for the surface.

Black spots began to move among the blue-green shadows, but I kept swimming, willing my body to relax. I'd been around water my entire life. There was a pool in the community, as well as a small fishing hole. My sister and I had snuck out more than once to visit them when the heat was unbearable, and sleep refused to come quickly.

Sneaking out of the house after curfew hadn't been easy, but time and time again, Ashlynn and I had gotten past the guards without being seen. She was the one who'd taught me to swim and, later, how to hold my breath for increasingly extended periods.

It was training that had paid off not two weeks ago.

A guard had discovered my nightdress near the fishing hole and begun searching the grounds. Ashlynn had pulled me under as his flashlight skimmed over the water. The minutes had ticked by, and my vision began to blur, but the guard eventually moved on. When the water went dark, we'd kicked our way to the surface, desperately sucking air into our lungs. I'd been forced to sneak back into the house naked as my nightdress had been confiscated, but we'd never been caught.

You can do this.

I relaxed and let the waves I'd fought against moments before carry us lazily toward the shore. Then, using my legs and the last of my energy, I pushed us forward until the sandbar rose up beneath my feet. It was enough for me to propel the upper half of my body above the water with a strangled gasp. After several attempts, I managed to lift the boy's head too.

Exhaustion set in, but I kept pushing forward, dragging the boy onto the beach before collapsing across his chest with a groan. Waves lapped against the shore, punctuated only by the sounds of my ragged breathing.

I'd done everything I could. The rest was up to him.

Just as I began to fear I'd been too late, the boy jerked violently beneath me, coughing up mouthfuls of lake water. I gripped his shirt with both hands and weakly pulled him onto his side just as I'd seen Sister Sarai do once for Mama when she got sick in the bed.

"I've got you now," I panted. "You're safe."

His eyes remained closed, and I hesitated before pressing my fingers to his jaw. A jolt of something electric arced through my body like an errant lightning bolt had been cast down from the heavens.

I'd often felt a heat quietly simmering away within me, but with one touch, it had built to something like a wildfire. The blood left my limbs, redirecting all of its focus to the muscular organ galloping against my breastbone.

Feeling emboldened, I shifted closer, brushing the water droplets from his long dark lashes. He was, without a doubt, the most beautiful thing I'd ever seen. Up close, I realized he wasn't a boy, but something closer to a man. His jawline was dotted with stubble, and my fingers moved down, reverently tracing the outline of it.

"It's time to wake up now," I whispered softly.

As much as I wanted to stay with him, I had to go back. They were bound to be looking for me by now. But first, I needed to ensure he was going to be okay.

His eyelids fluttered at the sound of my voice before he managed to open them, peering up at me in confusion. Against the darkening sky, his blue eyes appeared almost gray. I continued stroking his cheek, enjoying the roughness against my palm.

Like sandpaper against satin.

"Are you good?" I blurted, immediately regretting the question. He was obviously a good person, or God wouldn't have placed me in his path. He would have been left to die under the dock.

Down the beach, a couple of teenage girls were laughing loudly as they jogged across the sand while their dog splashed through the water beside them.

He blinked several times before focusing on my eyes once again. I brushed the damp hair from his forehead, committing his every detail to mind before forcing out a stammered cry for help. Something brushed against the back of my hand, and I looked down, surprised to see his fingers moving delicately over my skin. His brows pulled together, and he frowned as if he hadn't expected me to be real.

Remembering Mama's story, I felt the need to confess, "I'm no angel."

He swallowed and opened his mouth just as the girls made it over. I allowed myself one final look before pulling my hand free and darting back into the trees to grab my book.

My shoes were like damp kitchen sponges beneath my feet, squishing loudly every time they came in contact with the earth. By the time I made it back into the clearing, the sun had dipped below the horizon. Not only had I missed dinner, but storytime as well.

It wasn't until I was squeezing through the hole again that I realized I hadn't gotten my answer as to whether Mama or Papa was right.

And it would be the next day before it dawned on me I hadn't stuttered once when talking to the boy.

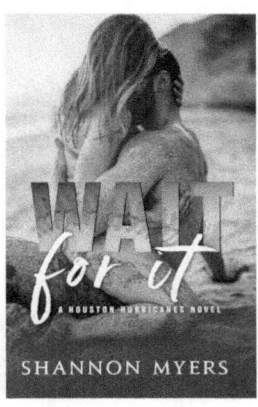

Our worlds never should have collided.

Not once. Not twice.

The pastor's daughter and a world-famous professional baseball player... we couldn't have less in common. His arrogance reminds me of my father—until it doesn't. Until he makes me feel more than I ever have before.

I can't remember the night of the accident or who I was running from.

But I'm starting to believe Killian Reed might be my only salvation... my way out.

Ten years ago, I saved his life. Now, it's his turn to save mine.

One click WAIT FOR IT now!

notes

Whew. It's raining on my face. Okay, deep breath, everyone.

Operation Annulment was jam-packed with information. I debated whether to cover some of what happened in *Operation Fit-ish* in this book, but I felt it was essential to get the back story on Kate and Nate for those who may not have read Dakota's story.

Many of the characters in Fit-ish also feature heavily in this storyline, so it made sense to include as much detail as possible. And with that ending, it wouldn't have made sense to do it any other way.

As with every book, I research everything, but please forgive any inaccuracies you may find. Sadly, I'm only human...not a Marvel superhero.

This book was a lot of fun to write. I've always wanted to wrap up Jess's storyline, and this seemed like the right book for her. It gives us closure after the David situation in the *From This Day Forward* series.

Fun fact: The soap opera As The World Turns featured an incredible couple known as *CarJack*. Carly and Jack Snyder were two of my favorites, and I loved referencing them in this.

Detective Mike Sullivan's story can be found in the Silent Phoenix

MC series. It delves into his upbringing and why he is the person he is. This series also features cameos from Kate and Dakota.

Thank you for continuing to read these books and making my dreams come true.

also by shannon myers

(Killian and Ari's Story)

Wait For It

Fictioned Series

(Hayden & Jake's Story)

Protagonized

about the author

Shannon is a born and raised Texan. She grew up inventing clever stories, usually to get herself out of trouble. Her mother was not amused. In junior high, she began writing fractured fairy tales from the villain's point of view and that was the moment she knew that she was going to use her powers for evil instead of good.

After an unplanned surgery in 2014 and a long pity party, she decided to pen a novel about the worst thing that could happen to a person to cheer herself up. She's twisted like that. Thus, From This Day Forward was born and the rest, as they say, is history.

She resides in the Texas desert with a posse of men (nothing like she'd imagined in her fantasies) and a plethora of fur babies.

Find her online at: http://shannonshaemyers.com
Or in her fan group: https://www.facebook.com/groups/
630229377127363/

facebook.com/shannonmyersauthor
x.com/shannonsmyers
instagram.com/shannonsmyers

www.ingramcontent.com/pod-product-compliance
Lightning Source LLC
Chambersburg PA
CBHW050338030726
47503CB00008B/2502